Keri Arthur is an award-winning author of thrilling paranormal romances. She's a dessert and function cook by trade, and married to a wonderful man who not only supports her writing, but who also does the majority of the housework. They have one daughter, and live in Melbourne, Australia. Visit her website at www.keriarthur.com.

Also by Keri Arthur

Riley Jenson Guardian Series:

Full Moon Rising
Kissing Sin
Tempting Evil
Dangerous Games
Embraced by Darkness

The Darkest Kiss

KERI ARTHUR

PIATKUS

PIATKUS

First published in Great Britain in 2008 by Piatkus Books
This paperback edition published in 2008 by Piatkus Books
First published in the US in 2008 by Bantam Dell
A Division of Random House Inc., New York

A CIP catalogue record for this book
is available from the British Library

ISBN 978-0-7499-3925-0

Data manipulation by Phoenix Photosetting, Chatham, Kent
www.phoenixphotosetting.co.uk

Printed and bound in the UK by CPI Mackays, Chatham ME5 8TD

Piatkus Books
An imprint of
Little, Brown Book Group
100 Victoria Embankment
London EC4Y 0DY

An Hachette Livre UK Company
www.hachettelivre.co.uk

www.piatkus.co.uk

I'd like to thank:

Everyone at Bantam for doing such a great job on
this book—most especially my editor, Anne;
her assistant, Josh; and finally, my wonderful
line editors and cover artist.

A special thanks to Miriam, my agent,
Karenne for all her hard work on my newsletter,
and the Lulus for their wonderful support
over the years.

The Darkest Kiss

Chapter 1

Being thrown out of a tree wasn't my idea of fun.

Granted, countless nestlings all over the world went through this every year, but they only had to do it once, and for them it was simply fly or die trying.

I wasn't a nestling, and I wasn't built to die. Not easily, anyway. I was dhampire—the offspring of a newly turned vampire whose dying seed somehow created life in the werewolf who raped and then killed him—and my bones were extraordinarily strong.

Being pushed from a tree couldn't kill me like it did those countless nestlings. But God, it could still *hurt*.

I mean, werewolves weren't designed to fly, and muscles used to being either a wolf or a woman were having trouble with the mechanics of being a bird.

Not that I particularly *wanted* to be a bird. And

particularly not the type of bird I could now become. I mean, a seagull? A rat of the sea? Why that? Why not something more dignified and fearsome—like a hawk or an eagle? Something with useful weapons like talons and a hooked beak built for tearing?

But no. Fate had thrown me a seagull. I'm sure she was up there laughing at me right now.

Of course, I probably *could* become something else. The drug in my system that had caused the initial change into a gull would probably allow me to take other forms, but I wasn't about to risk it. The other half-breeds who'd been injected with ARC1-23 had changed into so many different forms that they'd lost the ability to become human again, and that wasn't a problem I was willing to face. Especially not when I'd already felt that moment of confusion, right after I'd first attained gull shape, when the magic that allowed me to shift shape had seemed to hesitate, as if it couldn't remember my human form.

That had terrified me.

So, much as I hated being a gull, I was going to stick with it, practice its form, until being a gull was as natural and as ingrained into my psyche as the wolf and the woman.

Maybe then I would play with other shapes.

Maybe.

"Riley, you cannot stay on the ground forever," a deep voice rumbled from above. "Learning to fly is a matter of perseverance. And height."

I muttered something unpleasant under my breath and rolled onto my back. A dozen different aches assaulted the muscles along my shoulders, spine, and arms, and made me long for the heat of a nice, deep bath. Though even a bath wouldn't do much for all the bruises I was beginning to collect.

Not that a bath was in my immediate future anyway, if old Henry had his way.

He was sitting in one of the top forks of the gum tree high above me, his bright red shirt contrasting sharply against the cheery yellow flowers that dotted the tree. His silver hair gleamed like ice in the dappled sunlight, and his nut-brown skin was as weathered and worn as the bark of the tree itself.

He wasn't Directorate personnel, but rather a friend of Jack's. He was also a hawk-shifter, and his family apparently had ties with Jack's that went way back. I'd tried some gentle questioning in an effort to glean something useful about my boss, but Henry had so far proved an unwilling gossiper.

"Riley," he warned again.

"Henry," I said, mimicking his cross tone. "I'm not going to have an inch of white skin left if you keep this up."

"Jack says you must learn as quickly as possible."

"Jack hasn't been thrown out of a tree a million times."

He laughed—a rich, merry sound that had a smile tugging at my lips despite my grumpiness.

"It's only twenty today. It took Jack a good thirty or so times a day—for a week—before he got it."

Jack might be a vampire now—thanks to the blood ceremony he'd taken over eight hundred years ago—

but he'd been born a hawk-shifter and had the advantage of coming from a family of shifters. If it had taken *him* so long to learn, then heaven help me.

I raised my eyebrows and pushed up into a sitting position. "You taught Jack?"

"I am not that old, little wolf. No, it's just something of a legend in our roost. Few hawks are so slow to learn." He laughed again. "There are some who say that's why he's bald. He lost his hair because he landed on his head too often."

I grinned. "Well, I'm glad to know it's not just us seagulls."

"You have spent most of your life as a wolf. It's natural that you would find the ways of flying difficult." He shook the rope tied to the branch near his legs. "Come."

"If it was as easy as coming, I'd be a natural." I rose, and bit back a groan as a dozen fresh aches erupted across my torso and legs. Damn, I was going to be black and blue by tonight. Not that it really mattered. It wasn't like I had anyone to go home to anymore.

Pain rose like an old ghost. I quickly shoved any thoughts of Kellen back into the box labeled "do not think about," then reached for the rope and began to climb. It had been two months since we'd split. I should be getting over it by now. Should be getting over him.

But I wasn't, and I wasn't actually sure I ever would. I'd loved him, and he'd walked away. And not for the reason I'd most expected—the fact that I was infertile, and a half-breed. No, he'd walked away because I was a guardian and wouldn't give it up. And the fact that I *couldn't*, thanks to the drug and the havoc it was still wreaking on my system, hadn't made a difference.

He'd walked away. Become just another man who couldn't accept what I was. Another man who'd managed to smash my heart.

I'd had just about enough of the whole damn "love and relationships" thing. So much so that, since our split, I'd been keeping pretty much to myself. Of course, I was a werewolf, so the moon heat would always ensure sex was a part of my life. But that one week was about it for me and men. It seemed that love and I were never going to find a happy medium, and as much as I still wanted the whole picket fence ideal, I just wasn't up to coping with the whims and foibles of men right now.

Chocolate, coffee, and ice cream where far more reliable when it came to providing a good time, and at least *they* would never disappoint me.

I just had to thank the fast metabolism of a wolf for the fact that I hadn't put on any weight over the last few months. If I were human, I'd be the size of a house.

I reached Henry's branch and edged carefully past, sitting down and letting my feet dangle. My fingers were clamped around the branch tightly and I avoided looking down. Since my last fall off a cliff—the same one in which I'd gained my gull shape—my stomach had been getting a might queasy at even the slightest hint of a drop. Though I suppose that jumping repeatedly out of this tree and landing face-first on the ground below—and not breaking any bones—was going a long way toward curing a little of my unease.

I took a deep breath and blew it out softly. "So, explain it all to me one more time."

"A bird does not fly by simply flapping its wings," he said patiently. "Hold your arms out now, and try moving them really fast."

I did, feeling like a fool. Luckily, we were on Henry's estate up in the Dandenong hills, and well out of the way of curious passersby.

"Now, try turning your arms as you move them. More air motion happens as you twist your arms, does it not?"

I nodded, though to be honest, the difference was negligible. But then, maybe I'd hit the ground one too many times and my skin just wasn't up to feeling anything anymore.

"This is how it works with a bird. On the downstroke of the wing, the leading edge must be lower than the rear edge. And it doesn't just move down, it moves down and back, providing lift and forward movement."

"Yep, got that totally." Not.

He clipped me lightly over the ear. "Enough of the smart mouth, young woman. You can do this. You just need to think."

"All the thinking cells are either too bruised or knocked senseless," I muttered, edging a little farther along the branch so he couldn't hit me harder.

Anyone would have thought I was a teenager back at school again. I used to get clips over the ear for my smart mouth then, too.

"Think," he said. "Down, back, then up. Not up and down. Now change."

I blew out a breath, then shifted position and called to the magic that lay in my soul—the magic that had been altered to supply the form of the gull as well as the wolf. Power swept through me, around me, changing my body, changing my form, sweeping me from human to gull in the blink of an eye.

"Go," Henry said.

I spread my wings, closed my eyes, and jumped. Felt myself falling, felt the old familiar sense of panic roll through me, threatening to overwhelm. To freeze.

So I tried to concentrate on moving my wings instead. *Down, back, up, down, back, up.*

And miraculously, I was no longer falling. I squeezed open an eye, saw the ground sweeping past underneath me, and opened the other eye. I was *flying*.

"That's it," Henry said. "You've got it, my girl!"

"Woohoo!" The sound came out as a harsh-sounding squawk rather than any actual word, but for once I didn't care. I was *flying*. And it was such an amazing, powerful feeling.

Unfortunately, it didn't last long enough. Maybe I was so wrapped up in the sensation of flying that I actually forgot to fly, because suddenly the ground was approaching at the rate of knots and I was tumbling through the grass and twigs and dirt again.

I shifted to human shape and spat out a mouthful of earth. "Well, crap."

Henry laughed. He was lucky that I wasn't up there

with him, because I would have damn well pushed him off the branch.

"It's not funny, Henry."

"No, it's hysterical. Most fledglings at least learn to land with some dignity by this time. I fear you and Jack are two peas in a pod."

I rolled onto my back and stared up at the blue sky that seemed as impossible to reach as ever. "If all this makes me go bald like him, I will not be happy."

"You flew, Riley," he said, amusement still evident in his voice. "It might not have been for long, but you flew. Soon you'll get a grip on the mechanics of it all."

"Even with my coordination? Or lack thereof?"

"Even with."

I grunted and hoped like hell he was right. When I glanced at my watch, I saw it was nearly three. I'd been at this whole falling thing for nearly six hours, and I'd just about had enough.

Of course, a crash course in flying was the least of my problems. Jack wasn't happy that I'd waited so long before telling him about the change, and lately he'd been taking every opportunity to chew me out. According to him, a broken heart was no reason for stupidity. I was beginning to think he'd never been in love. Or that it had happened so long ago that he'd forgotten the pain of it.

"I think I'll call it quits for the day, Henry. My bones are feeling a little battered."

"Go on up and help yourself to a shower, then. I think I'll go for a fly myself, stretch some of the kinks out of my wings."

"I'll see you tomorrow?"

"You will, my girl, you will."

He shifted shape and stepped off the branch, swooping low past my head before soaring up into the blue. I watched his brown and gold form until it disappeared, and couldn't help the touch of jealousy. I wanted to fly like that, I really did, but I was beginning to doubt it would ever happen.

With a sigh, I dragged my battered body to its feet and walked over to the tree to retrieve my clothes. The magic that allowed us to shift shape didn't always take the best care of the clothes we were wearing, so I tended to shed my outer layer for these lessons and just wear strong cotton undies and a T-shirt. Of course, that meant more scrapes and bruises than I would have gotten if I'd worn jeans and thicker tops. But, like most weres and shifters, I healed extraordinarily fast. Jeans and tops weren't as easy to fix or replace. Not when I had a brother who kept blowing the family budget.

I grabbed the bundle of clothes and headed back to Henry's tree house. Not that it was actually a tree house—just an old wooden house built on stilts, so that the living areas were high in the canopy of the surrounding trees. The light that filtered in through the windows had a pale, green-gold look, and the air was always rich with the smell of eucalyptus and the songs of birds. I loved it, despite my fear of heights. It had to be heaven for a bird-shifter.

I rattled up the stairs and made my way to the bathroom, taking a quick hot shower before getting dressed. Brushing my hair took a little longer than usual. It had grown amazingly fast in the last few months, and now streamed in thick red layers to well past my shoulders. The only trouble was it tended to get horribly knotted, especially when falling out of trees onto leaf-littered ground.

Once it was tangle-free, I swept it into a ponytail to keep it that way, then collected my purse and car keys and headed out. But I'd barely made it back to my car when my cell phone rang.

I knew, without a doubt, that it would be Jack. And it wasn't my strengthening skill of clairvoyance that told me that.

It was experience.

Jack always tended to ring when I least wanted or needed to work.

I dug through the mess of my purse until I found my vid-phone. "You gave me a week to learn to fly," I said, by way of greeting. "It's only been three days."

"Yeah, well, tell it to the bad guys." Jack's voice was etched with a tiredness that matched the dark bags under his eyes. "The bastards seem to be going out of their way to be pains in the asses lately. Just like some guardians I know."

I'd already apologized a hundred times for not telling him about the bird thing, so if he thought he was going to get another one, he was out of luck. Falling to the ground a gazillion times had knocked any sense of regret out of me. Besides, as much as I liked Jack—both as a boss and as a vampire—he could give the rest of us lessons when it came to being a pain in the ass. "So what have you got for me this time?"

"A dead businessman in Collins Street. The Paris end."

I raised my eyebrows. The so-called Paris end of Collins Street was filled with beautiful old buildings and mega-rich companies and businessmen. They had to be, just to be able to afford the rent there. It certainly wasn't the sort of place you'd expect us to be called into. Though I suppose when death came calling, it really had no respect for wealth or location.

"So are we talking a street death, or inside a building?"

"Inside. He was found in his office by his secretary. No signs of a break-in, and no obvious signs of foul play."

I frowned. "So why were we called? It sounds more like one for the regular cops than us."

"It's ours because the victim was Gerard James."

Who was obviously someone I should know, but didn't. "So?"

"So Gerard James was the head of the Nonhuman Rights League—the party intending to run several nonhuman candidates in the next state and federal elections."

"And his death is a political hot potato, so the cops have hand-balled it to us?"

"Precisely."

Meaning the pressure would be coming down from on-high to solve this case quickly. Great. "I gather he's not human himself, then?"

"Nope. He is—was—a hawk-shifter."

"Does he have family in Melbourne?"

"Elderly parents living in Coburg. Gerard's a self-made man, and there were rumors of a contract being taken out on him several months ago."

"Well, there are probably plenty of humans out there who'd go to great lengths to stop nonhumans getting into government."

"The rumor was investigated and appeared unfounded."

So why was he now dead in his office? "Have you called in a cleanup crew?"

"Cole and his team are there already. Kade will meet you out the front of the Martin & Pleasance building in half an hour."

I glanced at my watch. It was nearing three-thirty, which meant the daily traffic snarl had already began. "It'll take me longer than that to get there."

"Not if you speed."

Amusement ran through me. I had a somewhat checkered driving history—the last car I'd actually owned I'd driven into a tree, and to this day I have no recollection of the event. Though given I ended up in a madman's breeding center immediately after it, I very much suspected *that* particular accident wasn't my fault. But I'd had several mishaps in Directorate cars since that were, hence my surprise at Jack's order. Hell, it was only last week he was lecturing me about it, saying that any more accidents might send his budget into the red.

"If you're ordering me to travel fast in a Directorate vehicle, this *must* be urgent."

"Just don't wreck the car any more than you already have." He hesitated, then added, "Or yourself."

"Gee, thanks for caring, boss."

"Riley, just shut up and get there," he said, and hung up.

I shut up and got.

It took me a good forty minutes to get into the city, then another ten to battle my way through all the traffic to the Paris end of Collins Street. I might have had permission to go super fast, but this particular Directorate car didn't come equipped with lights or sirens. Which was a damn shame—I would have loved roaring through the city streets scattering pedestrians and cars alike. Although with my driving record, that probably wouldn't have been such a good idea.

Kade was already waiting in front of the building, his jean-clad butt resting against the trunk of the car, his muscular arms crossed, and his long legs stretched out before him.

Just the sight of him sent pleasure shooting through me. I might be reluctant to get emotionally involved with anyone right now, but I was still a wolf, and still capable of admiring a good-looking man. Kade was that, and a whole lot more. He was a horse-shifter, and his coloring was that of a bay—a rich, mahogany bay that came complete with jet-black hair and wicked, velvet-brown eyes. And he was built like a thorough-bred, with broad shoulders, slim hips, and those wonderfully long legs. Legs that could hold a girl just in the right place as she drove him deeper and harder inside.

I blew out a breath, lifting the hair off my forehead,

and tried to ignore the excited bouncing of my hormones. Even if I *was* back on the sexual merry-go-round, Kade would still have been out of bounds. Jack had made it perfectly clear the day Kade had finally finished training that he didn't want workmates becoming bedmates.

Which didn't stop Kade flirting one bit, but neither he nor I had pushed it any further. Jack was mad enough at me as it was.

I tugged my keys out of the ignition and climbed out. He made a point of looking at his watch, then said, "That was the longest half-hour on record."

"Jack was expecting miracles. There was no way— short of flying, and trust me, that ain't happening yet— that I was ever going to get to the city in half an hour. Not from the Dandenongs, anyway." I hit the lock button on the remote, then walked over.

His gaze skimmed my body, a caress of warmth that sent little tingles of desire shooting across my skin. In many ways, it was a damn shame that I couldn't play with Kade, because he was the one man who'd be totally safe. When it came to the two of us, he wanted nothing more demanding than sex. He didn't care that I was a half-breed, that I couldn't have kids, that I was a guardian, or that my DNA might be changing for the worse, not the better. He didn't demand that I stay away from other men, that I be with him, and only him. All he wanted was to have a good time, while the good times lasted.

And I really did wish I could reciprocate—but it just wasn't worth the hell my life would become if Jack found out. I'd only seen him truly angry a couple of times, and I had no wish to go there more than necessary. An angry Jack was not a pleasant thing to behold, nor be around.

"Do you know how boring it was, waiting here?" he said, voice warm and rich, and so very sexy. "There wasn't even decent scenery to admire."

A smile tugged at my lips. "Lust after, you mean."

Amusement crinkled the corners of his velvet-brown eyes. "Admire, lust. It's all the same."

"Whatever. But I refuse to believe that in a street filled with offices—and therefore tons of secretaries and workers—there wasn't a single pretty girl who walked by."

"Well, maybe one or two. After all, I do have a couple of phone numbers tucked into my pocket that need to be checked out." He raised a hand and lightly brushed some hair from my cheek. His fingers were warm against my skin and a shudder that was all pleasure ran through me, but I resisted the urge to press into his caress and stepped back instead.

His lips twitched. "Jack," he said heavily, "is a pain in the ass."

"Oh, he'll be more than that if we get down and dirty, trust me." I stepped to one side, waved him on, then added, "So what has Jack told you about this case?"

"Probably the same as you. We've got a dead shifter whose political aspirations have made him too hot for the regular police." He glanced at me as he opened the building's glass door and ushered me through. "I'm betting he brought a bit of tail into the office and had a heart attack while showing her the official briefs."

I raised my eyebrows. "How old was he?"

"Forty-five."

Not what anyone would call old, especially for a shifter. "Has he got a history of heart problems, then?"

"No, but he's got a bit of a reputation as a playboy. And even the fittest playboy can go down if he overexerts himself, and one thing our boy wasn't was fit."

I dug my badge out of my purse and showed it to the cops on duty as we headed toward the elevators. Our footsteps echoed on the marble floors, and the sound seemed to be amplified by the high ceilings. It had to be hell on the ears when there was a full complement of office staff going through here.

"But if it was just a heart attack, we wouldn't have been called in."

Kade snorted softly and hit the elevator button. "Yeah, we would have. Anytime a politician dies in suspicious circumstances, there's an investigation. But in this case, they'd want to be doubly sure there was no foul play. Him being the first nonhuman politician and all."

"All the while cheering that the political threat he represented has very neatly been taken care of, no doubt."

"No doubt. Gerard James wasn't about making friends, and I really doubt he had many of them, either in the political field or out of it. Not that it mattered— not to those who cared what his party was about."

I raised an eyebrow. "Are you a supporter of the Nonhuman Rights League?"

"Hell, yeah." The elevator doors slid open. He pressed an arm against the door and ushered me inside. "I liked what they were trying to achieve."

"Which was?"

"Getting us nonhumans into state and parliamentary offices so that we might actually have a voice in the things that are decided for us."

"Yeah, like the humans are ever going to want that." I punched the fifth floor button, which was the top floor, then glanced at Kade. "So if he didn't have many friends, why was he so popular with the public?"

"Because it was all about image, and he was good at that. He might have been an obnoxious bastard behind the scenes, but in the political arena—and on the social circuit—it was all smooth sophistication and friendliness."

"So if he was obnoxious and a playboy, why didn't the human politicians make political hay out of that?"

"Oh, they tried, but Gerard had a very good publicity machine behind him. They were able to twist derisive comments to his advantage."

I glanced at the floor indicator, seeing we'd barely reached three. This had to be the slowest elevator ever made. "How?"

Kade shrugged. "In the case of the ladies, by focusing on the fact that many of the women he went out with were human, and making the attacks feel race-related."

"Clever."

"But still an asshole. Wouldn't have stopped me from

voting for him, though. I want a fairer world for my kids to live in, and I think he could have helped achieve that."

Well, there was no law saying you had to like a politician to vote for them. If there was, there'd be no one in parliament. But could one lone politician make that much of a difference? Somehow, I doubted it.

I looked up at the floor indicator, saw we were almost there, then asked, "How's Sable doing, by the way?"

Sable was his lead mare, the one mare he'd managed to keep from the herd he'd gathered before he'd been captured and slung into a madman's breeding labs. Which was how I'd actually met him—I'd been slung into the same lab. We'd escaped together, and it was only after that I'd discovered he wasn't an innocent bystander snatched up into the scheme, but rather part of a military investigation into an arms theft who had somehow stumbled onto the breeding labs.

Like Kade, Sable was a horse-shifter—a stunning, leggy black mare whose every movement spoke of class and sophistication. I'd only met her once, but I'd seen her enough on TV. The woman was a phenomenon, with her show rating through the roof and five of her eight books on herbs and healing still amongst the country's best sellers.

Of course, she wasn't the only mare he now had. He'd collected at least seven others that I knew of, and was constantly on the lookout for more to add to his herd. The more the merrier was a stallion's creed, apparently. Why the hell we werewolves got branded as sex-mad lunatics and horse-shifters didn't was beyond me. I knew for a fact that Kade was sexually insatiable, and he didn't have the moon as an excuse like we werewolves did. Not that we used it as an excuse, of course. Sex was something wolves enjoyed indulging in, whether or not the moon was blooming full.

When their hearts weren't broken, anyway.

"Sable is very pregnant, very fat, and grousing about being forced to leave her leafy Toorak house to live with me." His sudden grin was all proud male. "Another mare confirmed she was pregnant yesterday, too."

"So that makes five of them now? Damn, nothing wrong with your little swimmers."

"With us, a sign of virility and strength is not only the size of the herd, but the number of foals. I fully intend to have the biggest herd in Melbourne."

"Show-off." The old elevator came to a jumpy halt, and I grabbed the railing to steady myself. "Your Directorate salary is not going to stretch to feeding that many mouths."

"Doesn't have to. Herds work as a complete support system. Everyone contributes to support each other."

"What happens if you die?"

He shrugged. "My personal insurance will take care of them. And the Directorate insurance policy is quite generous."

That I wouldn't know, having avoided the whole "death while on duty" line of thinking. Which I guess was stupid, given the fact that a guardian's lifestyle wasn't exactly compatible with a long life—unless you were a vamp and all but indestructible. But there again, if something happened to me, I don't think Rhoan would be worried about money. Nor me, if the situation was reversed.

The elevator doors finally swished open and Kade ushered me out. The foyer was empty, but I could hear voices coming from the right, and one of them was familiar. I headed that way.

Cole looked around as we entered the office. He was a tall, gray-haired wolf-shifter with a craggy face and a sharp attitude—at least when it came to dealing with me. Though I have to admit, I probably deserved it. I enjoyed teasing him a whole lot more than was warranted. Of course, it didn't help that he kept saying he wasn't interested when I knew for a fact he was. Even though wolf-shifters tended to think of themselves as better than us werewolves, not even they could hide the smell of arousal.

"Oh, great," he said, his voice heavy but amusement sparking in his pale blue eyes. "Beauty and the beast have arrived."

"I'd ask which one of us is classed as the beast, but I'm afraid I might not like the answer." I stopped just inside the doorway and scanned the room. There was a huge desk, several sofas, and a gleaming coffee machine that appeared to have more than a dozen different selections. Gerard James was a man not satisfied with mundane choices, it seemed. "Where's the body?"

Cole thumbed toward another doorway. "In the main office. His personal assistant found him slumped across the desk at two forty-five this afternoon."

"That's a rather late start, isn't it?"

He shrugged. "Apparently it was a one-off starting time."

One-off because he knew he was bringing someone back to the office, perhaps? Maybe someone he didn't want to be seen meeting? Though if that were the case, the office would be the last place you'd think he'd bring someone. The press would most certainly be keeping an eye on his comings and goings, regardless of the time.

"Has he been dead long?"

"It's a little hard to tell. Rigor mortis can set in faster on those who have been active before death."

"And was he? Active, I mean?"

"Very," he said, voice dry. "As a rough estimate, I'd say the time of death was around six this morning."

"Where's the PA now?"

"Down on the third floor, in the cafeteria. There's a lady cop with her. I figured it's the least the lazy bastards could do after fobbing this off on us."

"Meaning that you don't think there's anything suspicious?" Kade asked.

"At first glance, no." Cole shrugged. "But in this job, you never can be sure until a full examination has been made. And I've been wrong before."

"No," I said, putting on my best shocked face. "Tell me it isn't so."

The grin that tugged at his lips transformed his face, pulling it out of the ordinary and into the "oh my" class. "Why don't you get your skinny ass into that office and do some work for a change?"

"Skinny ass?" I raised my eyebrows and looked at Kade. "Do you think my ass is skinny?"

"Darlin', I think it's lush enough to kiss. But you won't let me."

"No, Jack won't let you. He's the spoilsport, not me." I looked back at Cole in time to catch him rolling his eyes, and grinned. "So what are you doing out here if the body is in there?"

"Collecting body fluids. Seems our boy had something of a sexual marathon last night."

Bang went my theories about illegal meetings. Literally.

"Can I pick it or what?" Kade said, voice smug. "Is his sexual partner around? We might need to talk to her. Or him, as the case may be."

"Her, I would think. There's a hint of perfume in the main office that's definitely feminine, and it's not the secretary's scent. There's no sign of the wearer, though. I've asked for the security tapes to be delivered to us." He bent down and began swabbing the desk. "Whoever she was, she obviously had access to the security codes. The whole place was locked when the secretary came in."

"Maybe she used his keys." Though why would she run if he just had a heart attack? It wasn't against the law to have sex in the office, though it was perhaps politically insane.

Of course, it could be that his partner in crime was somebody else's wife. That would certainly explain the disappearing act.

Cole glanced at me. "The keys are still on the desk."

"Oh."

"Yep, this is a weird one." He paused, then added

with that cheeky glint in his eyes, "Which I guess is why Jack sent you two."

"Keep the insults up, and you know I'm going to mess up your crime scene."

"You probably will anyway." His amusement faded as he nodded toward the main office. "Don't brush against the door. We've yet to get prints off it."

"They had sex against the door?"

"Apparently so."

I glanced at Kade. "Are you sure this guy wasn't a were rather than a shifter?"

He grinned and pressed his fingers against my back, pushing me forward. "Nope. He's just your run-of-the-mill, oversexed politician."

"Why can't any of them keep it in their pants?"

"It's the whole power and availability thing."

"Which doesn't go with the whole 'in the public eye and trying to win votes' thing."

I walked through the second doorway, stepping over a large coffee stain and abandoned cup sitting just inside the door before stopping. The two men in Cole's team—a bird-shifter and a cat-shifter whose names I didn't know, and who didn't seem in the least interested in introducing themselves—were both present; one examining the office chair, the other carefully taking pictures.

Gerard James himself was buck-naked and sprawled, arms spread wide, across the desk, his shiny-white butt facing the window for all the world to see. Or at least, for those in the offices opposite. I was betting the embarrassing pictures would be front page news tomorrow morning.

The scents of sex and lust lingered on the air, and underneath it was a hint of a jasmine and orange. A feminine scent, as Cole had suggested. But there was something else, something that made my nose twitch and my psychic senses tingle.

Not death, but something very like it.

I frowned and looked at the body, waiting for the energy of the dead to stir past my senses. Waiting for his soul to come out and speak.

It didn't.

In fact, there was an odd feeling of emptiness to the whole room, as if someone had come in here and sucked out all the warmth. Removed any lingering remnants of life.

I shivered and rubbed my arms. Clairvoyance could be a pain in the ass, sometimes—especially when it wasn't giving me anything more than spooky little "something is wrong" feelings.

Kade stopped behind me, the heat of his body pressing into my spine. "There is an odd feel to this room."

I looked up at him. Kade was sensitive to emotions rather than souls or death, so if he was feeling something in this room, it had be very strong. And it would also be something very different to whatever I was sensing. He was also telekinetic, which had proven to be extremely handy when he was fighting vampires that were naturally faster than him. "In what way?"

He frowned, his gaze sweeping the room before

coming back to rest on the body. "There is a strong sense of ecstasy and lust in here."

"Well, there would be, if they did it against the tables, the walls, the doors, and whatever else bit of furniture they could get a grip on."

His velvet gaze was half-hooded and his lush mouth pursed. Not really listening, not really hearing, just concentrating on whatever it was he was feeling. "This is more than that. It's like he was on a high, and couldn't come down."

My gaze went to Gerard. "Drugs?" It certainly wouldn't be the first time a politician had been caught using an illegal substance. And it might just explain the stupid risk he'd taken, coming into his office and leaving the blinds wide open.

"I wouldn't sense a drug high, but I'm sensing this." He frowned. "There is something entwined in the high, something I've never felt before."

"What do you mean?"

He hesitated a moment, then his gaze came back to mine. "Something very old, very powerful, and extremely deadly has been in this room."

Chapter 2

$\mathscr{I}$ raised an eyebrow in surprise. "Well, it's obviously not a dead something, because otherwise I'd be feeling it."

My clairvoyance was tuned to souls and dead things—which was probably why I'd been sensitive to the presence of vampires, even when my clairvoyance hadn't yet been forced out of the closet by the ARC1-23 drug.

I stepped closer to Gerard's body, and caught a stronger whiff of the woman's perfume. The jasmine and orange scents were sharper, but mixed in amongst them were notes of lilac and roses. I frowned. "I know that perfume."

"I didn't think you wore perfume." Kade's reply was almost automatic. He stepped around me, his nostrils flaring as he pulled some rubber gloves from the box sitting on the edge of the desk.

"I don't, but I walked past the Chanel store the other day, and some lady was testing something that smelled just like this."

Of course, I hadn't hung around to find out just what it was. That much perfume coming out of such a confined space had just about blown my olfactory senses. And the next time I walked past that shop, I'd be doing so from the safety of the other side of the street. I grabbed some gloves and snapped them on. Kade was bending over the body, studying Gerard's neck.

"What have you seen?"

"Scratch marks."

I moved around the desk to look. Gerard's shiny butt loomed large. Fitness and careful eating had obviously *not* figured on his agenda. Still, some of the most powerful men in history had also been some of the most unappealing when it came to physical attributes. In life, it was the power of these men that attracted. In death, that power was never obvious.

"What sort of scratch marks?"

"Cat, I think." He pointed to the three slashes etched deep into Gerard's neck. "The wound smells fresh."

The scent of blood, though faint, was evident this close to the body. I leaned closer still, and lightly pressed one of the wounds. They opened a little at my touch, showing how deeply the claws had sliced into flesh. "The wounds haven't healed, so he didn't shift shape at any time before his death." I glanced up at Kade. "You think it possible his partner was a cat-shifter?"

"Well, I doubt he has a pet cat. Bird-shifters and feline pets have something of an aversion to each other."

I glanced at the wound again. "Those cuts are definitely from cat claws, not human ones, so why would she even be in cat form if they came here to fuck themselves silly?"

Amusement glinted in Kade's eyes as his gaze met mine. "Maybe he just wanted to play with a bit of pussy before he got down to business."

"As puns go," I said heavily, "that sucks. It would be interesting to view the security tapes, and see if there's any record of her entering or exiting in either form."

"Why?"

"Just a feeling. She didn't report his death, wasn't here when the PA found him, and the place was apparently locked up tight. All of which smacks of secrecy. So, why would she let herself be seen coming into the building?"

"Assuming, of course, we *are* dealing with a female."

That perfume definitely seemed female-oriented, but given I didn't even use the stuff, I could hardly claim to be an expert. "Were there any rumors about Gerard being gay?"

Kade shook his head. "But politicians are great at covering that sort of shit up. And the positioning of the body is suggestive."

My gaze skated down his spine to his butt. "Not if she was underneath him at the time of the death, and merely moved him enough to get out."

He stripped off his gloves and dumped them into the disposal unit. "I don't think we're going to uncover much here. You want to head over to his apartment and see if there's anything—or anyone—there?"

"You do it. I'll go talk to the PA."

He nodded and walked out of the room. I took a final look at Gerard, waiting a little longer to see if his soul would come out to play, then shrugged and headed into the outer room.

Cole looked up. "Leaving so soon?"

I smiled. "I'll stay if you really want me to."

"I'm afraid I don't."

"You lie, wolf man."

He didn't deny it, which was a nice change, but his blue eyes were still cool. He was a man not easily swayed by hormonal attraction—not that I really wanted to get anywhere, particularly not at the moment—but half the fun was in the trying. I'm not sure what I'd actually do if he ever said yes. Beside the shock such an event would cause, there was Jack's ruling to consider.

I flung a hand in the direction of the main office. "You noticed the scratches on his neck?"

"I did."

"Want to send me the full analysis and autopsy report when it's done?"

"I will."

"Thanks. I'm off to chat to the PA—what's her name, by the way?"

"Rosy Ennes. You can let her go once you've spoken to her."

"Thanks, I will."

I headed down, taking the stairs rather than the

elevators, not wanting to risk another of those stomach-churning stops.

The smell of coffee hit as soon as I pushed open the door and I breathed deep. It wasn't a particularly fresh smell and it had a slightly burned edge, but any coffee was drinkable when you were as addicted to the stuff as I was.

I looked around for the two women, spotting the blue of a police uniform in the far corner, then headed over to the counter, grabbing two white coffees and a couple pieces of chocolate cake. Once paid for, I picked up some sugar and walked across the room.

"Can I help you?" the cop said, green eyes as cool as her voice.

"Riley Jenson, Directorate." I dumped the coffees and cakes on the table, then dug my badge out of my pocket and showed her.

She didn't look impressed. No surprise there. Though the police in general were thankful for our presence—particularly given it freed them from dealing with the worst of nonhuman excesses—there were still pockets who considered us little more than licensed killers. Which, in many ways, was nothing but the truth. It looked like this woman might be one of those.

Either that, or she just wasn't taken in by my charming personality and easy-to-get-along-with ways.

"I wasn't aware the Directorate now had day-shift guardians," she said, inspecting the badge more carefully than necessary.

Like anyone in their right mind would want to fake a guardian badge.

"New squad, announced several months ago." I shoved the badge back into my pocket and resisted the urge to suggest that maybe she should start reading internal memorandums a little more often. "I'll take over here for the moment. Thanks."

She sniffed, then rose and moved away. I sat down in her seat, my nostrils flaring as I sampled Rosy's scent. She smelled of lavender and eucalyptus, and also very human. I shoved a coffee and a piece of cake toward her. "Here. You look as if you need this."

She ignored the cake and wrapped her hands around the Styrofoam cup, her smile as wan as her lined features. I'd presumed—wrongly—that someone like Gerard James would have a young and attractive personal assistant. Someone that was easy on the eye as well as efficient at her job. From the little Kade had said, he'd just seemed that type.

But Rosy had to be in her late fifties—and with no makeup and her gray hair cut into an old-fashioned bob, she looked a good deal older. Maybe it did his political image good to have an older assistant or maybe she was simply damn good at her job.

"I'm afraid I have to ask you about this afternoon, and finding Gerard James." I lifted the lid off my coffee container and tossed it lightly into a nearby trash can. "You can take your time. There's no rush."

She nodded, but for several seconds she didn't say anything. She just sat there with her hands wrapped around the coffee cup and her eyes cast downward.

"Rosy?" I said gently.

She jumped a little. "Oh, yes." Her voice was quivery, but she continued. "It was a little after two-thirty when I arrived at the office."

"Do you always start so late?"

"No, but last night he was at a fund-raiser, so he gave me the morning off. We were going to work late to make up for it."

"So the office was all locked up when you came in?"

"Yes." She took a sip of coffee, then added, "I have a set of keys, because I'm usually here before him. He likes—liked—a cup of coffee to be ready as soon as he arrived."

"What time was he due in, then?"

"Not until three, but he's usually fifteen minutes early." She hesitated, her pale blue eyes sparkling with unshed tears. "I went into his office to put his coffee on the desk as usual. And that's when I saw—"

She stopped and took a large gulp of air. Her hands were trembling so hard the coffee was threatening to spill over the sides of her cup and scald her fingers. I reached out, gently plucking the Styrofoam cup and placing it back on the table. But I couldn't help wondering if the depth of her reaction was due just to shock, or if it was something deeper. Something that wasn't actually sexual, because from everything I'd heard about Gerard James, I very much doubted if Rosy would be his type. But that didn't mean Rosy couldn't have had a thing for him. It certainly wouldn't be the first time a PA had fallen for her boss. And, after all, there was probably little more than ten years or so between them. Not much, in the scheme of things.

"Was there anything unusual, or out of place, that you noticed?"

She shook her head. "Just him, on that desk." Her lip quivered, and a lone tear tracked down her pale cheek. "It was such a shock, seeing him like that, you know?"

"I know." I hesitated. "Did you notice his clothes anywhere?"

I certainly hadn't, but maybe Cole's crew had already bagged them.

"No," she said, "but they're probably hanging in the bathroom. He was always neat like that."

Even when in a mating rut? I found that hard to believe, but there again, he was a politician. They were a breed far different to the rest of us. "What function did he attend last night?"

"It was at the Crystal Palace in St. Kilda. Some charity fund-raiser he was asked speak at."

"Do you know who his date was?"

Her snort was disparaging. For the first time, I saw something more than sorrow in her face. "Alana Burns. She was one of the Toorak Trollops."

Amusement twitched my lips. No need to ask Rosy what she thought of the "Trollops," because it was right there in the tartness of her voice. "Who are?"

She waved a hand, coming perilously close to knocking over her coffee. I reached forward and slid it out of the way again. "They're a dozen or so single or divorced Toorak ladies who make themselves available to attend all the best functions. With only the best-bred men, of course."

"So they're high-priced hookers?"

She frowned. "No. Money doesn't change hands, as far as I know. Can you imagine the scandal that would have caused Mr. James? No, they're just well-bred, well-connected sluts, pure and simple."

I smiled, but I had to wonder if she'd voiced such sentiments to her boss. Somehow, I suspected not. "And did he go out with Alana often?"

"Quite a few times, although I think he was getting a little tired of her."

I took a sip of coffee, then asked, "Why?"

She hesitated. "He generally preferred to keep things casual."

And if Alana had started making demands and had gotten the wrong reaction, it might just explain his murder. Dumped women didn't always resort to chocolate. Some of them got angry—and others got even. "How did he usually dump his lovers?"

"With flowers the next day. I usually order them, which is how I knew he was getting tired of Alana. He asked me to check the prices on the roses."

Well, at least he didn't dump her with daffodils. "But they went out last night?"

"Yes. I rang her that afternoon to confirm the date, as I usually do. She was in a complete snit." Rosy sniffed. "Most of those women think they're too good to be dealing with the common folk."

And maybe the Trollops weren't the only ones with a chip on their shoulders. "Was Alana the first Trollop your boss dated?"

"No." She wrapped her hands around the coffee again and slid it toward her. "I kept telling him they'd get him into trouble one day, but he liked the contacts they could give him."

"Who else did he date, then?"

"There were several of them. He was with one for about a year, but she got very clingy and he called it off."

Meaning she probably wanted a commitment. Poor woman. I wondered whether she'd received the roses, or if she'd simply been shown the door. "What was her name?"

She frowned. "Cherry something. It'll be in the files—although I believe she's changed address, so those details won't be right. It's filed under T."

This time, my grin broke free. Rosy definitely had more fire in her than first appeared. "Are Alana's details there, too? I need to speak to her."

"Yes."

"Is there anything else you can tell me? Anything that might be useful?"

I reached out telepathically as I asked the question and linked lightly to Rosy's mind. Her thoughts were a confusion of sadness and grief for her boss as well as worry about her age and whether she'd actually find another job. I couldn't find anything resembling lies or half-truths, or anything she was concealing. So I gently withdrew.

She took a sip of coffee, then frowned. "Like what?"

"Well, had he been sick recently? Had he received any threats? Had anything unusual happened in the last week or so?"

"No. To all of that."

"Then for the moment, there isn't much more you

can help me with." I waved the cop back over, then added, "I'll get the officer to take you home, if you like."

Said officer didn't look too happy at being relegated to chauffeur duties, but Rosy looked pleased. "That would be lovely. Thank you."

I picked up my coffee and the uneaten bit of cake, then said my good-byes and got out of there. I munched the chocolate cake as I walked back up the stairs, leaving a trail of crumbs behind me.

Cole looked up as I reentered the office. "You expect me to just fall into bed with you, and yet you didn't even have the decency to get me a cup of coffee? Women these days. So selfish."

I grinned. "Yep, it's all about me and my appetites, buddy boy, not yours."

Amusement briefly touched the blue of his eyes. "What can I do for you now?"

"You seen a Rolodex?"

He waved a hand toward the desk. "Second drawer."

I dumped my coffee on the desk, then put on some gloves before opening the drawer and retrieving the Rolodex. Alana's address was indeed listed under T for Trollops. In fact, there were a total of seven women listed. Gerard had obviously been making his way through the Trollop ranks. I jotted down all their names and addresses, then retrieved my coffee and nodded a good-bye to Cole. I was almost out the door when I remembered what Rosy had said about clothes, and stopped.

"Cole, have you found Gerard's clothes yet?"

He answered without looking up. "Yeah, they're neatly stacked up in the bathroom."

"Really?"

I couldn't help the surprise in my voice, and he looked up with a smile. "Yeah. I suspect our boy is a bit of a neat-freak. Both offices are extraordinarily tidy."

"Except there was nothing neat about what they were doing last night."

"Well, no, but then, not even a politician would expect sex to be neat." He paused to pick up a strand of hair and place it in the bag. "The bathroom window is broken, though, which is odd."

That raised my eyebrows. "So if our killer was a cat-shifter, she could have escaped that way?"

"If it wasn't for the five-story fall to the pavement, yes." His voice was edged with exasperation. "It'll be in my report. If I ever get to finish my report, that is."

I knew a hint when it clubbed me *that* hard. So I turned around and headed back downstairs.

Once in my car, I switched on the onboard computer and typed in Alana's name, looking for anything we had on her. As luck would have it, there was practically nothing. The worst thing she'd ever done in her life was being late to pay a speeding ticket. The Trollops might be hard-loving, life-enjoying women, but it seemed this one, at least, was basically law-abiding.

I double-checked that the address we had listed was the same as the one in the Rolodex, then started up the car and headed off.

To say Toorak was a well-to-do suburb would be the understatement of the year. Only millionaires and over could afford to live there—though in recent times, some of the more affluent had been moving out to the trendier beachside suburbs like Brighton.

The only time I came to Toorak willingly was to visit Dia—a psychic who was on the Directorate's payroll who'd become a friend—or to go window-shopping along Chapel Street. Actually buying anything more expensive than a coffee was out of the question—the Directorate didn't pay us *that* well—and even the coffee came with a higher than normal price tag in this suburb.

The strident blast of a horn brought my attention back to the road, and I swerved to avoid an oncoming car. Ignoring the rather animated gestures from the driver, I flicked the computer over to satnav, and let it guide me to Alana's.

It turned out she didn't live in one of the leafy acre blocks that populated the money end of Toorak, but given her apartment was near the Yarra River end of Kooyong Road, it would still carry a million dollar price tag. At least.

I climbed out of the car and looked up at the building. It was only three stories high and modern in design, all concrete and windows. The floors weren't built directly onto each other, but at slight angles, giving everyone a view and the building an ill-stacked look.

Not ugly, not stunning, just another building that would probably get knocked down and replaced by something bigger and grander in another twenty years. That seemed to be the way in Toorak of late. Even Dia had received offers for her beautiful old house—apparently the plan was to knock it down and build grand-looking apartments that could be flogged for millions each. Dia had so far resisted the temptation—for which I was grateful, because I loved her place. It was such a warm and relaxing home to visit—especially when compared to the bombsite that was my apartment. A good housekeeper I wasn't. Neither was my brother—though he tended to be far tidier than me.

I locked the car and headed in. My phone rang as I jogged up the front steps, and I stopped at the top to dig it out of my purse.

The minute I hit receive, a sharp voice said, "How many times have I told you that the Directorate is not your personal answering service?"

I grinned. There was no mistaking that voice—it belonged to Salliane, the vamp who'd taken my place as guardian liaison and Jack's main assistant. "And how lovely it is to hear your dulcet tones again."

"Bite me, wolf girl," she snapped back. Obviously, Jack wasn't in the room, or else she'd be all sweetness and light. Sal wanted to get into Jack's shorts something bad, and I guess she figured bad-mouthing the boss's favorite guardian while he was in hearing range wasn't going to help her efforts.

Of course, I pretty much figured nothing would—not only was there his own ruling to consider, but Jack had been holding firm for months now against some pretty sultry onslaughts, and I very much doubted giving in was in the cards in the near future. But it was fun watching her try. And fail.

"Sal darling, nothing in this world would get me to bite you. And what's this about personal messages?"

"I've got one here from a Ben Wilson. He says it's urgent and asks if you could call him immediately."

I frowned. "Ben Wilson? I don't know anyone by that name."

"He says otherwise."

Which didn't exactly help. I shifted from one foot to the other and watched a woman in ultra-high, ultra-red stilettos toddle past. My nose twitched. She smelled of rum and cigarette smoke. "Is that all he said?"

"No, he said something about remembering Shadow, whatever the hell that is."

The name clicked. Ben was Shadow, a big, black wolf who managed Nonpareil, a stripper business that catered—as both strippers and studs—to human and nonhuman parties alike. I'd met him briefly while investigating a case a few months ago, and while we'd shared an attraction, I'd been with Kellen at the time and had promised to remain faithful to him.

Fat lot of good it had done me, too.

I blew out a breath, pushed away the lingering remnants of heartache, and said, "Did he leave a phone number?"

"He did. But this is the last time I'm relaying personal messages."

"It's not personal. It's business." Which wasn't exactly a lie, because I actually had no idea what Ben wanted. I doubted if it would be personal, though. Not after all this time.

She grunted. "Not believing that for an instant, wolf girl." She rattled off a phone number. "He also said you can contact him via the office if there's no answer on his cell."

"You're such a sweetie, Sal."

"You know where you can shove being a sweetie," she said and hung up.

I chuckled softly. Jack had told me numerous times to stop being such a bitch around Sal, but baiting that woman was just too much fun to let it go.

I dialed the number she'd given me. It rang several times, then a deep voice said, "Ben Wilson speaking."

"Ben, it's Riley Jenson, returning your call."

"Thank you for calling back." There was more than a touch of relief in his rich tones. "I know you don't know me or anything, but I'm in need of some help, and you're the only guardian I know."

Well, at least I'd been right before. It *was* business. I wasn't sure whether to be relieved or disappointed, then wanted to smack myself for even thinking the latter.

"What sort of help?" I said, perhaps a touch more sharply than I'd intended.

He hesitated. "One of our strippers has just been murdered."

"Then call the police."

"I have. They're treating it as low priority."

"Why?"

"Because Denny was a known participant in the BDSM scene, and his death looks like sex-play gone wrong."

"And if he was into that scene, they might just be right."

"Except for the fact that Denny only dabbled in

BDSM. What really got his rocks off was asphyxio-philia."

I frowned. "Which is?"

"Erotic asphyxiation. Only he wasn't found hanging from his neck, he was found hanging by his wrists, with his back and stomach stripped."

"He got off by trying to kill himself?" That didn't sound like very much fun to me. There again, neither did having my back and stomach beaten so badly that the flesh peeled away.

"He didn't do autoerotic asphyxiation. He was always—*always*—with a partner."

Something Ben couldn't actually be sure of, unless he was there each and every time. And as frank and as open as wolves were about sex, most of us didn't go blathering to all and sundry about each and every sexual exploit. "Did police find any indication of a partner in the apartment?"

"No, although there had to be one given the state of his body."

"So what do you want me to do? Try and find the partner?"

"I want the truth of what happened. Finding the partner would be a good start, yes."

"I'll need to get in his apartment." Smell the smells, see if his soul was hanging about for a chat. Though not all souls did, as evidenced by Gerard.

"I have a key. I can let you in."

I raised an eyebrow. "Do you have a key to all your employees' apartments?"

"No, just those who are into the more dangerous stuff."

"You mean there're sexual fetishes more dangerous than trying to strangle yourself?"

"Maybe not as dangerous, but certainly walking the edge, yes."

I walked across to the apartment building's main doors and pressed the buzzer for apartment 1B. While I waited for Alana to answer, I asked, "How long ago did he actually die?"

"Yesterday. He didn't turn up for work today, so I called in on the way home. That's when I found him."

So at least twenty-four hours had passed, if not more. I wrinkled my nose. The chances of the dead man's soul hanging about were slim. Even if he was there, the odds that I'd actually understand him were practically nil. To date, it seemed that the fresher the kill, the stronger I could see or hear the soul—and vice versa.

"The police took your statement, I presume." I pressed the buzzer again, then stepped back and looked up. No one answered, and there didn't seem to be any movement or sound evident from either of the first floor apartments.

"Yes, they did. You can double-check it if you think I've been lying about anything."

I smiled. "Oh, I will, but not because I think you're lying. I want to see what the cops and coroner all thought."

"I didn't think coroners worked that fast."

"It depends on the situation." And in this one, it could be days before a full report came out. He was right on one thing—BDSM deaths stood side by side with suicides at the bottom of the priority list when it came to cause-of-death examinations. Still, they'd have initial impressions, and those would be in the case notes. "Where are you now?"

"Home."

I gave the intercom buzzer one final push. Still no answer. Alana was either out or working. "Can you get to your mate's place quickly?"

"Be there in fifteen." He gave me the address, then added, "I really do appreciate this."

"You owe me a coffee. And I hope you realize there may be nothing I can do."

"I know."

"Meet you there, then." I hung up, then shoved my cell back into my purse and headed down to my car. Ben's dead friend lived in Prahan, which wasn't that far away, even with the late afternoon traffic going nowhere fast.

I got there with a few minutes to spare. Ben was nowhere to be seen, so I leaned against the trunk of my car and studied the building. It was one of those boring brick designs that were put up in the latter part of the twentieth century—a basic straight up and down affair with few windows and little imagination. Someone had recently painted it cream, and there were neatly trimmed hedges along the front and the sides, but the greenery didn't do a whole lot to relieve the blandness.

Not a place I could live in, if only because the apartments didn't look particularly large. It would have made me feel like a caged animal.

The roar of a motorcycle caught my attention. I looked around to see a leather-clad man on a big, mean-looking bike come roaring up the street toward me. He gave me a wave when he saw me looking, then slowed and drove the bike into the parking spot behind my car.

I smiled and walked back to him. "Fancy entrance," I said, as he took the helmet off.

Ben patted his bike affectionately. "Haven't given this old girl a run for a while. It's nice to be on her again."

I looked at the bike. It didn't look anything particularly special to me. "It's a bike."

Amusement gleamed in his bright blue eyes. "No, it's a 1975 GL1000 Gold Wing. Some of this baby's features were way ahead of her time."

"Well, I'm charmed to meet her," I said, voice dry. "Now, do you want to take me up to your mate's place?"

His grin was as sexy as all hell as he climbed off the bike, his teeth a stark contrast to his rich, black skin. "Not into motorcycles?"

"No." But my treacherous hormones were certainly into all that leather. He was a tall man—nearly a foot taller than me, and at five seven, I wasn't short—and powerfully built, with chiseled features and thick black hair. And all that wonderful black leather fit like a glove, emphasizing and enhancing his muscular build.

He undid the stud at his neck, then lowered the jacket zip, revealing a dark blue T-shirt underneath. My nostrils flared, sucking in the musky scent of man mixed with just the faintest hint of perspiration.

Very nice indeed.

"I think you need to come for a ride on one of my bikes. That'll change your tune."

The image of pressing close to his leather-clad body as we roared through the streets on his noisy machine had my pulse rate tripping—but I wasn't sure if it was excitement or panic. I mean, I liked looking—a lot—but I didn't feel ready for anything more right now. A quick dance with a stranger during the moon heat was safe enough for both my wounded heart and my emotions.

This wolf was not.

I stepped back, and waved him on ahead. "Cars are safer."

"That's the problem. There's no direct thrill."

"There is with sports cars."

"It's not the same, trust me." He glanced down at me, eyebrow raised. "And how can a guardian afford to get around in a sports car?"

"She can't. But I've been in them."

"Not the same." He began climbing the building's outside steps to the first floor, leaving me rather ideally placed for some butt-viewing action. "Denny's apartment is the end one. He hated having neighbors on both sides."

"Did the cops talk to the neighbor he has got?"

He shrugged, making the leather jacket ripple rather nicely. "They weren't exactly telling me much." He threw a grin over his shoulders. "But that could have something to do with me calling them pricks who wouldn't know a murder if it slapped them in the face."

"Could be," I agreed dryly.

We reached the end of the balcony. He stopped and opened a door that looked freshly painted. The air that flooded out was filled with the scent of roses and death.

I stepped past Ben into the apartment. It wasn't exactly a huge place, but it was neat and bright, thanks to the white walls and the skylights. The first room was a living room and kitchen combined, and the whole area was extraordinarily clean. Even the sink gleamed.

I scanned the scenery photos on the walls, wondering if he'd shot them himself, then said, "Where was he found?"

"In the first bedroom."

I walked around the L-shaped sofa and headed toward the first door. The smell of death was sharper the closer I got to the bedroom, and my skin crawled. Not because of the death scent, but because there was something else here, something that felt wrong.

I stopped just inside the doorway, briefly noting the blood splatters on the walls and the wide dark stain on the carpet before my gaze was drawn to the heavy-looking hook hanging from the ceiling above the stain.

"That where it happened?" Stupid question, but sometimes they just had to be asked.

"Yes."

Ben had stopped right behind me, and the thick, warm heat of him flowed over me, drowning my senses and sending desire prickling across my skin. Not what I needed right now.

Or later, for that matter.

I turned around and lightly pressed my fingers into his stomach. Felt the steel of muscle underneath the cotton T-shirt. "You need to step back. You're over-whelming my senses."

"I think that's the nicest thing a woman has said to me in a while."

He didn't move, but then again, I wasn't pushing very hard. Not yet.

I snorted softly. "Somehow, I'm doubting that."

"You'd be surprised." He took several steps back. The richness of his aroma abated enough to allow more of the room's flavors in. "We strippers are taken for granted more often than not."

"I thought you didn't do much stripping now." I turned around and took a step forward, distancing my-self a little more and trying to catch the source of that tenuous, unsettling scent.

"I don't. But I wasn't always a manager."

"So how long have you been in the profession?" I took another step forward. That strange scent got a bit stronger, reminding me more and more of a vampire's scent—only if the killer *was* a vampire, then he was one who smelled like no other vampire I'd come across.

"I've been in the business since I was seventeen. There wasn't a whole lot else a kid with little schooling could do. Even apprenticeships need minimum grade levels."

The closer I got to the bed, the stronger that odd smell got, and the more certain I became it was vam-pire. A vampire that smelled like no other, but a vam-pire all the same. And he'd been here recently. I stripped off the bed covers and bent to sniff the sheets.

The scents of wolf and sex emanated off them, but

though the vampire stench was extremely strong near the bed, he—or she—hadn't been in it. Not that it meant anything. Someone who liked hanging themselves for kicks wasn't likely to be restricted to a bed for lovemaking.

I looked at Ben. "Were any of Denny's lovers vampires?"

He frowned. "Not that I know of. He had a couple of wolves he'd mentioned recently, but never a vampire."

"Well, one's been in this room. You can smell him near the bed."

He came into the room, filling the whiteness with his dark vitality. He drew in a breath, then his blue gaze met mine. "Something smells old. Off, almost."

I nodded. "Vampire."

He frowned. "Vampires don't smell like that."

"Maybe not the ones you associate with, but the ones I deal with, yeah, they do." I contemplated the heavy metal hook for a moment. There were no vibes of power in this room, no chill that indicated the other side was coming out to play. Maybe his soul had moved on, or maybe he simply didn't want to talk. "I guess the first thing we need to do is try and uncover the name of the vampire who was here. What clubs did Denny frequent?"

Ben smiled. "All of them. He liked to cruise."

"No favorite, then? No club he went to more than others?"

"Maybe. I don't know. I could ring up and ask Jilli. She might know."

"Jilli being one of the wolves he mentioned recently?"

"Yeah. She owns and runs a coffee shop near the Blue Moon."

I raised my eyebrows. "Not Chiquita's? They have the best blueberry muffins there. And the coffee's not bad, either."

"So this coffee that I owe you—shall I pay the fee there?"

I considered him for a moment, seeing the amusement and playfulness in his eyes, feeling the answering response low-down in my belly. Wondered when—if—I was ever going to get back to the business of being a free and easy wolf.

I didn't know, I really *didn't* know, and I knew part of that was the fear of getting hurt again. After all, my heart couldn't be broken again if I didn't put it out there. And yet, how much longer could I continue to ignore a side of myself that was a part of my soul?

"It'll probably be easier if I was there to talk to her, so yeah, that would be fine."

He raised an eyebrow, expression a little quizzical. "Why do I get the feeling that you're avoiding the intent behind that question?"

"Because I am." I turned and opened the drawer of the bedside table. Painkillers, books, and condoms. I pulled one out and showed it to Ben. "He fucked humans?"

"Yes. Not all the time, but he liked the challenge of the restraint they represented. He used condoms so there were no unwanted pregnancies."

Because a wolf didn't have to worry about STDs, thanks to our ability to heal all sorts of things during the shapeshift. "A condom is not one hundred percent safe."

"It's better than nothing." He considered me for a moment, then said, "So despite the fact I can smell your interest, you don't want to go out with me?"

I shoved the condom back in the drawer and slammed it shut. "Don't take it personally. I'm not going out with anyone at the moment."

"You're a wolf. That's a physical impossibility."

"Obviously, I'm not talking about the moon heat." I stepped around him and walked to the closet. Opening the doors revealed that Denny's neatness continued here. His clothes were all stacked via type and color.

"And I'm not talking about sex," Ben said. "Just coffee and a chat. Nothing more, nothing less."

I cast him a look over my shoulder, a smile twitching my lips. "I'm not believing *that* for a moment. You, wolf man, have loving on your mind."

"I can control my mind. And I don't do sex on first dates."

I just about choked on my disbelief. "Yeah. Right. Must have made being a stripper hard, then."

He waved a hand. "Stripping is different. So is sex for the need of it. Outside of work and the moon heat— or maybe even because of them—I prefer to take things slower. Get to know the girl before I fuck her."

Then he was a rare man in wolf ranks. I shut the wardrobe door. "How about we do the coffee and chat thing while asking if this Jilli actually knows anything, and see what happens from there?"

He studied me for a moment, then nodded. "Though I have to admit, I am curious about this sudden turn-about in your behavior. Last time we met, you were not so reluctant."

"Last time we met, I wouldn't have acted on my impulses, either. No matter how fierce the desire."

He nodded. "I saw that. I can also see that the reason here is different. It is a puzzle I shall have to solve."

"Try too hard and there's no coffee. I'm not in the mood to be psychoanalyzed right now."

I walked around to the hook. The vampire scent was strongest here, which did suggest he might have been involved in Denny's death. "Why would someone want to kill Denny?"

"I don't know. He wasn't the type to have enemies."

Everyone had enemies, even the nicest of people. My gaze went to the thick metal hook. I just couldn't imagine someone willingly tying a rope around their neck and cutting off their oxygen almost to the point of death just to get their rocks off. But then, I couldn't ever imagine finding joy in being beaten so badly the flesh on my back hung in raw strips. Yet I'd seen that done, and had felt the sheer and utter pleasure the women had gotten from it.

To each their own, I suppose.

But even here, the point where he had died, there was no feeling of energy. No sense of the dead coming back. Denny had obviously moved on to the next level in his life.

I stepped around the dried bloodstain and checked the bedside table on this side, but there was nothing more enlightening than socks. I faced Ben again. "There's really nothing more I can do here at the moment. I'll need to read the police report and talk to his girlfriend before I can decide what to do next."

If there *was* anything that could be done next.

Ben looked at his watch. "Jilli does the day shift, so I doubt we'll catch her there now."

"Well, great, because I actually do have a job to do. Phone her, and make an appointment for tomorrow." I reached into my purse and took out a business card and a pen. After scrawling my cell phone number onto the back of it, I handed it across. "Ring me when you get a meeting time."

He glanced at the number then shoved it into his back pocket. "Thanks for coming out, Riley. I really do appreciate it."

I waved his thanks away. "As I said, it may yet turn out that there's nothing I can do."

"But you tried. More than the cops are doing, I fear."

There was no point in answering, simply because he was right. The cops wouldn't be chasing a BDSM session gone wrong as hard as they would a straight-out murder. It was a simple fact of policing life that priorities had to be given.

We left the apartment and rattled down the stairs. A couple of older men were near Ben's bike, one of them kneeling, as if inspecting the internals. I smiled. "You've got fans. Or your bike has."

"Beautiful bikes always get admirers. It's par for the course." He shrugged. "I'll see you tomorrow?"

"You will." I half-waved a good-bye, briefly watching—and enjoying—the sight of him sauntering toward the two men, then climbed into my car and drove off.

As I headed back into the traffic, I grabbed my phone and rang Kade.

"Hey, horse man," I said, when he answered. "What's happening out your way?"

"Nothing of interest at Gerard's place. I'm going back to the Directorate to hassle Cole for his initial report. There might be something helpful in there."

Hassling Cole didn't work. I'd tried it. "So no sign of a cat, real or shifter, at Gerard's?"

"Not a hair." He paused, and in the background, the music changed from dance to rock. "What are you doing?"

"The secretary told me who he was dating last night. I'm heading over to talk to her now."

"You want me along?"

"No, I'll be all right. I'll meet you back at the Directorate. Have a coffee ready for me. The real stuff, not that black muck we have in the machine."

"Your wish is my command," he said, voice deepening and oh so sexy.

I snorted. "Not going to work, my friend."

He laughed. "I can but try. See you soon."

I hung up and headed on. The traffic was so bad it took me another twenty minutes to get back to Alana Burns's apartment. Pressing the buzzer once again had little effect and there was no security guard handily sitting inside the small foyer to harass.

I stepped back and studied the balconies. There was a small concrete wall that separated the front stairs from the drive that led into the underground parking lot, but even if I stood on that, it was still a hell of a jump to the first balcony.

But maybe it wasn't so far for an inexperienced seagull to fly.

Excitement and doubt fluttered through me. Flying from a drop was a whole lot different than flying upward, but I had nothing to lose by trying. Nothing except more bruises.

I grabbed my cell and my badge out of my purse, shoved them into my pocket, then dropped the bag behind a potted bush, well out of sight. Then I clambered onto the wall and called to the magic in my soul. It swept through me, changing muscles and bone and body, until I was once again that dreaded seagull. I paddled along the wall a little bit, then looked up at the balcony.

It looked like a long, long way.

I could do this. It was just a matter of concentration. I adjusted my tail feathers and raised my wings, beating them as fast as I could to get the lift I needed. *Down, back, up, down, back, up.* And suddenly, I was going up, cutting through the air. Flying.

I felt like cheering. I concentrated on not falling instead.

I fluttered up and over the railing, then spread my tail feathers to act as a brake. But the change was too sudden, and I dropped too quickly, splattering chest-first against the concrete.

"Ow," I muttered, even though it came out little more than a harsh squawk. I rolled onto my back and shifted to human form. My chest still hurt. More bruises, no doubt.

Even so, I couldn't help a silly grin. I'd flown. Even if my landings needed more work, I'd actually *flown* rather than simply making a guided fall. Maybe this whole flying gig wasn't as bad as previously thought.

I climbed to my feet. As usual, my jeans had made it through the shift just fine, but my shirt had been shredded. They were usually pretty useless after a shift to wolf, but the destruction here was even worse.

Maybe it had something to do with trying to squash everything into a smaller form. I didn't know, but maybe Jack or Henry would.

I pulled off the now useless remnants of my bra and shoved it into my back pocket, then tied the torn edges of my shirt together. I wasn't going anywhere except back to the Directorate once I finished here, so the state of my clothing didn't really matter. Now I just had to get into the apartment.

I walked toward the glass sliding door, and that's when it hit.

The smell of death.

A death that was old and as rotten as hell.

Chapter 3

*I*f the smell was *this* bad out here, I'd hate to think what it was like in the apartment.

Unfortunately, it was my job to find out.

I peered through the glass and tried not to breathe too deeply. The only thing I could see in the small living area was dusty furniture and yellowing newspapers sitting on the coffee table—both indicators that someone hadn't been living in this apartment for quite a while.

So either Alana was no longer living here—and if she wasn't, why had she answered Rosy's phone call yesterday?—or she *was* here, and in a very bad way.

Which I guess went with what the smell was suggesting.

It also suggested that maybe it wasn't Alana who'd dated our dead politician.

I blew out a breath, then gripped the handle of the

sliding door and pulled back with all my might. I had
the strength of both a werewolf and a vampire behind
me, and the little metal clip holding the sliding door
closed didn't stand a chance. The door crashed back
with enough noise to wake the dead, and the force of it
sent a shudder recoiling up my arm.

But it was nothing compared to the smell that assaulted my senses. My stomach rose in a rush and I
gagged. The stench was *vile*.

Whoever—whatever—was dead in this apartment
had been that way for some time. Although the air
rushing out of the apartment was hot—the heating had
obviously been left on high, so maybe that had helped
accelerate the decomposition of whatever it was laying
inside.

I stepped back until I was breathing fresh air again,
then took a deep breath and dashed inside. It was only
ever going to be a quick look. I couldn't hold my breath
longer than a minute or so.

I ran into the first room off the living room. It turned
out to be a spotless kitchen. No junk in the fridge, no
unwashed dishes, no trash in the basket. Nothing that
would account for the smell. The next room was a bathroom, and once again it was spotless.

The third room . . .

That's where I found her, laying half-dressed on the
bed with one arm still in the sleeve of a sweater—as if
whoever had killed her had caught her in the middle of
either taking it off or putting it on. She only wore
panties on the bottom half, and her body was heavy and
bloated and . . . horrible.

Bile burned up my throat, and I raced outside, gulping in fresh air and trying not to vomit. God, unpleasant didn't even begin to describe *that* experience.

It wasn't like I hadn't smelled death before. I had. Hell, I was a wolf, and the wild part of me actually enjoyed rolling in stuff that would make my human half scream in revulsion. But I'd never smelled a death that old before. Or that deep into decay.

I shuddered, then got out my phone and rang Jack.

"Parnell here," he said, voice neutral. The tone he reserved for official speaking moments like press conferences. Given who our dead man was, it was an even-money bet *that* was exactly where he was. "What can I do for you?"

"Jack, it's Riley. I'm over at the apartment of Alana Burns, the woman Gerard James supposedly went out with last night. Only she's dead, and has been that way for at least a week, if the putrefaction is anything to go by."

"Hang on a sec." A muffled conversation came down the phone line, then footsteps. "Okay, we'll have to make this fast. I've got a room full of reporters waiting for an update. What's this about a dead woman?"

"Her name is Alana Burns—if it *is* her body inside the apartment. According to the secretary, Gerard James went out with her last night."

"Or someone pretending to be her."

Exactly. "James's secretary rang Alana to confirm the afternoon of the date. She mentioned Alana being in a snit, so she definitely talked to someone. And it very definitely wasn't the woman dead in the apartment."

"Interesting." He paused, and I heard voices in the background. "Has Cole requested the security tapes?"

"Yes. He was still at Gerard's office when I left, though. I think he's going to be there a while."

"Get another cleanup team out to the apartment, then go talk to the people at Marrberry House. They were running the charity function that Gerard attended last night. And keep me updated. I have the press and the politicians hounding my ass over this one."

"Will do."

I hung up, then dialed the Directorate. A less-than-cheery Sal answered. "What?"

Her voice was flat, and didn't even hold the usual spark of annoyance when she knew it was me calling. Something had obviously gone wrong since the last time I'd talked to her. "If I didn't know you were a vampire, I'd seriously suspect you were PMSing."

"That's because I have to deal with assholes all day. What do you want?"

Okay, that jibe I could fully understand—and hey, I *could* be a pain in the ass when I wanted to be. Just as every other guardian on the books could be. "I need a cleanup team at my current location. I've found a ripe one."

"Charming." In the background came the sound of typing. "Okay, I've dispatched Mel and her team. Should be there in fifteen. Anything else?"

"Can you send me the address of Marrberry House? It hosts charity functions, apparently."

"I know that, moron." She paused. "Sending their details through to your car's onboard now."

I blinked. Sal was usually superefficient, but this was brilliant service, even by her standards. And the bitch in me couldn't resist commenting. "You're horribly professional this evening. Maybe you need to get premenstrual more often."

"I haven't eaten," she said and hung up.

I stared at my phone for a moment, eyebrow raised. Why hadn't Sal eaten? The Directorate kept a supply of synth blood for the vampires in their employ, so there was no reason for her to go hungry. Although maybe she was one of those vamps who preferred their blood fresh, straight from the vein. She definitely seemed the fussy type. I was tempted to ring her back and see what was going on, but it wasn't like we were friends or anything. Talking to me was the last thing she'd probably want.

I shrugged and put the phone away, then leaned on the balustrade again and waited for the cleanup team to arrive. Mel turned out to be a tall, dark-haired woman with a fabulous figure and who wore red stiletto boots underneath her more sensible jeans. A woman after my own heart, obviously.

She strode up the pathway, saw me waiting, and stopped. "Riley Jenson?"

I nodded. "I'm afraid I've a rather ripe one for you. The victim seems to have been dead for at least a week, but the heating has been on full, so that guess could be way off."

"Any obvious signs of death?"

"I didn't get close enough to find out."

She smiled. "A guardian with a weak stomach. Nice to know there is such a beast."

"Now *that* sounded like something Cole would say."

Her smile grew. "He and I went to school together, and I'm best friends with his sister." She looked around as her team—a potbellied man and a woman who was rake thin and almost insect-like—arrived, then added, "You want me to send you a copy of the report as soon as it's done?"

"That would be great. Oh, and the building's front doors are locked. I'll unlock the apartment doors before I leave."

"Marshall will get these doors easy enough. Anything else I need to know?"

"We need the ID ASAP. She may be linked to another case we're investigating."

"We'll make it a priority."

"Thanks."

She nodded and disappeared from my view. I took a deep breath, then dashed inside and unlocked the front door. Then I ran back out, did a one-handed leap over the balcony, and dropped back down to the concrete.

Mel and her team had already gotten inside. Maybe Marshall had been a thief or a locksmith in his pre-Directorate days.

I collected my purse then headed back to the car. The information on Marrberry House had arrived, so I scanned it quickly, gleaning as much information as I could without reading the full thing. It seemed they ran a number of functions over the year, with their major beneficiaries being the Royal Children's Hospital and the Peter MacCallum Cancer Foundation. Last year they'd raised nearly half a million for the two organizations.

I really couldn't see how they could help our investigations, but being the good little guardian that I sometimes was, I drove over and had a chat with the organizer of last night's events.

Turns out I was right—he couldn't help me much. But he did give me a photo they'd been planning to use for publicity purposes—one of Gerard with a striking blonde at his side.

It was hard to say whether she was the woman I'd discovered dead on the bed, because the body had been in such a state of decay, but the height looked the same, as did the blonde hair.

So if it was Alana Burns I'd discovered in the apartment, then who was this? And why would she go to so much trouble to date—and then kill—Gerard James?

Unless Cole picked up something in his investigations, they just might be unanswered questions. Which wouldn't make Jack a happy little vampire at *all*.

I tossed the photo on the seat, then rang Kade to tell him I'd changed my mind and was heading home. I might have promised Ben I'd check what the police files had to say about his friend's murder, but I really wasn't up to doing any more this evening.

I found a parking spot not too far up the street from our apartment building, and hoped like hell the local vandals had gotten tired of their spray-painting binge. Last time I'd brought a Directorate car home, it had ended up green and red. Jack had not been happy.

The night air was cool and surprisingly fresh, free of the usual tint of fumes from the nearby freeway. Maybe the wind had been blowing the other way before it had died earlier this evening, because right now, all I could smell was the faintest hint of humanity, mixed with the sharpness of paint coming from the new pizza parlor they were building a few doors down from our place. If they did a good meat-lovers' pizza, they'd have me and Rhoan practically living on their doorstep.

I pushed open our building's old glass and wood front door, and rattled up the stairs. We lived on the sixth floor, in one of the bigger apartments the old converted warehouse had, and on clear summer days had a view right out over the western suburbs. It would have been nicer if it had been views of parks or even the bay, but we wouldn't have been able to afford the place if it had. Anything remotely resembling a decent view cost big bucks these days—even if the building was as rundown as this one.

I grabbed my door key from my purse and opened the apartment's front door. Then stopped.

There were dark mutterings coming from the direction of my bedroom, and there were clothes strewn *everywhere*. Over the floor, across the old leather couches, patterning the rugs scattered over the wooden flooring, even hanging off the old red-plastic light features.

Neither my brother nor I were the tidiest of people, but the house had definitely been in a better state when I'd left this morning.

I raised my voice and said, "What the hell have you been doing, Rhoan?"

He came stalking out of my bedroom, his face almost as red as his hair and his gray eyes flashing fire. "I'm looking for a shirt."

I looked pointedly at all the shirts strewn across the floor and furniture. "What shirt in particular?"

"The pink one."

"The one you hate?"

"Yes."

"The one you swore you were going to trash only a couple of weeks ago?"

"That would be the one." He stalked across the room and upended a basket of clean laundry onto the coffee table.

"Can I ask why you're looking for this shirt, and only this shirt?"

"Because Liander gave it to me to celebrate our anniversary and I need to wear it tonight."

I frowned. "I thought he gave you a watch for your anniversary?"

"He did. He also gave me an outfit. He wants me to wear it tonight."

"Why?" I stepped inside and closed the door, then dumped my purse and keys on the nearby lamp table.

He gave me an exasperated look. "It's the premiere of the movie, remember?"

Understanding dawned. Rhoan didn't usually attend the premieres of any of the movies Liander had been involved in, simply because he preferred to remain out of the limelight. But this one was important. This one was the first movie in which Liander's company had been totally responsible for *all* the movie's effects. Which

meant Liander had been on tenterhooks for the last
week, hoping and praying that the movie—and his effects—were well received. Which had made dealing
with both him *and* my brother a party.

As the scattered clothes would attest.

I shook my head and walked into Rhoan's bedroom.
Like the living room, it looked as if a cyclone had hit it.
No doubt my bedroom would be the same—though
why he'd think I'd be stealing pink shirts was anyone's
guess. Pink and me were not compatible.

Of course, seeing as we were twins, the shirt didn't
actually suit Rhoan, either, but at least his skin was a bit
more tanned than mine. It helped.

I ignored the open robes and went directly to his ar-
moire, sliding out the bottom drawer. I knew from experience—and my own packing habits—that this was
where all the unwanted clothing usually ended up.

Sure enough, there it was, shoved right at the back,
under the fluorescent pink and lime green socks I'd
given him for his last birthday. I thought he'd adore
them, as he usually loved all things bright. Obviously I
was wrong.

I dragged out the shirt and slammed the drawer
shut. "Would this be the shirt you're looking for?" I
said, holding it up on one finger as I walked out.

"Yes. Thank God." He walked across the room and
grabbed it from me. "Where'd you find it?"

"In the dead clothes drawer."

"Ah." He paused, then added, "I like the socks.
Really."

"About as much as I like those shiny yellow snakeskin shoes you gave me." My voice was dry. "What time is Liander getting here?"

"He said he'd pick me up about seven." He glanced at his watch. "Damn, I'd better move it. You sure you don't want to come along?"

I shook my head. "Zombies, trolls, and whatnot running around creating havoc is not my style." And I got enough bloodshed and havoc in my day job. I didn't need to explore it any further on the big screen. "Give me a nice romantic comedy any day."

He gave me a quick hug. "You're just a girly-girl at heart, aren't you?"

"Takes one to know one, bro."

He snorted. "I am the man of my relationships, thank you very much."

I glanced at my watch. "And if the man doesn't hurry, the wife will beat you up for being late."

"Good point."

He rushed back into his bedroom and I headed into the kitchen to make myself coffee and a toasted sandwich. I wasn't the world's greatest cook, but I could usually manage the basics without burning the place down.

But I'd barely even sat down on the sofa to eat it when my cell phone rang.

"Phone," Rhoan called out helpfully.

"Gee, thanks," I said, barely resisting the urge to throw a cushion his way. I picked it up. "Hello?"

"Riley? It's Ben. I need your help again, and quickly. A friend of mine has just called, and he's in trouble. As in, dead-in-a-few-minutes trouble."

"The cops?"

"He said it was a vamp. The cops won't help."

I blew out a breath, and wondered what the odds were of two of his friends being attacked by vamps. "Give me the address." I picked up a pen and scrawled it down on the overdue electricity bill sitting nearby. "Got it. I'll be there in ten."

By which time, if it was a vampire, his friend might well be dead.

"It'll take me longer, but I've told Ivan I'd be calling you for help. He's expecting you."

If he was still alive, that was. I hung up, picked up my ham and cheese sandwich as well as my badge and car keys, then headed out.

I could smell vampire as soon as I got out of the car. The night air had gone from crisp to cold, and the rotten smell of unwashed vamps seemed to cling thickly to the night.

I pocketed my keys and studied the apartment block as I walked up the pavement. It was one of those high-rise brick and glass affairs that the government had built some fifty years ago in an effort to relieve the low-income housing crisis. Of course, governments tended to work with minimal budgets—except when it came to their own comforts—so the resulting buildings were neither pretty nor truly functional. Add tenants who didn't really give a damn about the place, and you were basically left with a large hovel. One with many smashed windows and doors, and decorated by multi-colored graffiti.

It wasn't the sort of place I expected a friend of Ben's to live.

I walked past the front of the building, heading for the main entrance. The stink of vampire grew stronger, until the cloying, unhealthy smell all but surrounded me, filling every breath and clinging to my clothes.

This wasn't a human low-income building. Not any longer.

Which was unusual. Vampires tended to be solitary souls, and except for those who had newly blooded young to look after, they rarely lived together. Surely the fact that this lot *were* would have come to the attention of the Directorate, but I couldn't remember seeing any mention of a vamp encampment this close to the city. But I guess if the vamps were behaving themselves, they might have avoided Directorate scrutiny.

Footsteps whispered across the night, the sounds so soft regular hearing wouldn't have caught it. They were pacing me, watching. Worse still, the raw taste of their excitement and blood hunger tainted the air.

Young vamps, I thought. Great. I dug out my badge, holding it toward the building as I kept on walking.

"Directorate, folks. Mind your own business, or there's going to be a heap of trouble."

I didn't bother raising my voice. They were close enough that they'd hear me, even though I couldn't see them through normal vision. And I didn't *want* to see them through infrared. Just knowing how many there were might get a little scary.

The blood hunger abated a little, but I had to wonder what had them so worked up. If they were old enough to control their hunger, then why had the sight of me caused it to rise so sharply?

I could only think of one thing that would cause such a reaction—blood. The scent of fresh blood was a call few vampires could ignore, and with the young it stirred the blood hunger to life, making them react hungrily to even the slightest beat of life.

And yet the night seemed free of that scent. Or was the aroma of vampire overwhelming everything else?

I didn't know, but I had a suspicion I'd soon find out. And if Ben's friend was a wolf and living with this lot, then he was a braver soul than me.

The vamps were still following me, and my skin crawled with the sensation. I breathed through my mouth, and pretended to ignore them. Though, being vamps, they'd hear my accelerated pulse rate. I was just hoping they'd take it as readiness for action, not for any sort of fear.

Of course, if they decided to attack en masse, I was one dead puppy no matter what. I might have a vampire's strength and speed, but I'd still be one against dozens. Not great odds, in anyone's book.

I loped up the steps and through the smashed glass front doors. The yellow light of a solitary bulb broke across the darkness, making the corner shadows seem even deeper. Thankfully, there were no vamps in those shadows. Not yet.

The building had two elevators, but neither of them seemed to be working—one was sitting on the fifth floor with the floor light flashing, and the other had no numbers lit at all. I hesitated, switching to infrared before looking down the left, then the right, corridors. As I suspected, it was pretty scary. There had to be at least twenty vamps crowded against the walls, their eyes glinting brightly and their sharp canines prominently exposed.

I still couldn't smell blood, but a vampire's sense for life's nectar was far sharper than mine. And it was obviously still calling to them.

This would not be a pleasant place to be if things got out of control.

I flicked the small stud in my ear, turning on the two-way com-link—which had been inserted when I'd been going into a madman's lair, but was now standard equipment for all guardians. Jack didn't like losing his people, and the com-links also doubled as trackers.

The vamps melted back into the deeper shadows as I headed for the stairs, so hopefully that was a sign they didn't want any trouble.

But I wasn't about to take a chance on that.

"Hello, anyone listening?" I said softly.

"What now, wolf girl?" Sal's tone seemed even sharper than normal, coming though the tinny confines of the com-link.

"What, are you pulling a double shift or something?"

I ran up the stairs as I spoke, heading for the fourth floor. Thankfully, the vamps didn't follow, though the scent of them didn't lessen any. Meaning there were plenty more ahead.

"Yes," Sal snapped. "I am. Now what do you want?"

I used to get awfully bitchy when I had to sit double shifts, too. Combine that with hunger, and it definitely explained her attitude. "I'm investigating a possible vampire attack at my current location. We got anyone in the area, in case I need backup?"

"What, teacher's pet needing backup?" She sounded positively cheerful at the thought. "I think you've just made my night."

"I'm so glad." Not. "What have you got on this apartment block?"

Keys tapped, then she said, "Not a lot. It's an old government housing development that has been listed for demolition for the last ten years. It's become a squat for itinerants and the homeless, apparently."

"Well, it's now the home of a rather large vampire community. A youngish one, too."

"Impossible. Vampires don't pack like you wolves do."

"Well, tell that to the vamps here."

She grunted. "There's nothing in the files here about it."

"Then you'd better make a note and let Jack know. He may want to investigate."

"It's noted. Talvin's nearby if you need him."

"Thanks. I'll yell if I do."

"Don't yell too late, wolf girl. Talvin doesn't appreciate picking up the bits."

"Well, I don't appreciate *being* bits."

I slowed as I neared the fourth floor landing. The unwashed scent still clung to the air, and my infrared sight picked out several vamps hovering down the right-hand corridor, the heat of their bodies standing out sharply against the surrounding darkness. I looked left. No vamps.

Fortunately, Ben's friend lived in apartment 41 which, according to the signage on the walls, was the very last one on the left. My boot heels clicked sharply against the threadbare carpeting, the sound echoing across the thick air, as steady as a heartbeat. Just not my heartbeat.

The closer I got to apartment 41, the more tense I became. The soft scent of blood was now beginning to perfume the air, but there didn't seem to be any unusual noises coming from the apartment. No sounds of fighting, nothing to indicate anything was out of order.

Maybe Ben's friend had simply gotten a little paranoid about living amongst all these vampires. Or maybe he'd cut himself shaving and had panicked about the consequences.

I stopped when I reached the door, then flexed my fingers and raised a hand to knock.

That's when I heard it. A soft, hair-on-the-back-of-the-neck-raising moan.

The sort of moan that came from the dying.

I stepped back, raised a foot, and kicked the door open. It smashed back against the wall, sending dust and plaster flying. The thick smell of wrongness and vampire rushed out, overwhelming my senses and making me want to gag. Or maybe that was a reaction to the sight before me.

A naked man hung from a ceiling rafter—not from

his neck but from rope around his wrists. Rope as bloody as his shredded back and butt.

The man causing all the damage was the source of both the vampire scent and the wrongness. And his scent was one I recognized.

"I told you—" he began, as he swung around, then stopped. His expression changed from one of annoyance to surprise, then, without the barest flicker in his bloodshot brown eyes to warn me, he turned and bolted for a doorway at the rear of the living room.

I sprinted after him, the smell of blood, sweat, and fear heavy in my nostrils as I ran past the naked man. The wrong-smelling vamp had disappeared into what looked like a bedroom.

I ran into the room just in time to see him leap for the window. Glass shattered, spraying outward into the night as he plunged through and down.

The drop wouldn't kill a vamp. It might damage him, but vamps were a resilient lot. Unfortunately, in this case.

I cursed and spun around. I might be able to take a seagull's shape, but hitting the ground from the height of a fourth floor window would be a hell of a lot harder than hitting it from the top branches of a tree. And while I had flown briefly—and successfully—today, I didn't feel like putting my life on the line to test out my new-found skills. As I ran past the bloodied and still-bound Ivan, I said, "He's running. I'll be back in a minute."

"Wait," he said, voice hoarse. "Wait—"

I didn't. The vamps out in the corridor had drawn closer, perhaps lured by the sharper scent of blood.

"Touch him and you all pay the price!" I dragged my badge out of my pocket again, and thrust it in front of me. I didn't know if it would actually help, and I couldn't afford to hang around and find out. Not if I wanted to stop the vamp.

Because a vamp willing to go to such extremes of torture before tasting his victim's blood was a vamp who would *not* stop at just one victim.

Once upon a time, I might have taken care of the living before chasing after the dead, but I'd learned the hard way that such actions generally only resulted in more deaths—and I had enough of those on my conscience right now.

I just had to hope the vamps in this building feared the Directorate more than they wanted to taste Ivan's blood.

I pounded down the stairs and out the shattered glass doors. Even against the thick reek of vampire that clung to the night, the odd scent of my quarry was easy enough to pick up. I raced across the barren ground of what once might have been a playground, and out onto the street. The vamp was nowhere to be seen, but his scent pulled me on.

"Sal, the vamp is on the run." Headlights swept across the darkness, tearing away the shadows. The vamp became briefly visible—stringy hair flying, his legs almost a blur, arms pumping. "He's about half a block ahead of me. If Talvin's near, can you call him in as backup?"

"Will do."

The car moved past, the headlights sweeping onto

me. I threw up a hand to protect my eyes and kept on running. I was getting closer. Slowly but surely.

He swung right into a side street. I reached for more speed, not wanting him out of my sight for long, and felt the twinge of protest in my bruised and battered leg muscles.

I ran into the side street. The rich smell of barbequing meat filled the night, making my mouth water. The vampire was nowhere to be seen, but his lingering scent suggested he'd crossed the road and wasn't that far ahead. I flicked to infrared, and realized the strength of the scent was misleading. His body was a fading blur up ahead. Fuck, he was fast.

I upped my own speed again, and the twinges in my legs became outright pain. I ignored them and ran on.

The vamp swung left into another side street. It was almost thirty seconds later before I skidded around the corner. Who'd have thought a vampire with such skinny little legs could have so much sustained speed?

Under the glow of infrared, the street was empty of life. I frowned, looking left and right, seeing the glimpses of life in the houses along either side of the street, but nothing that indicated my would-be murderous vampire was anywhere near.

I couldn't have just *lost* him. No vampire could move *that* fast.

Yet his scent was not only fading fast, but dispersing in all directions. As if he'd stopped, and something had scattered the smell of him.

I looked upward. No vampire in the nearby trees, no unusual shape in the sky. Not that vampires could actually fly—not unless they'd been a bird-shifter in life, anyway.

Though with the sheer wrongness of his scent overwhelming everything else, it *was* possible for me to have missed the scent of shifter on him.

But if he was a bird-shifter, why hadn't he flown away when he'd jumped out the window? He could have gotten away much easier and cleaner.

Unless his intention all along had been to drag me far enough away so he could go back and finish what he'd started?

"Sal," I said, as I turned and ran back as fast as my aching legs would allow. "My target has flown the coop and I've lost him."

"Well, shit, Riley, that's slack."

No doubting that. "He's five ten, gaunt build, with brown eyes and stringy hair. Can you put out a bulletin? I've got a bleeder in an apartment block of vamps to attend to. Send an ambulance ASAP."

"What about Talvin?"

"Can you ask him to patrol the building's grounds? Just in case our rogue decides to return?"

"Will do."

The graffiti-strewn building felt no safer going in the second time than it had the first. The vamps still hovered, their hunger stinging the air.

At least there was no sense of a feeding frenzy. No overwhelming aroma of blood filling the air.

I pounded back up the stairs, wondering if I was even going to be able to walk tomorrow after everything my poor muscles had been through today.

The vamps on the fourth floor had stayed back, as ordered. I slowed as I neared the end apartment again, my breathing short, sharp gasps that filled the air. I raised an arm to swipe at the sweat trickling down my cheeks and entered the apartment.

Ben's bloodied friend still hung by his wrists, and the odd-smelling vampire was nowhere nearby. Relief filtered through me. For once, fate hadn't chucked me a curveball.

"Please," he croaked, "get me down."

"There's a knife in the kitchen?"

He shook his head, sending droplets of blood flying from the cut on his cheek. "Not strong enough. Bedroom."

I raised an eyebrow, though given his living arrangements, I guess it wasn't such a bad idea. Personally, I'd be keeping a few handy stakes within reaching distance, too.

I found several large hunting knives in the bedside table, along with several smaller throwing knives. I picked the biggest and headed back out.

To find we were no longer alone.

"Fuck," Ben said, his expression both shocked and angry as he stopped just inside the doorway. "I didn't expect this."

"No," I agreed. I waved the knife in the direction of his friend. "You want to support his weight while I cut him down?"

He moved forward quickly, his big arms going around the waist of his smaller friend and taking the weight off Ivan's torn and bloody wrists.

Ivan groaned, though I wasn't sure whether it was in relief or pain. I dragged a kitchen chair up to them both and climbed up.

"There's an ambulance coming. It should only be a few minutes."

"Good," Ben muttered. "But what about the vamp who did this?"

"Lost him."

"Shit."

"Putting it politely, yes."

I raised the knife and began to cut. The blade was razor sharp, and sliced through the thickly twined layers of rope with little effort. Ivan didn't say anything, and his gaze seemed a little unfocused. Maybe shock was starting to set in, either through blood loss or the sheer trauma of what he'd been through. His body had been shredded front and back, the rents jagged and uneven. No knife had caused them, that's for sure.

The last of the rope strands gave way. Ben carried his friend over to the ratty-looking sofa and gently put him down. Ivan hissed, his expression contorting with pain.

"Sorry, mate," Ben said, then looked at me. "You think he's going into shock?"

"Yeah." I glanced at my watch. "The ambulance shouldn't be far, but maybe we should give him some water to sip. If it's the blood loss causing the shock, we need to replace some of his fluids."

"I'll go get some." He rose and walked past me, smelling of blood and anger.

I knelt down in front of Ivan. He didn't react, so I touched his swollen fingers. He jumped, and his gaze swung to mine, momentarily filled with fear before he realized who it was and that he was still safe.

"I need to know what happened," I said softly.

He licked his lips and swallowed heavily. "He came in about an hour ago. Said he needed to talk."

"So you know him?"

He shook his head. "But he looked vaguely familiar, and Vinny had cleared him, so I thought he'd be fine."

I frowned. "Who's Vinny?"

"The head of the vampire group living here," Ben said, as he came back into the room. He squatted down beside me, the heat of him rolling over me, thick with the scent of barely controlled anger. He dribbled some water onto Ivan's lips, then looked at me. "Ivan's undergone the blood ceremony to become a vampire, which is why he's living here with Vinny and the vamps."

Confusion swirled through me. "Taking the ceremony doesn't mean he's going to die straightaway. Not unless he intends suicide."

And I very much doubt that had been his intent here. He wouldn't have called Ben for help, if that were the case.

"He's got cancer. Inoperable. He's been given a year to live, at most."

"Ah." At least that explained his living arrangements. It made sense to be close to his maker if he went sooner than expected. I glanced at Ivan. "So Vinny might know who the vampire is?"

He closed his eyes, took a shuddery breath, then whispered, "I don't know. But there was no intervention."

And *that* was the cruncher.

The majority of vamps tended to be protective of their young—or soon to be young—at least until they were old enough to control the bloodlust and know the tricks of the trade, so to speak. They had to be, because the Directorate held them accountable for their young's actions. It was only once they had a handle on being a vampire that the young were let loose into the big wide world. Vampires tended to be territorial, and two fully grown vamps generally couldn't live together. Which made what was going on here a whole lot stranger. They simply couldn't be all young ones. No vampire alive could control *this* many young.

Or so I'd thought.

Ben gave Ivan a few more drops of water. I waited until he'd swallowed, then asked, "Why did you invite him over the threshold if you didn't know him?"

"Because he went through Vinny. I thought he was okay."

Seems Vinny had a few answers to provide. And maybe it was Vinny, rather than my badge, that had kept the younger vamps at bay. Which meant, given the number of vampires living in this old building, he had to be fairly powerful.

But it was interesting that our rogue vamp had known enough about this building and its occupants to go through the protocol. Unlike me, who'd just charged in.

Of course, that's what us guardians were supposed to do. Charge into places the dead feared to tread. Lucky us.

"Has Vinny got a last name?"

"Castillo."

Hopefully, Sal hadn't become bored by proceedings and was now doing a check to see what we had on one Vincent Castillo.

"Did your attacker say what he wanted to talk about?"

"No, he just started attacking, telling me he'd make me pay for hurting him."

I raised my eyebrows. "So you do know him?"

"No. He was fucking crazy. I've never seen him before in my life, I swear."

I could sense no lie in his words, but that didn't mean there wasn't. I mean, why would a vamp go to so much trouble to get in here just to attack a complete stranger?

"So if he attacked you straightaway, when did you get the chance to call Ben?"

He closed his eyes. "I didn't."

I looked at Ben, who said, "Maybe the shock and blood loss is affecting his memory."

Maybe. And maybe he was telling the truth and something strange was going on.

Footsteps echoed down the hall, and as I looked toward the doorway, a voice said, "Ambulance officers. Who needs the help?"

"Down here," I shouted.

The footsteps drew closer, and a second later two men appeared. "Well, that was a hairy experience," the first man said. "Never been in a place where so many vamps haunted the shadows." He glanced at Ivan, and clicked his tongue. "The vamps do this?"

"No. They just didn't stop it."

"Vamps tend to be like that," he said philosophically. "It's all about their needs, not others'."

And that, I thought, as I rose to get out of his way, was the best summation I'd heard of vamps for quite a while.

I followed Ben across the living room. He crossed his bare arms, his blue T-shirt straining across his chest as he leaned a shoulder against the wall. He must have left the bike leathers at home in his haste to get here, but the T and the jeans were a damn fine look.

I tried to concentrate on the business at hand. "Does Ivan work at Nonpareil as well?"

Ben shook his head. In the bright living room light, his blue eyes looked almost sapphire with the anger that still overwhelmed his scent. "He's an investment advisor."

"Then how did you two meet?"

"We go to the same gym, and became friends a few years ago." He hesitated. "Why?"

"Because I think it's odd that two people you know have now been attacked in an identical way."

He frowned. "Why would either of the attacks be related, let alone related to me?"

"Well, you'd have to tell me. Why would someone want to get back at you by attacking your friends? Because one thing I'm sure of is the fact that they're related."

His frown deepened. "Impossible. I mean, Ivan and Denny didn't even know each other. And why do you think it was the same killer going after them both?"

"Because I recognized the vampire's scent. The vampire who was in Denny's bedroom—and who might well have killed him—is the same vampire responsible for stringing Ivan up by his wrists and slicing him open."

Chapter 4

*H*e stared at me for a moment, his expression neutral. But his blue eyes were even darker than before, and the sense of his anger increased. This time, it was aimed at me.

"Are you sure?" he said eventually, and the effort of control was evident in the burly, thick notes invading his rich tones.

"Yes."

"Then why in the hell did you let him go?" He said it with such force that it blew the sweaty strands of hair away from my face and had the ambulance guys looking around sharply.

I waved a hand to tell them it was okay, and met Ben's anger head-on. "Because he was a fucking vampire who jumped out the window and then probably flew away. I'm many things, Ben, but I haven't quite learned to fly yet."

He looked at me for a moment, then took a deep breath and released it slowly. "Sorry. You're doing me a favor by even being here, and I shouldn't be taking my frustration out on you."

I smiled and touched his arm lightly. Warmth tingled though my fingers—a reaction not so much to the heat of his skin, but to simple contact. I might have denied my need for it over these past few months—well, as much as any wolf could—but the hunger would always be there.

And I was beginning to doubt whether it could be restrained for much longer.

"It's okay. I'm well acquainted with the need to lash out when people you care about are hurt." Hell, I'd done it myself often enough.

Amusement crinkled the corners of his eyes. "I don't care about them *that* way, if that's what you're implying. They were just good friends—people I could trust—and that's rare in this cynical world of ours."

"True." I let my hand drop from his arm, but my fingers still tingled from the contact. I resisted the urge to clench them in an effort to retain the sensation for that little bit longer. My hormones didn't need that sort of encouragement. "I think my next call of duty should be our local vampire master. Are you going to accompany Ivan to the hospital?"

"I'd better, at least until his family get there."

"Keep me updated, then."

"I will." He touched my cheek lightly, briefly. "See you tomorrow."

"You will." I stepped away from the lure of his closeness, then turned and walked out the door. Once back in the darkness of the corridor, I said softly, "Hey, Sal, you got any information on one Vincent Castillo?"

"No details on either a Vinny or Vincent Castillo. If he's the head of that little shindig over there, he's kept himself under our radar."

Which wasn't to say that Jack didn't know about him, just that there was nothing on record. "You want to ask the boss about it when you see him?"

"He's not coming back in until tomorrow, but I'll leave a note."

"Thanks, Sal."

"Don't thank me, wolf girl. Thank the gods I'm feeling helpful right now."

I grinned. No doubt she'd be her regular snarky self tomorrow, but that was okay. I don't think I could handle too much of the super-efficient, super-pleasant Salliane.

I touched the com-link lightly, switching off voice but not tracking. It was doubtful the vampires would attack us now—if for no other reason than the fact they'd draw too much attention from the Directorate.

The vampires at the other end of the corridor still hadn't moved. I strode toward them, noting for the first time the fact that all five seemed to have been turned around the same age. They all had that lanky, almost awkward look boys seemed to get in their late teens. They were all blonds, too.

I stopped in front of them and tried not to breathe too deeply. "I need to speak to Vinny Castillo."

They glanced at each other, then one said, "Top floor. You're expected."

"Great." Though I wasn't sure it was.

I headed for the stairs and began to climb. The unwashed scent of vampire began to fade the farther I went up, so that by the time I reached the eighth floor, it had all but disappeared. In its place was a mix of blossom and pine that reminded me of springtime and made my nose twitch with the need to sneeze.

I stopped on the landing and looked around. Darkness haunted the corridor to the left, but the right was lit by a series of red candles in stylized, rose-shaped sconces. The flickering light danced warmly across the graffiti-strewn walls, and gave the hallway an oddly forbidding feel. Given that Ivan still had power in his apartment, the candles were obviously for effect rather than a necessity.

At the far end of the corridor, a woman waited. Like the vampires on the floors below, she was young and gangly. But unlike them, her blonde hair had been recently washed, and shone like pale gold in the flickering candlelight.

Two things were obvious—Vinny liked them young and blonde, and it didn't seem to matter whether they were boys or girls.

I lowered a shield and reached out carefully, feeling psychically for those in the room beyond. I might as well have been trying to source out a big black hole. It didn't feel like there were psychic deadeners involved, nor did it feel like any kind of natural psychic wall I'd ever encountered. It was just a hole. Or maybe it was more like a black star, because it seemed to suck away any sort of mental resonance.

Even the kid at the door wasn't showing up on my psychic radar, though she didn't look like an old enough vamp to block even a weak telepath.

Weird.

I strode toward the guard. Little emotion showed on her pale face or in her dark eyes, but her wariness stung the air. She was dressed casually—jeans, sneakers, and a pale pink tank top—but there was a suspicious-looking bulge on her right side. I wondered if the bullets were the regular kind, or if they'd just happened to have some silver ones hanging about.

"I'm Riley Jenson." I stopped just in front of her and dragged out my badge. "I'd like to speak to Vinny Castillo, please."

Something flickered through her eyes. Amusement, perhaps. "You're expected."

She opened the door, revealing a plush room that was nothing like the rest of the building. The graffiti was nowhere to be seen here. Instead, the walls were covered by thick velvet drapes in a dark, dramatic red. The carpet was thick and lush, and the color of rich sand. And there were chandeliers, for heaven's sake— two big ones that sent rainbow-colored sprays of light scattering amongst the shadows. The rest of his gang might live in squalor, but old Vinny was living it up like a king.

I stepped inside. Saw the thickly stuffed black

leather chairs and sensuous-looking chaise sofas before my gaze was drawn to the small circle of people at the far end of the room.

Half a dozen toga-clad boys and girls—I refused to call them anything else, because not one of them looked to be older than seventeen—stood around a mahogany and leather chaise lounge. Draped over it was a woman.

A woman who reeked of power and sensuality.

I stopped. I couldn't help it. The force of this woman was unlike anything I'd ever come across. I knew vampires who were either close to, or older than, a thousand years, and neither of them had the immediate impact this woman had. And yet I doubted whether she was anywhere *near* their age.

Hell, I'd put money on the fact that she hadn't even reached triple figures yet—if only because a vampire with any sort of years behind them would surely be able to afford better accommodation for themselves and their get.

She wasn't anything stunning to look at. I guess she could be classed as average—not pretty, not ugly, just normal. A medium-height, medium-built woman with dark brown hair and chocolate-colored eyes.

But in her case, looks didn't matter. Her power lay in her essence. In her very nature.

Werewolves had auras that were totally capable of seducing anyone, willing or unwilling. We weren't allowed to use it on any other race but our own, of course, but that didn't mean it didn't occasionally happen. The energy she was putting out was similar to a werewolf's aura. It was all heat and need and desire, and it spun around me sensually, making my pulse race. My body hunger.

The desire to run forward, to caress her pale skin as the others caressed it—lightly, reverently—hit like a wrecking ball. Sweat began to dot my skin, and the thirst to touch her, kiss her, make love to her, was so strong that I took a step forward.

But it wasn't *my* desire, wasn't real, and I wasn't about to become some young vamp's plaything. Especially not a young *female* vamp's plaything. So I clenched my fists, digging my fingernails into my skin, using pain to overwhelm desire. In any other situation, I would have thrown up my own aura to battle hers— but I was standing in the middle of a den of vampires, and that might cause a whole lot more problems.

"Stop it," I said, voice sharp, "or I'll get the Directorate to do a sweep and clean out this whole damn place."

She laughed, a sound as rich and as warm as the room, and the swirling heat of desire abated. Not completely, but enough that it was ignorable. "I have no wish to antagonize the Directorate. Please, step forward, so that I can see you better."

I felt like saying that, as a vamp, she should be able to see me perfectly fine just where I was, but that could have been seen as churlish. Which I certainly could be on more than a few occasions, but I had a feeling that this was one of those times when it was better to play along.

At least until I got the feel of things.

I walked forward. The scent of blossom and springtime got stronger, mixing warmly with the heavy scent of desire still stirring the air. The toga-clad teenagers watched me with almost languorous expressions, but their pupils were extremely dilated. I would have guessed they were high on something, except for the fact that they were extremely still.

My gaze went to the woman. Maybe the only drug they needed was closeness to their maker. Maybe touching her was akin to a sexual or drug high. Just because I'd never heard of a vampire capable of getting someone off on the merest contact didn't mean they weren't out there. And hell, this woman had made *me* want her. If skin to skin contact with her was as powerful as her aura, then their expressions were understandable.

I stopped when there was still a good ten feet between us. This close, her skin looked almost luminous, as if the richness of the moon itself glowed from deep within her . . . and I blinked. Reapplied my nails to the palm of my hand. Saw that her pale skin was just that. Pale skin. Nothing luminous and beautiful about it at all.

Anger swirled through me. As a werewolf, I'd been taught restraint almost from the beginning. Oh, not sexual restraint, because to a werewolf, sex was life. But the aura was a different matter. From the time I'd been a pup, long before my aura had even begun to develop, we'd learned that it was wrong to force another—both morally and legally. The fact that a werewolf's aura could make the unwilling willing *didn't* make it okay, because the end result was the same—you were forcing an action on someone they might not have taken otherwise.

Of course, I *had* done it, as a guardian, just to gain

some advantage over a foe. But I'd never done it to force sex on someone otherwise.

This woman had been taught no such restraint.

"I did warn you to stop it." I turned on my heel and walked toward the door.

She laughed again, a sound that shivered warmly up my spine. "Please, I'll behave. You have questions about Ivan Lang, no?"

I turned around again. "Yes."

"Then I will answer them. But please, come closer. I had a degenerative eye disease before I was turned and, as a result, my eyesight is not good."

I studied her for a moment, seeing no lie in her brown eyes, and not sure if I would even if she were. "What is your real name?"

"Vincenta Castillo. Please, I assure you I will not play games with you again. Come closer."

I hesitated, then did. Odd to think that this woman had me wanting to run, and yet I'd faced things a thousand times stronger, and far more dangerous. Hell, I had a permanent reminder of one such encounter on my left hand, which was now missing a pinky finger thanks to the hunger of a death god.

She smiled. It was just an ordinary smile, which meant she was keeping her word. For the moment, at least.

"If Ivan has taken the ceremony to become a vampire, why didn't you protect him?"

"Because I was paid not to interfere in any way."

Surprise ran through me. "You took money over protecting your get?"

"Why wouldn't I? Look around you, guardian. These premises are more suitable for street scum than an upwardly mobile vampire. But I am young in vampire terms, and therefore have not yet accumulated the sort of money I require."

Meaning she was earning her cash legally? Somehow, I doubted it. A vamp with the sort of seduction skills she had could entice all manner of things out of her bed partners.

"So you were just going to sit back and let a rogue vamp kill Ivan?"

She gave an unladylike snort. The toga-clad kid nearest her shoulder trailed his fingers up her neck and across her cheek, in what I supposed was a soothing gesture. "He's not dead, is he?"

"Which comes down to luck as much as timely intervention on my part."

She smiled. It was both amused and calculated, and warned that there was a sharp mind behind all the sexual playfulness. "Ah, but your timely intervention wouldn't have happened had we not made a phone call."

I raised an eyebrow. "I thought you'd been paid not to intervene?"

"The operative word being 'me.' While he asked that I keep my fledglings back and control their hunger, he made no mention of them interfering with proceedings in other ways. So one made the call."

"One who sounded like Ivan himself?"

She nodded. "We knew about the stripper. He has been here several times to visit Ivan. He is a big man, a strong man. His presence might have been enough to scare off the rogue."

It might *not* have been, too. While Ben was a big werewolf, the rogue was a vamp, and vamps would win over regular weres each and every time. It wasn't just strength, it was speed.

"So did the rogue say why he wanted to slice and dice Ivan?"

She shrugged. "I tasted the need for revenge on him. More than that, I don't know."

"So you didn't ask?"

"It was a large amount of money. Not asking questions was part of the deal."

So was not offering Ivan help in any way, but she'd gotten around that little clause just fine.

"Why did you perform the ceremony with Ivan?" My gaze went briefly to the toga-clad teenagers behind her. "He's nothing like the rest of your get."

"As much as I love my toys, a vampire cannot exist on them alone. Ivan is a very good investment advisor. That will be useful in the future."

"If he's such a good investment advisor, why is he living here?"

She smiled again. Deep in her brown eyes, hunger flickered. Not blood hunger, but rather a hunger for money. Or power, which often came hand in hand with money in this wealth oriented world of ours. She might not be a force in the vampire world just yet, but she certainly intended to be. And I had a feeling she wouldn't particularly care how she went about it.

But couldn't that be said of all vampires? Most of

them couldn't ever be classed as the caring, sharing types.

"Simple," she answered. "He tithed me his apartment in Brighton as payment for the ceremony. He has enough money to live elsewhere, of course, but he remains close because his death is imminent. His choice, not mine."

"So if you hate this place so much, why not move into his apartment?"

She raised dark eyebrows. "It's a simple matter of logistics. We are forty strong here, and that number simply will not fit into a two bedroom apartment, no matter how luxurious."

"Isn't that a large number of vampires to have living together? And whatever happened to that whole 'vampires are territorial creatures and don't share' line I keep hearing?"

She smiled again. "Blood vampires are territorial. We are not of a bloodline. For us, the bigger the community, the better. Community nourishes us."

"So those who haunt the downstairs rooms are fed by the goings-on up here?"

"Something like that."

"So it wasn't the bloodshed that was stirring their hunger, but rather the emotions being broadcast?"

"Yes."

She shifted, placing her feet on the floor and sitting up straight. The teenagers behind her gathered together, so that their bodies were pressed tightly against each other. The contact sent an odd sort of humming flaring across the air. It didn't feel like the aura of their master, and yet it possessed a similar sense of power. Although maybe it didn't feel the same because it wasn't actually aimed at me. Maybe it *would* seem similar if it had been.

Either way, goose bumps skittered across my skin. I had a feeling that I wouldn't want to be here when feedings were happening.

But as much as I wanted to just get the hell away from this place as fast as I could, there was still a question that needed to be asked.

"Did the rogue vampire happen to mention his name?"

She smiled again. "I was wondering when you'd get around to asking that."

"Meaning yes, he did?"

"Of course. No one gets through my door without me first knowing their name."

"Then would you mind telling me it?"

Amusement played about her lips. "What are you going to offer in exchange?"

I looked at her for a moment, then said, "How about I not call the Directorate on you?"

"You've already reported our presence. There's another guardian patrolling outside, isn't there?"

"He's there to catch Ivan's attacker, should he decide to come back."

She waved a hand. "But the Directorate will come to investigate us regardless."

"They will. But investigating is not cleaning out."

"You would not ask them to go that far. You are not the type."

I raised an eyebrow. "Lady, you have no idea what type I am."

"I can taste it in the air, little wolf." She considered me a moment, then smiled. "You are honorable, in your own way. And at the moment, you are also very wary of what you sense in this room."

Mainly because what I sensed in this room was nothing like anything I'd come across before. "I can't pay you."

"I'm not asking for money."

"Then what are you asking for?"

"A kiss. Just a simple kiss."

There was nothing simple about a kiss. Not when it involved *this* vampire. "Why?"

"Because I want to taste you."

"I thought you weren't a blood vampire."

She rose from the sofa, her long skirt billowing briefly around her in cloud-like wisps of bloodred organza. Surprisingly, she was my height and build. She'd seemed so much smaller and daintier on the chaise lounge—another carefully placed illusion, no doubt.

"I am not a blood vampire," she said softly. "And I give nothing for free. If you wish the name, guardian, you pay with a kiss."

I stared at her, wishing I could read her mind. Wishing I knew her motives. Wishing I understood why the whole kissing deal filled me with such indecision. Hell, if it were a man asking the payment, I'd be doing it in a second.

So was it just the thought of kissing a female that was making me hesitate? Or was it more to do with the fact that I didn't know what she really was, or what she could do?

I'd love to say it was the latter rather than the former, but the truth was, I couldn't.

I didn't *want* to kiss another woman. It was as simple as that.

But I was a guardian, and sometimes guardians had to do things they really didn't want to do. Especially if lives were on the line.

I took a deep breath and blew it out slowly. "No feeding, no aura—or whatever that sexual heat thing of yours is. If I sense any of it, I'll shoot the fucking lot of you."

She smiled. "I think you mean that."

I think I did, too. I flexed my fingers, feeling the dampness on my palms and not liking it. "And no tongue," I added. "I'll bite it if I feel it."

She laughed, a warm merry sound that had lips twitching. Mine included. And *that* only made my wariness and need not to do this even stronger.

"One would think you've never kissed a woman before."

"I haven't."

She raised an elegant eyebrow. "What, not even as a friendly gesture of hello?"

I could've pointed out that I wasn't the social, friendly type, but I wasn't about to give her that much information. "Let's just get this over with."

"As you wish."

She stepped closer. My nostrils flared, sucking in her scent, tasting flowers and springtime and something else, something I couldn't quite define. Something that felt dangerous and exciting all at the same time.

She stopped so close that her wispy gown swirled around my legs, encasing them in a sea of red. I clenched my fingers, fighting the desire to step back, to escape the heat and feel of her, and watched her face. Watching the anticipation in her brown eyes grow as she drew closer.

Then her lips brushed mine. Tentatively, gently. They were surprisingly cool and soft, and not unpleasant, however much I wanted them to be. I didn't react, holding myself still, not wanting to prolong the contact.

She opened her eyes, stared deep into mine. "A kiss takes two people, guardian. React, or the payment will not be accepted."

Her lips touched mine again, and after a moment of hesitation, I moved into them, kissing her gently but thoroughly. It was a strange kiss, a passionless kiss, and yet it was a kiss that had my nerves tingling and pulse racing. It wasn't desire. It was fear of the unknown.

I had a bad, bad feeling that more than just lip-tasting was going on.

I pulled away, felt the coolness of the room caress my skin, washing away the heat of her. She smiled, and flicked her skirts away from my legs. "You do not taste like a wolf, guardian."

"You got your kiss, vampire. I want my name."

She considered me for a moment, then said, "Aron Young."

"Got that," Sal said into my ear. "Instigating search."

"Thank you," I said, more to Sal than Vinny. I

stepped back again, relishing the distance each step was giving me. "If he happens to return, Vincenta, please call the Directorate straightaway."

"I will. I'd hate to have the force of the mighty Directorate brought down on me." Her voice gently mocked. "I will see you again, guardian."

No, you fucking won't, I thought, and got the hell out of there.

*R*hoan still hadn't arrived back home when I woke the following morning. I picked up the storm of clothes that were still scattered everywhere, dumping them all back into their various baskets, then made myself a coffee and some breakfast and turned on the TV to see if I could catch a glimpse of him and Liander on the entertainment channels.

I didn't, but they walked in the door about ten minutes later, arms around each other, both of them half undressed and looking more than a little worse for the wear.

"You two," I said, around a mouthful of cereal, "look like shit."

Liander waved a hand and gave me a silly grin. "But we're feeling *fine*."

He tripped over the end of the rug as he said it, and would have fallen flat on his face if Rhoan hadn't hauled him upright. Though *that* effort caused the two of them to stagger sideways, missing the coat stand by the merest of inches. I snorted. Drunk as skunks, the pair of them.

I dumped my cereal on the coffee table, then got up and walked to the kitchen to flick on the kettle. "I gather last night went well?"

"Very. The effects are a hit."

Leather groaned as the two of them fell more than sat on the sofa.

"What about the movie itself?"

"You know what the movie business is like. Some will rave, some will tear it apart, some will equivocate." Liander waved a hand about airily, then leaned into Rhoan's arm. "The effects looked gorgeous, and that's all I was worried about."

Rhoan gave him a hug, then looked at me. "So, how did you fill in the evening while we were out partying?"

Of the two of them, he looked slightly less pickled. Though at least both of them could talk without slurring their sentences. I leaned a shoulder against the doorframe and smiled. "I went out and kissed a girl."

They both blinked owlishly at me for a moment, then Rhoan said, "What?"

I didn't answer straightaway, making them coffee first, then sitting back down and reclaiming my breakfast. "The girl was a vamp who wasn't a bloodsucker, and I kissed her to get the name of a rogue who was beating up an accountant."

"So what was it like?" Liander asked. "Kissing a girl, I mean?"

"Not in the least bit arousing." Which was the truth, and yet not the *whole* truth. I picked up my coffee and took a sip. The fact was, the caress of her lips had haunted a good part of my dreams, but the cause was trepidation rather than desire. Even my dreams had been filled with the certainty that something more than lip-locking had happened.

Rhoan untangled himself from Liander and leaned forward. "Why would you kiss a vamp to get information? Why didn't you just read her mind or beat it out of her?"

I waved my spoon at him. "It's not polite to run around beating up women."

"It is when they're vamps who could beat the shit out of most normal people."

"We're not normal people." We weren't even normal in the nonhuman sense of the word. According to Jack—who apparently kept an eye on such things—we were the rarest of the rare. Who'd have thought, after all those years of getting beaten up because we were half-breeds?

He waved the comment away. "They don't know that. So why kiss her when you didn't want to?" He hesitated a moment, then added with a cheeky grin, "Or did you?"

"I'm still hetero all the way, bro. Trust me on that." I took a sip of coffee, then added, "I tried reading her mind, but it felt like falling into a black hole."

"So why not use threats or force? If she's withholding evidence, you're entitled to."

I shrugged. "Beating her up would have been an exercise in stupidity. She had forty of her get living with her and those sort of odds are a little overwhelming."

"Forty?" He frowned. "How does any one vampire

control that many fledglings? And how would they even manage to all live together?"

I finished off my cereal, then dumped the bowl back on the table and said, "She wasn't a blood vamp, but rather some sort of emotional vampire. Apparently living together is a requirement for suckers who feed off emotion."

"There're vamps who feed off emotion?" Liander said. "That's a somewhat horrific thought."

I raised an eyebrow. "No worse than blood vamps, really."

He snorted. "It's hard to miss a blood vamp feeding off you. Bet the same couldn't be said of an emotional vampire."

He had a point. Especially if all emotional vamps had an aura as strong as Vinny's.

"You reported their presence to Jack?" Rhoan asked.

"Yep."

"Good." He paused to sip his coffee. "So why were you even there rescuing this accountant? Did it have something to do with that phone call you got last night?"

I nodded and explained why Ben had rung, then added, "Which is why I kissed the vamp. To get the name before he attacks someone else."

"So it's not someone connected to this Ben fellow?" Liander asked.

"Ben doesn't seem to think he's the connection, but I haven't talked to him since getting the name. Could turn out that he *does* know this Aron Young."

Which wouldn't be a good thing, because Young's

actions had earned him an execution order. Vamps involved in the torture of others didn't live all that much longer than those actually killing—simply because one crime usually developed into the other anyway. And if Ben was a good friend, he'd come under Directorate scrutiny as well.

Liander frowned. "That name rings a bell."

I raised an eyebrow. "You know someone called Aron Young?"

"I didn't say that. I just said it rings a bell."

"I'm sure there's more than one Aron Young out there," Rhoan said dryly.

Liander sniffed. "Well, of course there is. I'm just saying the name seems familiar."

"Well," I said, grabbing my cup and bowl as I rose. "Let me know if you remember. Meanwhile, I'm heading into the Directorate. You want me to let Jack know you're going to be late?"

"No need." Rhoan's voice was decidedly smug. "I've got the day off. Some of us do occasionally think ahead and prepare."

"And this would have to be a first for you."

He threw a cushion after me. It thudded into a wall, missing by miles. For some reason, it sent the two of them off into fits of laughter. I shook my head and left them to it.

Thankfully, the car had survived the night without additional decoration from the local goons. I threw my gear in, clipped my cell phone onto its hands-free holder, then pulled into the traffic and headed to work.

The phone rang well before I got there and my heart

sunk. The number said it was either Jack or Sal, and a call at this hour from either one could never be a good thing.

I pressed the receive button and said, "You know I can't stomach bad news before I've had my second cup of coffee."

"Well, ain't that just too bad," Jack said, sounding tired and just a little frustrated, "because I've got another one for you."

I slowed the car as the lights ahead turned to red. "I take it you mean another dead naked politician flashing his butt to the world?"

"Not quite. This one is a naked shoe-store owner flashing his butt to all and sundry."

That raised my eyebrows. "Human or nonhuman?"

"Non. Werefox, to be exact."

The killer wasn't restricting himself to any one race, then. "Where was he found?"

"In his store, by his employee. Apparently the dead man and a friend were getting hot and happy in the store window, and that's where he died."

So we had a killer who liked to do the deed in exposed spots, and who obviously had no qualms about being seen. Either that, or it added to the thrill. "Let me guess—his friend is nowhere to be found again?"

"Spot on."

"So why are you so sure it's connected? Beside the fact that our killer is something of an exhibitionist?"

"A feeling, nothing more."

And I'd put money on Jack's feelings over most people's certainties any day.

"Kade's heading there now," he continued. "I want you there ASAP to see if you can sense anything."

"I didn't sense anything useful at James's office." And if my job at the Directorate started to be nothing more than visiting murder scenes to try and sense departing souls, then I'd rather quit.

Which was quite a statement considering I never actually wanted to be a guardian in the first place.

"Still worth trying. I'll send you the address." He paused, and in the background I heard paper rustling. "We checked out that nest you found last night, too."

I raised my eyebrows. "That was fast."

"Emo vamps can be quite dangerous. We had to assess the situation."

"So they really *do* feed on emotions rather than blood?"

"Yes. And they have the ability—and the tendency—to amp up emotions. In certain situations, that can get extremely dangerous."

"This one seems to feed off sexual energy."

"Sexual emotions tend to be the rawest, and therefore more satisfying to emo vamps, but they'll make do with lesser emotions like fear, anger, and pain when they have to."

Which is why there'd been such a strong sense of hunger in the building when I'd walked in—they'd been feeding off what was happening in Ivan's apartment.

And I wouldn't have been surprised if that had been part of the reasoning behind Vinny allowing the vampire to visit Ivan.

"What's your impression of Vincenta Castillo?" Jack asked.

I hesitated. "She's one to watch. I think she has great plans for herself and her fledglings, but I don't think she's done anything to cross the line just yet."

"Interesting."

His voice was dry, and my eyebrows rose again. "Why?"

"Because our inspector gave a glowing report."

I grinned. "Was he young and blond?"

Jack paused. "Young, yes. Blond, no."

"She razzle-dazzled him, boss. He wouldn't have known what side of his pen was up when he was taking notes."

"Young Clark has strong shields. Even an emo vamp shouldn't have been able to affect him."

"*I've* got strong shields, and I felt her pull."

"Then we'll keep an eye on her, for sure. Have you written up a report about last night?"

"Nope. I was intending to do it when I got in this morning. Did Sal get anything on Aron Young?"

"We found three. We're still trying to get a current address on two of them."

"At least there's not hundreds to investigate."

"True." He paused for a moment. In the background, someone was murmuring. Paper moved, then he added, "Sal mentioned you were investigating some BDSM case?"

Meaning Sal had listened in on my phone call—there was no other way she could have known, because I hadn't yet written the report. "It's related to last night's case—same vampire."

I wasn't a hundred percent positive of that, of course, but I wasn't about to let Jack know that.

"I'll hunt up the police report on it for you, and hurry the search on Young. If this is the start of a murder run, we'll need to get onto it straightaway."

"Could you also get a check done on a Ben Wilson? He's a black wolf who manages the Nonpareil stripper business. As far as I can see, he's the only real link between the two men."

"Will do."

"Thanks, boss." I hung up, then changed lanes and headed over to South Yarra and the address Jack had given me—which just happened to be in the heart of trendy Chapel Street.

Obviously, whoever was killing off these people had a taste for power and money. And perhaps a need for the high that exhibitionism could give. Which in itself would suggest some sort of were. While the danger of public sexual acts—and the high such risks gave—were not the sole province of weres, we weres were certainly willing to take it further than most races.

It was impossible to find parking near the shoe shop in Chapel Street, so I parked in nearby Garden Street. And made sure an "Official Directorate Vehicle" sign was visible through the front window, just in case the parking inspectors got a little trigger-happy with their ticket machines.

I pocketed my keys and headed back to Chapel Street. The shoe shop was easy enough to spot—it was the one with the cop cars out front and the black plastic sheeting over the windows.

Kade was nowhere to be seen, so I ducked under the tape, showed my badge to the patrol cop, and headed in. And discovered Chapel Street shoe shops weren't like ordinary shoe shops. For a start, the shoes were well spaced rather than crammed together in soldier-like rows. Then there were spotlights over the display racks, high-back comfy chairs, and plush carpets.

And a dead naked guy in the front window.

His thick thatch of red hair was the first thing I noticed. He was leaning over a waist-high shoe display, his butt facing the window, arms and head flopping down the back of the metal stand, with pretty-colored stilettos and boots scattered all around his feet.

"Puts a new spin on eye-catching window displays, doesn't it?" Cole said, stripping off bloodied gloves as he stepped out of the window.

I frowned at him. "Whose blood?"

"His. Seems our killer got a little heavy-handed with the scratches this time." He nodded toward the victim's torso. "Got scratches on his chest, genitals, and legs."

"What type of scratches?"

"A cat of some kind. She's a big one, though."

"How big is big?"

"Twice the size of a regular cat, at least."

"So are we looking for something the size of a puma or something more like a tiger?"

"Something the size of a tiger, at least."

I stepped closer. The metallic tang of blood perfumed the air, as did the scents of sweat and sex. But underneath those were notes of jasmine and orange. The same scents that had been evident in Gerard James's office.

My gaze ran from the dead man's neck to his back and down his legs. There were scratches scattered across his pale flesh—big, thick, ugly scratches that had taken more than a little skin with them.

"It can't be the same cat that scratched James," I said, glancing around at Cole. "This one has massive paws."

"I think it is, but I won't know that until I do some DNA tests."

I raised my eyebrows. "You found more than the victim's DNA this time?"

"Found it last time, too. I'm hoping the saliva found on James's cock will match that found on this man."

"And that's the only DNA of our mysterious lady friend that you've found?"

"Nope. And it appears our murderess is in heat."

That raised my eyebrows. "Then why would she be killing her mates? That's more a spider habit than cat, isn't it?"

He smiled. It was a nice smile, a smile that lit up his whole face. "Maybe they *really* disappointed her."

"Then let's hope her future dates have brushed up on their technique a bit more." Or that we caught her before those dates happened. The violence in her attacks seemed to be escalating, and I really didn't want to imagine what she might do to the next man. "We've got a witness this time?"

"Henry Rollins is the gentleman who found him. He's waiting in the back storeroom, if you'd like to talk to him. There's also another potential witness, but it might be best to let Kade deal with him."

I raised my eyebrows. "Why?"

"He's as drunk as a skunk and smells like vomit." His gaze met mine, blue eyes twinkling. "And we all know what a delicate little nose you have."

"Thanks. I think."

I turned and headed for the back of the store, but had only gone three or four steps when Kade finally arrived. I didn't have to actually see him to know he was there—his sheer, masculine scent overwhelmed just about everyone else in the room.

"About fucking time you turned up," I said mildly, over my shoulder.

"Hey, I had to stop for coffee."

"For everyone, I hope," Cole commented.

"I didn't think you boys were allowed to drink on the job. In case of spillage, etcetera."

I pointed an imperious finger and tried to be stern, despite the smile teasing my lips. "If you didn't bring us coffee, you can just go out on the sidewalk and interview the witness the cops are holding."

"Geez, is bossiness inbred in wolves or something?"

"Yes," Cole and I said together, then shared a grin. I have to say, I was liking this relaxed version of Cole a whole lot more than the sourpuss I'd first been introduced to months ago. Although maybe he was opening up more because we *had* gotten to know each other a bit better through our on-the-job sparring.

I continued on into the back storerooms. There had to be a small kitchen in the back somewhere, because I could smell coffee. And it wasn't top shelf stuff, if that smell was anything to go by. Either that, or the percolator needed a good cleaning.

But underneath that almost burned aroma, other scents ran. Leather and man and, softer still, orange and jasmine.

And underneath them all, a scent that made my wolf soul twitch.

Cat.

It was faint, but it was there. Our murderess had definitely come this way, though the scent wasn't strong enough to suggest she was still here.

I came across the cop first—a tall man with blond hair leaning casually on one of the shelves. He straightened when I approached. "Directorate?"

I nodded, looking past him as I showed him my badge. Rollins was huddled on a kitchen chair, pale hands wrapped around a coffee mug. "Has Mr. Rollins said anything?"

The cop shook his head. "I just gave him a coffee to calm his nerves."

"Thanks." I slipped past him and walked over to Rollins. He didn't react, so I squatted down in front of him. "Mr. Rollins? I'm afraid I need to ask you some questions."

He looked up, brown eyes haunted. "I saw her, you know."

I raised my eyebrows. "You saw the woman who killed your boss?"

"Well, she was with him in the front window when I

arrived, so yeah, I presume it was her that murdered Frank."

"Did she see you?"

He snorted. "Hell, yes. She paused and waved at me. There was blood smeared all over her hands and skin."

"She was naked, then?"

He nodded.

Not only a killer, but a brazen one, who seemingly *didn't* have any fears about getting caught. "Where were you?"

"Sorta standing in the middle of the road, a little shocked. I mean, it's not every day you see your boss and a babe making out in the window."

No, I guess not. "Were you the only one watching?"

"There was a drunk." He shrugged. "Most of the traffic kept zipping by. One of them almost ran me over. People in cars generally don't take much notice of what's going on around them."

And if they *had* glimpsed the naked woman, would they actually have believed it? Or would they have thought it a mannequin? "What happened then?"

"She jumped out of the display area and I presume she walked to the back of the shop. There were no lights on in the store, so I couldn't be sure, but she certainly didn't come out the front."

"Did you enter the shop?"

He shook his head. "I called the cops, and waited out the front. If she could kill Frank—and he wasn't responding to me banging on the window, so I had to presume he was dead—I wasn't taking the chance of confronting her alone. I mean, I'm half Frank's size."

Wise man. I waited while he took a sip of coffee, then asked, "Is there another exit beside the front door?"

He shook his head. "Only the window above us."

I looked up. The window in question was maybe one foot square in diameter, and wouldn't have been large enough for a woman or a cat the size of a tiger to get through. But the latch was undone and the woman had gone, so this *had* to be her exit point.

Which meant we had a shifter who could actually alter the size of her beast. Interesting.

"Did you see her well enough to give us a description of her?"

He nodded. "She was tall and willowy, with large breasts and a lush mouth. Blondish hair, long fingers."

I raised my eyebrows again. "Long fingers?"

"I'm a pianist. I notice hands." He hesitated. "I'm sure she lives around here somewhere. I've seen her on the street a few times."

"But you don't know her name?"

"No. Sorry."

I squeezed his hand then rose. "There'll be another Directorate officer in here in a moment or so to take a full statement and work up an image ID, then we'll send you home."

He nodded. "Thanks."

I left him to his coffee and walked back into the main shop area. Cole looked up as I entered. "Anything useful?"

"He saw the killer, so we'll need a full statement."

"Does his description match that of the woman James was last seen with?"

"Only in that they both had blonde hair."

He quirked an eyebrow. "It'll be interesting to see what the DNA comes up with then, because the MO is the same for both murders."

"Except for the amount of blood shed and the size of the scratches." I walked over to the victim and squatted down, studying his neck. Like Gerard James, this man had three small scratches near the pulse point of his neck. But why—especially given that larger claws had been used on the rest of his body? I shifted a little, and saw the lipstick smear across his lips. It was the color of dried blood—not a very nice shade. "If it *is* the same woman, do you think we're dealing with someone who can change the size of her animal?"

Cole raised his eyebrows. "It'd be rare."

"But there are wolves who can alter their human forms, so why couldn't there be shifters who can alter their animal one?"

"I don't know. I'll do a search and see if I can come up with anything."

"Good." I rose. "I think she escaped through a back window. I'm going to go around the back and see if I can catch a scent to track."

Cole nodded, obviously not paying a whole lot of attention as he picked up a hair and carefully placed it in a bag.

I walked out the front and looked around until I found Kade, then walked over. I could smell the drunk before I got anywhere near them, and his unwashed, sour puke aroma had me stopping several yards away. Kade glanced over his shoulder, wrinkled his nose and made a face, then continued his interview for another few minutes.

"Well," he said, when he finally joined me. "That was interesting."

"Interesting because he had lots of information, or because he smelled like something the cat chucked up?"

He smiled. "Both, actually. Our killer is apparently into spanking—and he swears that while she was human, one of her hands was that of a large cat."

"Which would at least explain all the blood and claw marks." I touched his arm, tried to ignore the urge to caress his warm, bay skin, and added, "She apparently escaped through the back window. I'm going to try and track the scent."

His steps matched mine as we headed for the small lane at the end of the group of shops. "He also said that near the end of the session, she seemed to be doing this weird sucking thing to his mouth, and that he suddenly seemed in great pain."

I raised an eyebrow, amusement twitching my mouth as I glanced up at him. "Maybe she bit his tongue."

"He seemed to imply it was more 'oh my God I'm going to die' type pain, but then, he's as drunk as a skunk, so who knows what he was really seeing." He took a mouthful of coffee, then tossed the container into the trash. "There are Japanese legends about soul-stealers—you think we could be dealing with something like that?"

"It would certainly explain why there's no souls hanging about afterward." Shadows closed in around us as we moved into the laneway. "But in the Japanese legends, the soul-stealers are foxes, aren't they?"

He shrugged. "There's no reason why there can't be soul-stealing cats, as well."

"True." It was certainly an idea worth chasing.

The ripe scent of rubbish left a little too long in the sun began to flavor the air, jostling for prominence with the sweet scent of the yellow roses climbing the fence that divided the lane from the house next door.

Kade stepped over a puddle, then asked, "You get anything useful from inside?"

"Cole thinks it's the same woman and that she's in heat, but the description our other witness gave us doesn't really match the woman Gerard James was apparently last seen with."

"Doesn't mean anything. She could have been wearing a wig, colored contacts, or anything like that. My witness certainly didn't get close enough to pick up those things."

"Mine, neither."

"Did he have small scratches on the side of his neck, like James did?"

I nodded and stepped over another brackish looking puddle. "Same place, same size."

"Then that's our constant. For whatever reasons, she's marking her victims."

"But is she doing it before, or after? You know, for all the blood in this murder, there didn't seem to be any blood related to those scratches. Yet they were open, unhealed wounds."

"Maybe it's some weird way of testing them before

she kills them." He shrugged. "We won't know for sure until we catch the bitch."

"Cats are queens. Only dogs are bitches."

He snorted softly. "She takes female humanoid form, so therefore the bitch tag can apply. Trust me, I live with a household of them."

I grinned. "And here was me having the image of you all being one big happy family."

"Oh, we are. But where a group of females gather, bitching can be found. I'm sure it's part of female DNA, just like the ability to sniff out chocolate wherever it may be hidden."

"You could be right." We reached the end of the shops and moved into the lane behind them. There were several cars crammed into the small space, leaving barely enough room between them and the brickwork to get through. None of the shops had rear entrances, which I would have thought would be against fire regulations. Even heritage-listed shops—which I didn't think these were—had to have a fire exit. Maybe the owner was paying someone under the table to get away with not installing them.

I stopped at the shoe shop window and looked up. The sun hadn't yet hit this wall, and the bricks were still damp from the early morning dew. Small paw marks were visible, sliding through the wetness partway down the wall before disappearing.

"She definitely came this way," Kade commented, then glanced at me. "You think you can track her?"

"We'll soon see." I stripped off my jacket and sweater,

handing them to him before calling to the magic deep in my soul.

Energy swept around me, through me, changing me into the form that had found me at puberty. The form that was a part of me in ways the seagull shape—no matter how comfortable I ended up being with it—never would be.

To my wolf nose, the world came alive with a myriad of scents and sounds. I trotted forward, loving the feel of cold dampness under my paws and the play of sunlight across my fur. The texture of the air was thick and rich, and after sorting through all the different and delicious aromas, I found the one I wanted.

Cat.

But it was mixed with the scents of orange, jasmine, and humanity. She'd fled in human form, not cat. Which was odd, because her feline form would have been less noticeable.

But it made her trail easier to follow.

Nose to the ground and tail held high, I followed, padding between the cars and out into the main lane. With Kade's shadow looming over me and his thick, rich scent teasing my senses, I ran back down the lane, leaping the puddle before moving out onto the main street.

The scent swirled, as if my quarry had waited and watched proceedings for a while before moving on. I ran down the street, following the trail over a road, past several more houses, then left into another street. The scent finally led into one of the houses.

I stopped at the gate and waited for Kade to catch up.

The house was a small, brick affair that probably cost a fortune despite the fact it didn't look wide enough to hold anything more than a small bedroom and a hallway. The front yard was almost nonexistent, but nicely kept, filled with sweet-smelling roses and abundant lavender bushes.

I looked around as Kade approached, then hit the gate with my paw. He opened it without comment, and together we headed up the steps to the front door. The scent of cat became stronger, but mingled with it was the metallic tang of blood and new death.

Not again, I thought, and shifted back to human form. Without saying anything, I motioned Kade around to the side of the house, then held up two fingers. He nodded and leapt the side fence, disappearing quickly and quietly. I glanced at my watch, waited the two minutes, then slammed a shoulder against the front door. It might have had locks, but they didn't stand a chance against a determined werewolf. The door crashed back against the wall, denting plaster and sending dust flying.

"Directorate," I yelled, "Come out with your hands up."

Chapter 5

No one bothered coming out, but the scramble of tiny claws against polished floors suggested our quarry had most definitely heard me. I ran down the hallway, following the sound of fleeing steps, trying to ignore the growing scent of death to concentrate on the smell of cat.

Hoping all the while she ran straight out the back door and into Kade's waiting arms.

The hallway ran the length of the long house, and finished in an open plan kitchen-living area. Windows lined the rear wall, letting the sunlight stream in and lending the white room a warmth it wouldn't have had otherwise. I couldn't see Kade in the garden beyond those windows but I knew he'd be near, waiting and ready.

I scanned the room, looking for the cat, and saw the

flick of a black tail just before it disappeared through another doorway. I ran after it, heard a creaking noise and a soft thump, and got there in time to see the small window in the laundry room closing. A second later I barreled into the washing machine, leaving a huge dent in the pristine metal front. It didn't do my knees a whole lot of good, either.

I cursed, but scrambled—well, limped—to the back door and flung it open.

Kade was little more than a warm red and black blur as he leapt the fence into the neighbor's yard. I shifted shape again and followed, my belly barely clearing the top of the wooden palings.

Kade was nowhere in sight. I sniffed the air, finding both his scent and the cat's, and ran after them—across an overgrown back lawn and over another fence. Kade was standing in the middle of the next yard, his hands on his hips and his expression one of frustration.

A second later I understood why. The scent of cat had multiplied and the scent we were chasing wasn't strong enough to stand out amongst the other half dozen cat scents now staining the air and the ground. I swore internally and nosed around, hoping against hope to catch the trail again. Instead, I found a white cat and a tabby, neither of whom were pleased to see me— a fact demonstrated by the way they hunkered down and hissed their little hearts out. I kept out of the way of their sharp claws and continued on, searching through the small garden bed and behind the old shed, but couldn't find anything.

I shifted back to human form. "Fuck, we've lost her."

"So it appears." Kade ran a hand through his sweaty dark hair. "I didn't even see her well enough to stop her kinetically."

I frowned. "She must have been moving fast if you couldn't freeze her. You can generally freeze vamps when they're blurring, can't you?"

"Yeah, but the trail of their emotions usually gives them away. I was getting nothing from her." He glanced at me. "Did you catch a glimpse of her?"

"Yeah. Her animal form is black, but she can obviously shift the size of her cat, because what we were chasing is not what killed that man in the shop window. Cole reckons her hands were at least tiger size."

Kade frowned. "I didn't think it was possible for shifters or weres to alter the size of their beast, let alone partially shift."

"Well, up until recently, I didn't think there was a wolf pack who could alter their human form, either, so who knows what else is out there?" I shrugged and adjusted my bra. Luckily, I'd gone for one that was Lycra rather than lace this morning, and as a result it had come through the shapeshifts in wearable condition. Which meant I'd definitely have to buy more for work situations. Running around with a bra on was infinitely better than running around without. "We better get back and check what—or who—is dead in that house."

"Our shifter is obviously killing these women to assume their identities, which means she probably looks a lot like them to begin with."

"Not necessarily. Maybe she can alter her human shape as well as her animal. After all, her cat is black, and yet the witnesses said she was blonde." I shrugged and clambered back over the fence. "Or maybe she's not even a shifter to begin with. Maybe she's something else entirely."

"But what else is there that can shift?"

"Who knows?" But if the spirit of an ancient god of death could be called into this time to create havoc once again, there was no saying what else was out there.

Or what else could be called into being.

A chill ran across my skin and I rubbed my arms. Kade must have caught the movement, because he retrieved my sweater and tossed it to me. I pulled it on gratefully, then caught my coat. Wearing it didn't seem to ease the chill, though.

Our footsteps echoed through the silent house as we made our way back up the corridor. The death scent was coming from the first room and my steps slowed as we approached. I'd seen a lot of bloodshed and killing over the last year—had even done my fair share of it—but it never seemed to get any easier to confront.

I hoped it never did.

I hoped the part of me that mourned the wanton destruction of innocent lives haunted my days—and nights—for as long as I remained in this job. Because it meant that I wasn't becoming my brother, wasn't becoming the unthinking killing machine that he could sometimes be, and that Jack wanted *me* to be.

We stepped into the room. A large bed dominated the small space. Like the rest of the house, everything was white—only here, the brightness was alleviated by dark red patches that adorned the walls, the bedspread, and the carpet near the bed.

Like the woman I'd found yesterday, this woman was laying half-undressed, slumped across the bed. Her lacy bra dangled from the stump of her shoulder, and her torso was crisscrossed with bloody gashes. Gashes made with claws bigger than your average black house cat.

"Christ, the press are going to love this. First James, then his lover, and now another member of Toorak's finest."

"The press won't get anywhere near the story if Jack has anything to do with it. He'll keep them focused on James."

"Press have a nose for these things."

"And Jack's had plenty of experience restraining them."

He grunted, but whether that was agreement or not was anyone's guess.

"She hasn't been dead all that long." He stopped near the body and looked down at her. "Why would the cat come back to this house when she'd already used the woman's face and knew she'd been seen?"

I shrugged. "Given that we're probably not dealing with a rational mind here, maybe she simply didn't think we'd trace her so easily."

I stopped beside him. Unlike her body, the woman's face was untouched, but the terror of her ordeal seemed frozen on her features. My gaze fell to her mouth, and I frowned.

"Is that lipstick?" I leaned closer to have a look. The

odor of death and new decay overrode the metallic scent of blood, but the scent of cat and that vague, orange and jasmine aroma was present as well.

"Where?" Kade said.

I pointed a finger to the smear of red across the woman's top lip. "It looks like someone wearing lipstick has been kissing her. The shoe guy had the same color on his lips."

"So she kissed this woman before she killed her, then stole her identity and killed the shoe guy. Maybe we *are* dealing with a soul-sucker of some kind." He studied her mouth for a second longer, then stepped back and looked around. "There's an awful lot of fear lingering in this room. Fear and anger."

"Anger?" I raised an eyebrow. "Same source, or different?"

"The anger is older. Deeper." He frowned. "When I sensed it in James's office, it felt ancient and powerful. Now it feels even more so."

I'm glad *he* was feeling something, because I wasn't. And really, that was beginning to bug me. Four murders, and not one soul left hanging about afterward? Granted, the woman I'd found yesterday had been dead for so long her soul was unlikely to be still here, but with the other three, I should have sensed *something*. Hell, I might have wished more than once to go to a murder scene and not sense the dead, but the reality of it happening was prickling my radar. Something was *very* off-kilter.

And, at least with these cat killings, it really did suggest that we were dealing with some sort of soul-sucker.

Goose bumps fled across my skin. I resisted the urge to rub my arms, and said, "So our murderer is somehow gaining power every time she kills?"

"That would be my guess, yes." His gaze met mine. "Which means we have to catch her soon, before she grows too powerful."

"If we can bring down a god of death, we can bring down this thing. Whatever she is." But I wished I sounded a little more confident. "What I don't get is why she's marking her victims first. I mean, why bother with three tiny slashes if she's going to cut them up so badly or rip off an arm? And why would she do that to this women and the shoe guy, and not to James and the first female victim?"

"Maybe it was some sort of test that developed into something more violent." His gaze raked the woman's body, and distaste flicked through his warm eyes. "And she didn't only claw here. She's nibbled."

My stomach did an odd sort of flip-flop. "What?"

"Here." He pointed to a small area near the woman's left breast. The skin had been torn open, and globules of fat and flesh were evident. "Those aren't claw marks around the wound. That's teeth."

"Why on earth would she be eating the flesh now when she didn't before?"

"What better way to induce fear than to actually eat bits of your victim?" He shrugged. "She seems to be getting more violent with each murder, so perhaps this is all part of the escalation."

I shuddered at the thought. I didn't want to think about the mess her victims would be in if we didn't stop her soon. "If that *is* a bite wound, then she was wearing a smaller form. And no one—not even a human—is going to stand around and let a cat nibble on their flesh. Besides, the woman was in the process of dressing—it would have been hard for the cat to sneak in a bite before the woman reacted."

"We don't know what other skills she has, besides her ability to shift her shape and size."

That was true. I glanced at my watch, and swore softly. I was late for my coffee appointment with Ben. "Look, I have to go chat to a man about another murdering psycho. You want to call in a cleanup team on this one?"

He nodded. "I'll go talk to James's secretary after that, see if he was the connection to the two women."

"Even if he was, how would they all be connected to the shoe guy?" It was easy enough imagining the women buying shoes there, but I highly doubt James was the type to be running around in high heels.

"With politicians you never really know." He reached across and flicked my nose lightly. "It's nice working with you, even if we can't have sex."

I grinned. "Ditto. Just be careful that cat doesn't come back and decide to make a meal out of you, too."

His warm brown eyes twinkled with sudden mischief. "Wouldn't be the first time a woman has decided to eat me."

"Yeah, but this one is taking more than a pound of flesh with her. I'm sure you wouldn't want that."

"No, and neither would my mares."

"I don't know," I said, trying for a reflective tone

rather than amused, but missing horribly. "I bet Sable is so far into her pregnancy she's now cursing your pound or two of flesh and hoping it'll disappear for quite a while."

"No doubt about it," he said with a smile. "But when she comes into heat again, it'll be a different story."

"She's not a baby machine, you know."

"She's a mare. That's what they do."

So much for the enlightened world of horse-shifters. I shook my head and left.

Thanks to morning traffic, it took me close to thirty minutes to get to Lygon Street. Parking was as difficult to find as ever, so by the time I entered Chiquita's, I was a good fifteen minutes late. The café was cozy rather than flashy in design, full of intimate tables and seating that wrapped around you and lent a feeling of privacy. Down at the far end of the room was one of those fireplaces that looked like logs but was actually gas, and the air was warm enough to almost instantly snatch the chill from my skin.

I didn't see Ben straightaway, but a moment later he stood and waved. I couldn't help the smile that touched my lips. Damn he looked *good*.

He'd dressed in blue jeans that molded around his strong legs and highlighted the sharp definition of muscles. The sleeves of his red shirt had been casually rolled to his elbows, and emphasized not only the width of his shoulders, but the rich blackness of his skin.

He smiled when our gazes met, his white teeth flashing brightly in the gloom. My hormones did several excited skips. I might have been off the casual bandwagon for several months now, but this man had me reconsidering my options.

Or maybe I was simply ready to get back into the hunt again. I might not be over the hurt of watching Kellen walk away, but the break had at least given my bruised heart time to mend a little.

Maybe I was ready to play again, even if I had no intention of taking it further than that for a while.

Of course, knowing fate's sick sense of humor, she'd probably consider that now would be the perfect time to fling my soul mate into the equation.

If he hadn't already walked away, a little voice whispered.

I shoved that thought back into the box where it belonged, and let a smile of appreciation play about my lips.

"You're looking nice this morning," I said, dropping my purse onto the seat before rising onto tiptoes to kiss the side of his cheek. His skin felt good under my lips— warm and slightly roughened with whisker growth— and the taste of him was musky. It was tempting, so tempting, to keep on kissing and tasting, but that *wasn't* what I'd come here for. No matter what my hormones were suddenly thinking.

"And you're looking a little ragged around the edges." With his warm hands on either shoulder, he stood back a little and studied me critically. "Had a rough morning, huh?"

"Yeah, and the bitch got away." I pulled back from his light grip and slid down onto the bench. The skin still tingled from the heat of his touch, and part of me wished that I could feel that warmth elsewhere.

I crossed my arms on the table, and tried to remain businesslike. "So, is Jilli working today?"

He nodded. "She'll come out and talk to us during her morning tea break." He paused and glanced at his watch. "Which is in another ten minutes."

"Then we'd better order some coffee." I picked up the menu and scanned through it, though I'd made up my mind before I even walked through the door. "And I hope your pockets stretch to cake. Chasing crazy bad people always makes me hungry."

"Anything the lady wants, the lady can have."

I looked up from the menu, saw the cheeky twinkle in his blue eyes, and smiled. "I thought you didn't do sex on the first date?"

"I don't. But if I take you out to dinner tonight, that would be a second date. Therefore, all bets are off."

I raised an eyebrow as the smile teasing my lips grew stronger. "And who said anything about wanting to have dinner with you? We haven't even experienced coffee together yet. It might all end disastrously."

He laughed. It was a warm, rich sound that overran the babble of noise and had those nearest to us briefly looking our way. "Wolf, you want me as much as I want you."

"Doesn't mean I'll take you."

He studied me for a moment, his smile fading just a little. Then he leaned across the table, took the menu out of my grasp, and wrapped his large hands around mine. "Someone has really hurt you, haven't they?"

Tears stung my eyes. I looked away, blinking furiously. After all this time, it shouldn't still hurt this much, should it? "We hurt each other. In the end, he chose the best option for him. I can't say I blame him."

"He couldn't have been a soul mate, then."

I met his gaze again. His dark features were full of a compassion that was surprising considering he was basically a complete stranger. But maybe he'd been in a similar situation.

I shrugged. "Our relationship had only just begun, but love was definitely part of the equation. It could have developed into more."

He was shaking his head before I'd even finished. "It might have been love—it might have even been a deep love—but it couldn't have been soul mate deep. Trust me on that."

"You say that with such certainty. Why?"

Something akin to grief—but deeper, darker—briefly twisted his features. He didn't immediately say anything, and for several minutes, the noise of the café flowed around us as he struggled with inner demons.

"Because I found my soul mate ten years ago." His voice was soft, matter-of-fact, cutting oddly through the shock that ran through me. He could have been talking about a football match rather than the one event every wolf lived for.

But if he had a soul mate, then he wouldn't be sitting here propositioning me.

Would he?

After all, having found his soul mate had never stopped Rhoan.

My gaze went to his. There in his eyes was a torment and suffering so deep it beat to death anything I'd ever felt in my entire life.

He smiled—a twisted smile that made something deep inside me ache—then added, "I lost her four years ago."

Again, shock ran through me. The soul-mate bond was unshakeable *and* unbreakable. In many ways, it was similar to the bond of a twin. I knew when Rhoan was sick, or in trouble, or hurt. I mightn't be able to read his mind, but I knew him, understood him, and probably better than I knew or understood myself. The soul bond was like that—only deeper. Much deeper.

To lose a soul mate was to lose part of yourself.

"Had you sworn your love to the moon?"

Because if they had, it was even more amazing that he was sitting here sane and whole. I'd always heard—always believed—that in a moon-sworn bond, the death of one partner meant the death of the other. That one could not survive as a whole without the other. If they did . . . madness was the end result.

Ben looked remarkably sane for a wolf who had lost his heart *and* his soul.

"We never performed the moon ceremony, simply because of the job. We both wanted to get out of the business, but to do that, we needed money. And to get money, we had to work."

"And neither of you could do anything else?"

He grimaced. "Nothing else paid as well."

I shifted my hands and squeezed his fingers lightly. As comforting gestures went, it was pretty poor, but then, what else was there? This man had lost his soul mate. There were no words, no actions, that could ever provide enough comfort after such a horrendous event.

"How did she die?"

His lips twisted. "A car accident. A stupid, fucking car accident. And no one's fault but the weather's."

"I'm sorry—" The words were out before I could retract them. They were stupid words, really, because they had no meaning when we were strangers and I hadn't even known his mate. So I added, "I'm sorry we got onto this subject. I'm sorry I made you remember—"

As if he would *ever* forget.

"Hey, I brought the topic up, not you." He shrugged, and it was almost as if he were shrugging away the cloak of his woes, putting it away for another day. I wondered how long it had actually taken to gain such control over the ache. "And to answer your original question, no wolf can walk away from a soul mate. It'd be like ripping out your heart and flinging it away—you can't survive if you do it."

"And yet you survived her death."

His laugh was bittersweet. "Yeah, I did. But only thanks to my ever-loving, goddamn nagging sister."

I raised my eyebrows. "How did your sister save you?"

"She refused to let me die." He shrugged. "Our pack is a small one, and the two of us were always close. I think that bond is the only reason I'm alive today."

I studied him for a moment, then asked, "So you did try to die?"

"Of course. My heart and my soul had left me. It

didn't matter that we hadn't sworn our love to the moon—she was my world. My reason for living. Without her—" He shrugged, and gave me that heart-breaking smile again. "Except my sister wasn't about to let me go so easily."

They had to have one hell of a strong relationship for her to be able to drag him back from the brink of death. I very much doubted the normal bond of siblings would have done so.

God, if something ever happened to Liander, would Rhoan choose death? We had a strong bond—a bond as strong as life itself—but I really didn't know if that would be enough to pull my brother back. No matter how badly he sometimes treated his mate, Rhoan loved Liander with every fiber of his being.

I licked my lips and said, "So you're still close to your sister?"

"She nagged me back to life. How could I walk away after something like that?"

The waitress arrived, and we ordered our coffee and cake. I glanced at my watch, wondering when Jilli was going to come out. Jack would get less than pleasant if I stayed and chatted for too long—especially when we had a badass running around killing humans.

"This wolf that walked away," Ben asked, after a moment, "what made you think he was your soul mate?"

I shrugged. "It was probably wishful thinking more than anything else. I cared for him—cared for him a lot—but we never really got it together enough to see if it could ever be more."

"And when you made love?"

I raised an eyebrow, amusement teasing my lips. "When we made love, a good time was had by all."

Amusement twitched Ben's lush mouth. "That goes without saying for a wolf."

"Then why ask the question?"

His grin was as sexy as hell and my hormones did another little dance. And really, I couldn't be sorry that my self-imposed exile from sex seemed to be coming to an end. I might still hurt, but what was the point in continuing to abstain from something that was so much a part of who I was?

I might not be ready to step out with my heart on my sleeve, but a good time was definitely beginning to hit my agenda once again.

"What I mean by that question," he said, "is what did you feel deep down? Besides arousal, besides desire?"

I'd felt lots of things when I was with Kellen, and some of those feelings had not been entirely my own. Quinn, I'd discovered, had found a way to use the sensual, sexy dreams we'd shared as a path into my deeper thoughts, placing a compulsion deep within to avoid the things he disapproved of. Like the wolf clubs. And Kellen.

"What I was feeling often depended on how I was feeling about our relationship at the time, or what else was happening in my life. Why do you want to know?"

"Because the first time I made love to Jodie, I knew she was the one. My heart, my soul, my life. We were inseparable from that moment."

I raised my eyebrows. I'd never felt that with anyone. Not even Quinn. "So it was love at first sight?"

He laughed, a warm rich sound that sent tingles of desire scooting across my flesh. "God, no. Quite the opposite, in fact. We worked with each other for six months and never got an inkling. And our first kiss was nothing more than the polite kiss colleagues share at Christmas. It wasn't until we actually had sex that things changed."

So did that mean the whole meeting-of-eyes-across-the-crowded-room moment I'd been dreaming of half my life was just that? A dream? Or was it simply a matter of different wolves, different situations?

I had to hope so. Fate had snatched away so many of my dreams of late that it would really hurt to lose that one as well.

I crossed my arms and leaned forward a little. His gaze flicked downward, caressing my breasts, and the heat of his desire flicked around me. My nostrils flared as I sucked in the scent, feeling it swirl its way through me. It was nice, so nice, after such a long absence. "So what was it like? That first moment, I mean."

"Well, there was no chorus of angels singing, if that's what you were expecting."

I grinned. "In this day and age, I think angels have better things to do than hang around chorusing while people mash body parts."

Amusement flirted with his mouth again. "It was more a feeling of belonging and completeness. From the moment that we made love, I could think of no other, wanted no other."

I definitely hadn't felt that with Kellen. Or Quinn, for that matter, even though there'd been a connection—a deep connection—between us. One that was richer and stronger than I could ever possibly explain. But did that validate my feelings that he wasn't the one? The fact that I'd walked away—or rather, sent him away—seemed to confirm that possibility. Not to mention the fact that even when we were together, I'd also had other partners. Much to his disgust, for sure, but still . . .

"It wasn't like that with us," I said eventually. "But I was hoping it was something we'd grow into."

"You don't grow into a soul mate," he said, the amusement on his lips clear in his voice. "It's just something that *is*. Or isn't."

"Trust me, nothing is *that* simple in my life."

"Love is."

"For you, maybe." I thanked the waitress as she brought over our order, then began tucking in to the thick, gooey chocolate cake. Which wasn't as delicious as the scent coming from the big wolf sitting opposite me, but still more than lived up to the standards of this place.

"So how does the whole sex and dating bit work for you now?" I asked.

He shrugged. "There will always be an emptiness deep inside, one that no amount of lovemaking will ever fill. But I'm a werewolf, and sex is still *damned* good." He gave me a grin that was so sexy my insides just about melted. "I can demonstrate just how good, if you'd like."

"You know," I said, glad my voice sounded dry rather than husky with the excitement that was buzzing around my insides, "as much as I enjoy a bit of exhibitionism, this is a little too public for me."

He laughed—a rich and luscious sound. "Well, I didn't mean right here and now."

"I'm glad." Time, I thought, to change the subject. "Have you heard from Ivan?"

He took a sip of coffee, then said, "Yeah. He checked himself out of hospital this morning."

I frowned. "Was that wise? That vamp's still out there and Ivan might still be a target."

"He seems to think that the worst is over." Ben shrugged. "He said Vinny will keep him safe."

I snorted. "Vinny sold him out the first time. Why wouldn't she do it again?"

"He believes she values him too much to give the vamp access again."

"If he believes that, he's an idiot." Vinny was hungry for both power and wealth, and I didn't think she was particularly fussy about how she got either.

He shrugged, then looked past me. "Ah, here she comes."

I twisted around. The woman approaching was typically wolf in build, but given she probably stood at five one, she was definitely on the small side. But she exuded a sense of authority and her brown eyes had a no-nonsense gleam to them.

She kissed Ben lightly on the cheek then her gaze came to me. "Riley Jenson, I presume?"

I nodded and fetched my badge out of my purse to show her. "Ben's requested my help in finding out why your lover Denny died."

"Yes, he told me that."

There was a brief flicker in her eyes, one that hinted at sorrow. Then it was gone, replaced by the no-nonsense gleam. Jilli might be sad about her lover's death, but she wasn't going to let it stop her from going about her daily business. Jack would have loved her attitude.

"Tell me, do you know if he had any vampire lovers?"

Little frown lines briefly creased her otherwise smooth forehead. "Not that I knew of. But we'd only been lovers for a few weeks."

"What about clubs? Which of those did he frequent?"

"All of them. Particularly the underground ones."

I raised my eyebrows and glanced at Ben. "There are still underground wolf clubs?"

"For people who have similar sexual needs to Denny. Such things are generally not authorized at the legal clubs."

Meaning they weren't places I'd want to frequent—though I would, if it meant getting answers. I glanced back to Jilli. "When did you and Denny last have sex?"

"The night he died."

"So it was you I smelled on the sheets?" My gaze went to her neck as I said that, but she had a turtleneck sweater on.

"Yes, but he was perfectly fine when I left him." She sniffed. "He was sleeping, in fact."

Her tone seemed to imply he had no stamina, and I resisted the urge to smile. "And there's nothing else you can tell me? Nothing he said or did that seemed odd to you?"

"No." She hesitated. "He did complain about being followed."

I raised my eyebrows. "When?"

"The night he died. He said he'd spotted some lanky fellow trailing him a couple of times. He'd tried to point him out to me the night before, but I couldn't see him."

Lanky—Ivan's attacker had certainly been that. And given the smell that had been in both apartments, it was looking more likely that my sense of smell was spot-on, and it *was* the same attacker.

"So did you believe he was being followed?"

She hesitated. "Denny wasn't into playing games like that. If he said he was being followed, then yes, I believe him." She glanced at her watch. "Is that all?"

"Yes. Thanks."

She nodded and marched efficiently off.

"Denny never mentioned anything like that to me," Ben said heavily.

"I wonder if he mentioned it to the police?" Wondered if Jilli had. I should have asked, but I guess it would be in the report if she had. I took a sip of coffee, then said, "Did Ivan visit the underground clubs?"

"No. Ivan is as straightlaced as they come."

"So that's probably not the connection, then." I studied him for a moment, then said, "What about you?"

Amusement gleamed in his eyes. "I know where they are, simply because I sometimes need to direct clientele there. Nonpareil does not cater to such needs."

"Just good old-fashioned sex, huh?"

"Not *just* good, thank you very much. Our standards are beyond excellent."

I grinned. "Not to blow your own horn, of course."

"Of course," he agreed, with the sort of look that had the blood surging through my veins.

Man, what I wouldn't give to be able to . . .

My phone chose that moment to ring, which was probably a good thing. I really didn't need to be thinking about what I'd like to do with this wolf. I grabbed my purse from underneath the table and dragged out my cell. The number wasn't one I recognized, which was unusual because this was a Directorate phone, and few people had the direct number.

I pressed the receive button and said, "Riley speaking."

"Riley? This is Vincenta."

Speak of the devil, and she calls. Something inside me went cold. "How did you get my number?"

"Ah," she drawled, amusement evident in her rich tones. "That would be giving away trade secrets, now, wouldn't it?"

The kiss, I thought. It had something to do with that goddamn kiss. That'd teach me not to follow my instincts.

I was getting a new number as soon as I got back to the Directorate.

"What do you want, Vinny?"

"Ivan has been killed. I felt his death a few moments ago."

"You felt it?" How was something like that possible? As far as I knew, the bond of a vampire and his—or her—get went no deeper than creator and child. There was a duty of care to get them through the first treacherous years of turning, a responsibility that most took seriously if they didn't want the Directorate hunting their asses. But to have the depth of connection to actually feel a true death?

"Vampires who feed off emotions are different from our blood kin," she said, rich voice holding just a whisper of anger. "I share part of myself on creation, and they share a part of themselves. It makes us one. Hence, I felt the moment of his departure from this world."

"How did it happen?"

I held my hand over the phone, and mouthed her name to Ben. Seriousness suddenly overtook the light amusement that had been lingering in his eyes. "Trouble?" he said softly.

I nodded.

"He was decapitated," Vinny said.

Decapitation was the one way to prevent someone who'd taken the blood ceremony from ever rising again. Hell, it was one of the few good ways to stop a regular vampire, too. It didn't kill them outright, but with a broken neck they couldn't move and couldn't feed, and death was usually the end result.

"Did the sensation of his death tell you anything else?"

"I didn't see his murderer, if that's what you're asking," Vinny said. "But then, I do not have to. This death came via Aron Young."

After his slice-and-dice efforts on Ivan yesterday, Young was the immediate pick for prime suspect. That didn't make him guilty, of course, and neither did the certainty in Vinny's voice.

"If you didn't see it, how can you be so sure?"

"Because I tasted the need for vengeance on his lips."

Which suggested her kiss was a whole lot more than just a meeting of lips—which is what I had feared all along. God, what had she tasted on mine? Part of me wanted to ask, but maybe it was better to just ignore the whole situation.

"You tasted that, and yet still let him see Ivan?"

"His money was good," Vinny said. "And I thought I could control the situation."

And her overconfidence had now not only cost Ivan his life, but his afterlife, too.

"You had the chance last night to tell me what you knew about Aron Young. This death is on your conscience, Vinny."

If she had a conscience, that is. Personally, I figured her conscience would only come into play when it suited her.

"I realize that," she snapped. "Which is why I've rung. Aron Young lives at 4 Havard Street, Glenroy. Kill him for me."

"The Directorate isn't your personal assassination squad," I snapped back, then hung up and flung the phone back into my purse. After a deep, calming breath, I met Ben's gaze. "Ivan's dead."

"I gathered that." He crossed his arms, his expression grim. "How?"

"Decapitated."

Understanding ran through his bright eyes. "So, no rebirth then."

"No." I hesitated, then added, "I'm sorry you lost another friend."

He smiled and reached across the table, taking my hand in his and squeezing my fingers lightly. "Catch this bastard for me."

"I will." I glanced down, suddenly wishing the hands that clasped mine with such warm strength could caress the rest of me and bring me back to aching, fierce life. I wanted that. Wanted it bad.

I just wasn't sure that I was ready for it.

Besides, I had a bad guy to catch, and as much I had never wanted to be a guardian, I had grown to enjoy many parts of the job. I couldn't now shirk responsibility to pursue pleasure.

I rose. "I'll ring you later. We'll finish this another time."

"I certainly hope so."

He released my hand, and my hormones let out a collective sigh of frustration. I ignored them and headed out.

Once I was in my car and back on the road, I switched on the onboard and contacted the Directorate. Jack answered.

"I need another cell phone number, boss."

"Yeah, like they're something I can just haul out of my ass and hand around willy-nilly."

I grinned. "I was under the impression you could do anything."

"You, my dear guardian, are testing even my limits."

There was an undercurrent of amusement in his voice, which meant he wasn't as grouchy as his words made out. A quick look down at the screen confirmed the fact. There was a decided twinkle in his eyes. Maybe he'd found himself a nice little blood donor last night. "So tell me why you need to lose a perfectly good phone number."

"Because it seems our emo vampire has acquired it. She rang me just now to tell me we've another dead body."

"You kissed her, didn't you?"

"Well, yeah, because it was the only way to get the information I wanted."

"Emo vamps siphon information through intimate contact."

"I figured as much when she called me. But it got me the name, so I can't say I wouldn't do it again."

I could almost feel his sudden grin. "Darlin', you've come such a long way since we first dragged you kicking and screaming into this job."

There wasn't much I could say about the truth in that statement, so I got back to business. "The accountant that was attacked last night was killed this morning, apparently. Vinny rang to give me the killer's address. I'm heading over there now."

"Did the vamp who attacked him last night feel very old?"

"I didn't get a whole lot of time to sniff him out, but I'd have to guess no."

"Then it can't be the same killer. It's after nine."

And young vamps fried at the slightest touch of

sunlight. "Then either he has an accomplice, or he's older than he seems."

"Just be aware of both possibilities when you go in there."

"Boss, I have been doing this for a little while now. You don't need to tell me the basics anymore."

He harrumphed. "You may know the basics, my dear, but you have a frightening tendency to ignore them."

"But that's what makes me a good guardian, isn't it?" I said, then hung up before he could comment further.

It didn't take all that long to get across to Glenroy. It was one of Melbourne's older suburbs, and had originally been the haunt of the working class. These days, it had become a wasteland of run-down and grimy-looking houses—and run-down and grimy-looking people. Which was odd really, considering the closeness to the city.

Using the nav-computer, I found Havard Street and parked several houses up from my target. Number four was a red-brick affair with a sagging roof and smashed front windows. It didn't look as if anyone was living there, but maybe that was the whole point.

I got my gun out of the secure box under the seat, then climbed out, locked the car, and walked down. The scent of decay bloomed in the air, heavily enriched with the smell of humanity. The house beside my quarry's looked to be in a similar state of disrepair, but there were clean-looking floral curtains adorning the windows, and a shiny new car sitting in the driveway. Not hard to guess where all the money had gone in *that* household.

With the heavy scents that already rode the air, it was hard to catch Young's. Even when I walked through the broken front gate, the wrongness that I'd come to associate with him failed to materialize. I frowned and stopped just short of the steps. Neither of the front rooms had glass, let alone curtains, so I very much doubted Young would be in either of them. Even if he *was* older than I'd been presuming, he still wouldn't be able to stand the amount of sunlight that was streaming in through those windows.

I flexed my fingers, then gripped the laser a little tighter and made my way around to the side of the house. A ramshackle wooden fence divided the rear yard from the front. I jumped it easily enough, then kept to the side of the house as I crept forward. The ground here was barren, and little puffs of dirt rose with each step, making my nose twitch with the need to sneeze.

I ducked past a window and approached the back of the house. There were fewer windows here, but again, none of them were curtained or boarded—which was extremely unusual for the haunt of a newer vampire.

Dirt and cobwebs caked the back door, but the old metal handle gleamed in the sunlight. The dirt around the handle was smudged—as if fingers had brushed it when opening the door.

So obviously, someone *had* been through here recently. I just had to hope it was a vampire, and not some poor hobo looking for shelter for the night. Because if it was the latter, he was about to get a very big fright.

I walked up the steps and wrapped my fingers

around the handle. Nothing seemed to be moving inside, and the smell of vampire remained annoyingly absent.

Hoping Vinny hadn't sent me on a wild goose chase, I twisted the handle and carefully opened the door. Cold air rushed out at me, filled with the aromas of rot and age. But wrapped within those scents was the slightest hint of vampire.

It wasn't exactly a fresh smell, but he'd at least been here. He might still be, for all I knew.

I edged inside, my back to the wall and finger on the trigger of my gun. This back room was small, and filled with cobwebs and yellowed newspapers. I flared my nostrils, seeking the scents beyond what was in this room. Still nothing strong. I crept past the stacks of paper and into what had once been a kitchen. What remained of the counters showed recent use. A newish kettle sat on a stove, and a jar of coffee and a cracked mug sat nearby.

Young—or whoever was living here—was going all out when it came to the luxuries, obviously.

I continued forward, into a hallway. The wooden floorboards creaked under my steps, the sound seeming to echo oddly through the silence.

There was another room to the right, but again, beside newspapers and rubbish, it was empty. As was the bathroom and the living room. The front room possessed a bed that appeared to have been used recently, if the crinkled state of the sheets was anything to go by.

And Young *had* been in here. His scent was faint, but nevertheless here—it seemed not even the breeze coming through the smashed windows could remove the foulness of it.

But why would a vampire have a bed in one of the sunnier rooms of the house? Or did he only use it at night, when he wasn't out torturing people for whatever sick reasons he had?

Whatever the reason, he didn't appear to be here now. I blew out a breath and lowered the weapon. What next? It wasn't usual for a vamp to have more than one bolt-hole, but Vinny has seemed pretty positive that this was his current address. I mightn't trust her, but I trusted the anger that had been in her voice. Trusted her need for vengeance.

I moved back into the hallway. *None* of these rooms were exactly dark—certainly not dark enough for a vamp needing to avoid sunlight, anyway.

So, if he *was* here, he'd have to have a daytime bolt-hole. I looked up at the ceiling. Old places like this had high rooflines, and it wasn't unusual for this attic area to be used as a storage area. And if it could fit junk, it could certainly fit a vampire.

I flicked my vision to infrared and studied the ceiling again. Nothing in the area immediately above me. I walked back through the house, gaze searching the shadows above me. It wasn't until I reached the kitchen that I saw the heat of life.

Only it didn't look big enough to be a vampire. It was more the size of a small cat.

Frowning, I retraced my steps until I found the hatchway, which was in the bathroom. After making sure the old cabinet would support my weight, I climbed up and carefully pushed aside the cover.

Dust and old spiderwebs drifted down from the darkness, and I brushed them away from my face. Spindly cracks of light ran across the roof high above, suggesting the old tin wasn't as waterproof—or light-proof—as it had looked from outside. After checking that the life source hadn't moved, I flicked the laser's safety on and shoved it in my pocket, then grabbed either side of the hatch and quickly hauled myself up. My gun was back in my hand before my butt hit the ceiling.

The red blur of life hadn't moved, but its oddly round eyes were regarding me steadily.

There was no smell of vampire up here at all. Just rotting wood mixed with the slightest tang of excrement. Not human excrement—not even vampire. This had an aroma that suggested some sort of animal had made itself at home here.

I switched back to normal vision and looked around. Despite the light creeping in through all the cracks, the edges of the roofline were still wrapped in shadows, and that's where my quarry—whatever it was—was hiding.

I rose and crept forward. Dust stirred, dancing in the streaks of light and tickling my nose. I sniffed, trying not to sneeze so I wouldn't startle whatever it was in the corner.

I was halfway across the roof when it moved, briefly coming out into the lighter areas before scampering off to the shadows at the other end. I smiled, and some of the tension eased from my shoulders.

It was nothing more dangerous than a brush-tailed

possum. The little marsupials had flourished in suburbs all across Australia, and while they were damn noisy at night—and often messy when they got into roof cavities—they weren't particularly dangerous unless cornered and frightened.

The fact that *this* one was living here suggested a vampire wasn't. While they were comfortable sharing living space with humans and most nonhumans, vamps seemed to send them scattering.

I blew out a frustrated breath, then made my way back to the hatch and jumped back down.

This place had proven to be one big, fat dead end. Young might have been here, but he wasn't now. Whether he would come back was the question—and though the kettle and coffee suggested he would, with crazy vamps you never could tell.

And I wasn't about to hang about and wait for him. Jack could get the night guys to run a watch on the house—there were more of them anyway. I needed to get back to the other investigation before our bloodthirsty cat found another horny male to beat and murder.

In the room ahead, a board creaked. Which wasn't usual in old houses, granted, but up until now, the floorboards had only creaked when I'd stepped on them.

I stopped. The creaking didn't.

Someone—or something—was in the house with me. My fingers tightened around the laser.

I couldn't feel the presence of a vampire. Couldn't smell him.

And yet the hairs on the back of my neck were standing on end, and the sudden sensation that trouble waited just around the corner sat like a weight in my stomach.

As it turns out, my clairvoyance had it all wrong.

Trouble wasn't waiting around the corner.

It was right behind me.

Chapter 6

I sensed him a heartbeat before he attacked, but that was enough time to move. I was *very* fast, and even though I didn't move all that far, it still saved my life.

The steel pipe that had been aimed at my head hit my shoulder instead. Pain exploded—a red-hot agony that reverberated up through my brain and right down my arm. My fingers went numb almost instantly, and the laser fell to the floor with a clatter.

Air stirred again.

I swore vehemently and dropped, scooping the weapon with my left hand and firing blindly behind me. Blue light flashed and plaster exploded, sending a cloud of white dust through the air. Then the boards creaked, and though I heard no footsteps, I sensed the vamp was moving away.

I swung around and ran after him. The room was

totally empty and even switching to infrared didn't help. Dammit, he *was* here somewhere, so why couldn't I see him? Hell, I couldn't even see the pipe he was using and *that* was just plain weird.

His scent got stronger as I neared the door that led out into the hallway. I skidded to a halt and fired, using a sweeping motion from left to right. Wood fiber joined the plaster dust and the stench of burned hair suddenly tainted the air. Several grimy, greasy tufts plopped to the floor just beyond the doorway. He swore, then moved, skittering away like a spider on all four legs—something I sensed rather than actually saw.

I edged out the door, my nostrils flaring as I tried to capture the elusive scent of him. Dammit, how could the feel of him—the smell of him—have been so strong last night and yet so faint now, no matter how close I got? For that matter, how the hell could he be invisible when he'd been perfectly visible last night?

And if he had this sort of power, why hadn't he used it last night rather than running?

It wasn't a psychic trick—not only hadn't I felt any attempts at psychic intrusion, but I wasn't exactly prone to falling for any sort of vampire wiles or tricks anyway. Not in the "now you see me, now you don't" sense that humans did.

It was almost as if he didn't *exist*.

Like he was a ghost.

Except no ghost that I knew of could grab a metal pipe and attempt to brain you with it.

I crept down the hallway, my back against the wall and my shoulder protesting every little movement.

I ignored it, concentrating on the tingling sense that was Young's presence, wishing I could pin down his location. He was close. That was all I could tell. Which was a fat lot of good if he decided to come at me with the pipe again.

Another board squeaked in the kitchen—and this time, the sound seemed to be moving away. The bastard was trying to get around me again.

Or he was trying to make me *think* that he was.

Given I wasn't sure, I stayed where I was, my left hand clenched firmly around the laser and my right shoulder aching like hell. Whether this was Young or not, the minute I sensed or scented him, the bastard was dead. Invisible vampires with a murderous bent didn't get second chances—especially not when they'd already tried to kill me.

My, my, an inner voice snarked, *haven't you changed your tune since becoming a guardian?*

Maybe I had—at least when it came to murdering psychos. But I'd still like to think the trigger-pulling impulse was generally more restrained in me than in my brother. That I *wasn't* the shoot-first, think-later guardian that Jack wanted me to become.

For several minutes, nothing happened. Sweat began trickling down my spine and I gripped the gun so tightly my hand was beginning to cramp. Not a good thing when holding a laser with the power of this one.

I flexed my fingers in an effort to ease some of the tension. In that moment, air stirred. I glanced to my right, caught a glimpse of a pipe whirring straight at my face, and threw myself down and forward.

I hit the wall opposite with a bone-jarring crunch and, for a moment, saw red as the pain in my shoulder caused a wave of agony that had my head spinning and my stomach twisting. The now-visible pipe hit the wall behind me and clattered to the floor.

I sucked in a breath that did little to ease the blinding ache and, in the process, tasted the foulness of vampire.

A foulness that was getting stronger with every second.

He was coming straight at me.

I dropped low and spun, lashing out with a foot. Saw a blur of washed-out color leap over it, then he was on me, hitting like a ton of bricks, the sheer weight of his attack forcing me backward. I hit a doorframe hard, and the pain in my shoulder intensified. Sweat broke out across my forehead and all I wanted to do was throw up. I swore and kicked out as hard as I could instead. My foot hit something solid, and there was a sharp crack.

"Bitch!"

The word stung the air, filled with venom. Then his weight left me, and suddenly his scent was fading again.

I pulled the laser's trigger. The bright beam shot out, slicing the air in front of me and continuing on, through another doorway before shattering yet more plaster and wood.

I didn't hit Young, but just for an instant, I caught a glimpse of a gaunt, ghostly face, thin lips stretched back into a snarl and yellowed canines glistening. I fired again.

Missed again.

Then he was gone, and the sense of wrongness retreated.

I was losing him.

I swore and pushed off the doorway, but the sudden movement had pain burning through every nerve ending and sent the room spinning around me. I grabbed at the wall to steady myself and took several slow, deep breaths. God, it felt like my whole damn shoulder had just gone into a spasm and it fucking *hurt*.

But I couldn't just stand here. I had to move, had to go after Young, no matter how much agony I was in. I couldn't let him get away.

I carefully shifted my sore arm and cradled it with my left, giving it some support as I walked forward. Young's scent was already drifting, dispersing on the air. What the hell was going on? How could a young vampire—and I still had no doubt that he *was* young—move around in sunlit rooms so easily?

And how the fuck could he be invisible?

That wasn't any vampire power I'd heard of. But then, I wasn't exactly up on vampire law and history. There could be a dozen different types of suckers, for all I knew. The emos had certainly been a surprise.

I followed the tenuous scent forward. It led straight out the door and into the sunshine. Any normal vampire would have burned right there and then, but not Young. I followed his trail out the gate and down the street, until the rising wind tore the trail apart and left me with nothing.

I'd lost him.

God, this day was *not* going well.

I sat down on a brick fence and carefully let go of my arm so I could press the com-link in my ear.

"Hello, anyone out there?"

There was a pause, then a deep voice said, "Liaison Benson here, Riley. You okay? You're sounding a little off."

"That's because I *am* a little off. Is Jack around?"

"Not in the immediate vicinity, no."

Damn. "Tell him I checked that address Vinny gave me, and it was our vamp's lair, but the bastard got away. Ask him what sort of vampire is immune to sunlight and invisible."

"Invisible?" I could hear the doubt in Benson's voice. "I know there's day-walkers, but they tend to be humans—"

"Yeah, I know all that," I snapped. "Just ask him."

"Okay. Anything else?"

The sudden lack of warmth in his tone suggested I'd offended him, and I sighed. A common problem with new liaisons was the fact they expected civility—and while I was generally more than happy to provide it, now was not one of those times.

Still, I'd been new once, too. So I said, "Benson, not only am I pissed off about losing my target, but I'm also sitting here with a busted shoulder. If I sound a little snappish, I'm sorry."

"You want medical assistance?"

"Just send someone to take me to the hospital. I can't drive like this, and shifting shape won't help." The bones would still be out, regardless of what shape I took. What hurt in one form was going to hurt in another.

"Janny's on her way home and is currently close to your location. I'll get her to detour and drive you to hospital."

"Janny? Where's she from?"

"She's part of Mel's cleanup team. You would have seen her yesterday. She's tall and thin."

Ah, the woman who had reminded me of an insect. "That would be great. Thanks, Benson."

"No problem."

He signed off. I switched the com-link to receive only, so that they wouldn't hear me swearing when the pain flared, and waited for my ride to arrive.

*I*t turned out my shoulder wasn't busted, but rather dislocated. Which meant that once everything was put back into place, the pain would vanish and I'd only be left with soreness.

The bad news, of course, was that I had to get the shoulder put back into place to achieve this result.

It was a process that hurt more than the actual injury did, and the wolf within came roaring to the surface in retaliation. It was a real battle to curb my instinctive need to batter the cause of all this pain away from me.

Once the doctor had gotten the ball back into the socket, the pain stopped almost instantly. An ache remained, but that I could handle.

"You should wear a sling for a day or two," he

commented, stepping back warily as I jumped off the table. "And ice it regularly to help with the swelling."

"I'm a werewolf, Doc." I grabbed my sweater and my gun from the nearby chair. "And the Directorate doesn't give time off for minor injuries like this."

"That's against the labor laws—"

I snorted softly. "Like either the Directorate or the bad guys give two hoots about the labor laws." Hell, I couldn't even see many humans being overly worried about the noncompliance of the laws at the Directorate. Not when it was being done to protect their butts. "Thanks for patching me up, though."

He nodded, and I got out of there as quickly as possible. Hospitals were high on my list of *un*favorite places—mainly because, like cemeteries, they held far too many ghosts. And I'd had more than enough of *those* today.

I found Liander waiting at the bottom of the hospital's front steps. He was dressed in dark jeans and an aqua shirt, and his silver hair was streaked with a blue that matched his shirt. His scent spun around me, rich and warm. Much like the man himself. I smiled a greeting.

"Hey, makeup man, what are you doing here?" I gave him a kiss on the cheek, then linked my good arm through his. "And don't you look smashing."

He grinned, silver eyes twinkling. "I just came from a series of interviews about the special effects. Drumming up interest in the new movie and all that."

"So why are you here? Not that I'm complaining, mind."

"Rhoan rang and said you might need a lift. I wanted

to talk to you anyway, so here I am." He glanced down at my arm. "How's the busted shoulder?"

Someone at the Directorate had obviously contacted Rhoan. Jack might be the only one who knew we were brother and sister, but everyone knew we were from the same pack, and living together. And they knew better than to keep injury information from Rhoan—even if he generally knew if I was hurt before they did. "It wasn't busted, just dislocated."

"Ow." He screwed up his nose. "I think that's more painful than a break."

Having had a few breaks in my time, I'd have to disagree. Dislocation might be fucking painful, but so was a busted limb.

"So what do you want to talk about?" I said, as he guided me to the right. "Not that useless brother of mine again, I hope. You know I have little influence over him."

Liander smiled. "Your useless brother has been rather well behaved of late. No complaints, either in or out of the bedroom."

For which I was glad. The last couple of years had been pretty rough for Liander when it came to the relationship between him and my brother, and he deserved some good times for a change. "So what's the problem?"

He unlocked the door of his old Ford, then said, "You remember that name you mentioned? The one I said sounded familiar?"

"Aron Young?"

"Yeah. I remembered where I knew it from." He motioned me to sit, so I did. He slammed the door shut, then ran around to the driver's side and climbed in. After starting up the car, he added, "I've got pictures at home, if you'd like to see if it's the same man."

"I would, but I need to pick up my car from Glenroy, first." I gave him the street name, then shifted in the seat so that I was facing him and said, "So tell me all."

"He was briefly in the same school as me." He glanced in the rearview mirror, then pulled out into the traffic. "Tenth grade, at Beechworth Secondary College."

I raised my eyebrows. "You went to a state school?"

He nodded. "The Moore pack was a small one, and we certainly couldn't afford to set up our own private school. The cost of building and hiring teachers was just too much."

"And the local community didn't mind?" While wolves and other supernaturals might have become an accepted—even if sometimes not *liked*—part of city living, there were still pockets in country areas that preferred to keep their towns as free as possible from the nonhuman "taint."

A task that was harder in the alpine areas, simply because there were so many wolf packs up there. Mountains were a good place to run free and wild.

"Unlike some of the packs around, the Moores were well integrated into the local community." He shrugged. "We did community stuff, Dad coached the local football team, and Mom was heavily involved in church fetes. People forgot what we were, to a great extent."

"Sounds like it was a nice place to grow up." Better

than what Rhoan and I had, anyway. But then, that wouldn't have been hard.

"It was." He gave me a quick smile, then added, "Anyway, Young transferred into our school at the start of tenth grade. He was there long enough for the school photos, but disappeared a month or so before the end of the year."

"Was he pulled out or suspended?"

"Neither. He actually disappeared." He pulled to a halt at a red light and glanced at me. "There were rumors, of course. He got mixed up with some pretty bad elements, and there was talk he'd been involved in some sort of initiation gone wrong."

"Was he human?"

"Shifter. Some sort of bird." He shrugged. "I never had much to do with him, so I really couldn't say for sure."

At least that explained how he'd disappeared on me the night I'd chased him from Vinny's. When a nonhuman became a vampire, they took whatever shifting skill they had into *un*life. But if he could shift shape, why didn't he simply fly from the building from the very start? Hell, if he could disappear, why hadn't he simply done that rather than run? "Did the police investigate the disappearance?"

"Yeah. No charges were ever brought, and a body was never found. If something *did* happen, it was well covered up by everyone involved."

"What about his parents?"

He raised his eyebrows. "What about them?"

"How did they react to their son going missing?"

"From what I remember, furiously. But about a month after the disappearance, they picked up stakes and left town. We never saw them again."

"And there were no whispers around town about why they might have left?"

"Not that I can remember. But I was a kid, so I'd probably lost interest in the whole situation by then."

Which was one major difference between him, and me and my brother. We would have investigated. I had a nose for trouble, and I hadn't been afraid to use it—as the many scars that scattered my body would attest.

"Has the school photo got names attached?"

"Yep." He looked at me. "You think your Aron Young's recent spate of murders has something to do with this Aron Young's disappearance all those years ago?"

"I have no idea what to think. I don't even know if I have the right Aron Young. Right now, I'm just grabbing at straws."

"If it is him, it's a long time to hold a grudge."

"Maybe he needed time to build up courage." Or strength, perhaps. It couldn't be easy for a ghost to pick up solid objects. "Is there anyone up in Beechworth who might remember more about the case? Who was the cop on the case?"

"Old Jerry Mayberry was the local cop. He's retired, but still living up there, as far as I know." He gave me a half-smile. "Haven't been back up there for a while now."

I shifted in my seat and looked at him. "How did your pack react when they realized you were gay?"

"I got more grief from the local kids than I did from the pack." He shrugged. "I think it was a disappointment to my mom, more than anything, because she wanted grandkids. But my sister has had five in the last seven years, so that's one problem solved."

A little bit of envy swirled through me. Having a whole pack of kids had once been my dream, too. But that was gone forever—well, mostly. I still had viable eggs frozen, but I would never be the one to carry them. "Your sister has five kids? How come we've never met them?"

He laughed. "She comes down here to escape the kids, not show them off."

"But I'd love to meet them sometime."

He gave me an amused look. "Spend an hour with that lot, and the whole idea of being a mom will suddenly *not* seem so alluring. Trust me, they're a handful."

"Kids are. Hell, I was."

"Imagine you and Rhoan multiplied by about ten. That's how bad they are."

I grinned. "No one can be *that* bad."

"Okay, so maybe I exaggerate a little." The amusement in his expression and the twinkle in his eyes did little to deny the statement. It also showed just how much he loved those kids. "Seeing you're coming back to my place after you pick up your car, you want to stop for some lunch?"

"If you're going to cook it, I'll definitely eat it." My cell phone decided to ring at that precise point, so I added as I reached for it, "At least, I hope I can, if this isn't Jack with another problem."

Unfortunately, it was.

"Riley?" Jack said, as soon as I pressed the receive button. "We've got another one."

"Man or woman?"

"Woman. Another one of the names in James's Rolodex."

"You know, our murderess seems to be targeting those women as much as the men."

"Which is why I've sent Kade on to the murder scene, and I want you to go talk to Dia. Maybe she can shed some light on what is going on."

It was a *big* maybe. I liked Dia—a lot—but the information she saw generally tended to be vague, at best. She was far more accurate when it came to personal stuff—which is why I tended to avoid too much hand-to-hand contact whenever we went to coffee or lunch. My life so far had not gone the way I'd planned, and I didn't want to know that the future would go to shit, as well. Not knowing meant I could still hope. Still dream.

But even if she couldn't give us any direct psychic help, she *was* a part of the Toorak set, so she could at least give me information about the Trollops, as James's secretary had so charmingly called them.

"I've already rung her," Jack continued. "She's not home, but she said she'd meet you at the usual place in half an hour."

The usual place was an out-of-the-way nook in Brunswick that had some of the best coffee I'd ever tasted, and that didn't mind kids running around making noise. Which meant Dia had her daughter, Risa, with her. "I'll drive over as soon as I pick up my car. Did Benson pass on my question about invisible vampires?"

"Yeah, but I haven't had time to research the database yet. Personally, I've never heard of that particular skill in vamps, but it's not like I've been around long enough to meet all the different types."

"But you've been around long enough to be fairly high up the vampire ladder." And considering he'd been a vamp for over eight hundred years, you'd think he would have heard *something* in that time.

"Yeah, but that ladder is composed mainly of blood vamps, with a few emos scattered here and there. We generally don't get other types of vamps joining."

I raised my eyebrows. "Joining? I was under the impression the hierarchy system was a natural part of being turned." Meaning, young suckers started at the bottom of the ladder, and rose through the ranks as they got older and stronger.

"It is for blood vamps. And it was—is—a good method of keeping track of all blood vamps, and ensuring there is no war between the different bloodlines."

I wondered what bloodline Jack had come from—and whether he'd ever created his own fledglings.

Wondered whether Quinn ever had.

He didn't seem the type, but then, what did I really know about either him or his history?

"I still can't see how that works, you know. Vamps are just as hungry for power as everyone else." Probably more so. "What's to stop someone down the ladder bumping off those ahead?"

"The threat that his or her whole line would be erased."

"So it's not so much a matter of honor and respect, as Quinn said, but rather fear?"

"It often works better than respect." Jack shrugged. "Anyway, there's a database kept of our history—a record, if you like, of the vamps who have lived and died since the hierarchy came into place. I'll check it for any mention of a line of vamps immune to sunlight. But don't hold out too much hope. I'd imagine such immunity would have been greatly studied had it existed."

Or kept very secret indeed. After all, they wouldn't want humanity knowing there were some branches of vampires who could move around in daylight. Humans had enough trouble dealing with the nighttime versions.

"Once I talk to Dia, I might head over to Vinny's and see what she can tell me." After all, she'd kissed the sucker. Maybe she'd tasted what he was.

"Be careful," Jack said, and hung up.

"Bad news?" Liander asked.

"Yeah, looks like I'm going to miss lunch." I shoved my phone back into my pocket. "If you see Rhoan tonight, could you give him the photos? I want to check if there are any other links to that school and Young's disappearance."

"Will do." He paused, turning right into traffic, then said, "So, how badly are Collingwood going to defeat Carlton in this week's match?"

I snorted softly, and we got into yet another argument about the pros and cons of our favorite football teams. It filled the time.

He dropped me off at my car then continued on. I got my keys out of my pocket, but didn't immediately climb into my car. I walked back down the street and checked whether Young had crept home.

He hadn't—at least, not that I could smell anyway. Which mightn't have meant anything considering how little I'd caught his scent the first time.

Brunswick was only a ten minute drive from Glenroy, but by the time I found parking and got to the restaurant, I was a good twenty minutes late. I couldn't see Dia sitting in her usual spot on one of the outside tables, but as I neared the door, little Risa came bounding out of the restaurant and flung herself at my legs.

"'iley!" she yelled, wrapping her tiny arms around my left leg and hanging on with the grip of a boa. "Coke!"

I laughed and picked her up, ignoring the twinge in my shoulder as I spun her around lightly before holding her close. She smelled of soap and powder and warmth, and made me wish again for a child of my own.

"Hey, monkey," I said. "What does your mommy say about you getting Coke?"

Her amazingly bright violet eyes twinkled with mischief. "Mommy said yes!"

I grinned as I entered the café. Dia was in the far corner, sitting in a booth near the large play area the owners had provided for the kids. She was, as usual, both immaculate and stunning. Her hair was a pure whitish-silver that shone with an almost unnatural brilliance, and when combined with the luminous blue of her eyes and the white business suit she wore, she was hard to miss.

Of course, the blue of her eyes wasn't natural, same as her silver hair. Her true hair color was a mix of silver and brown, and her eyes were also naturally brown, ringed by blue.

Dia wasn't only a psychic, but a clone with Helki shapeshifting genes who was able to subtly alter her appearance as easily as I could become a wolf. The silver and blue suited her psychic business better—and enabled her to use her true form when she didn't want to be noticed. Little Risa had obviously picked up her father's coloring, although Dia never talked about him nor was there mention of him on Risa's birth certificate.

Few would have guessed Dia was blind. The sight she *did* have came through the presence of a creature known as a Fravardin—an unseen guardian spirit who'd been assigned protection duties by her clone brother, Misha. They'd failed in their duty to protect him, but only after a bloody battle that had taken many of their lives. After his death, they'd honored his wishes and continued to protect Dia. When she was outside the house, one of the Fravardin kept close—and by linking lightly to the creature's mind, Dia was able to move with a serenity and grace that denied her handicap. I had no idea where the creature was right now, but given she was looking directly at me, it had to be somewhere close.

"Mommy didn't say yes," she said dryly. "But Riley rarely takes notice of a no, anyway."

"It's only once a week." I slid into the U-shaped booth then placed Risa on the seat beside me. The little girl clambered to her feet and ran around the booth, white pigtails flying as she threw her arms around Dia's neck.

"Love Mommy," she said.

"That child has the world worked out already," I said, swallowing a laugh. "She's going to do just fine when she grows up."

"Oh yeah." Dia picked her daughter up and swung her over the table. "Go play until the drinks get here."

Risa ran off happily. Dia shook her head, amusement and love evident in her expression. "I've already ordered the coffee and cake. What's the problem?"

"I need to know about the Toorak Trollops."

She lifted a pale eyebrow. "How have the Trollops come under Directorate scrutiny? They're basically harmless."

"Yeah, but someone is bumping them off and stealing their identities to kill their lovers."

The amusement fell from her features. "God, there's been nothing along the gossip lines suggesting anything like that."

"We've managed to keep the press relatively quiet." They were still concentrating on the dead politician, and I think Jack was hoping to keep it that way. "What can you tell me about them?"

She wrinkled her nose. "They're actually not very nice people."

"Not nice how?"

"It's their attitude. Not only do they treat men as dumb playthings, but they go into relationships simply to see how much they can get out of it. It's become something of a game between them."

I smiled a thanks at the waitress as she brought over three plates of thick banana cake, then said, "I take it you mean gifts and money?"

"But also position. They try to outdo each other when it comes to bed partners."

"So a politician would be prized more than a shoe store owner?"

"Depends on who the politician and the shoe store owner are, but yes." She paused, looking at me steadily for a moment. "So the murder of Gerard James was not political, as the press have been saying?"

"Nope. Bad choice of a bed partner, we think."

She picked up a spoon and scooped up a piece of banana cake, munching on it for several seconds before saying, "I know both Cherry Barnes and Alana Burns were going out with him. Can't say I'd be sorry to see either of them dead and gone."

I raised my eyebrows. "And here I was thinking you got along with everybody."

She snorted softly. "In my line of work, I have to try. Doesn't mean I always succeed. Though if Alana has been murdered, it's odd that I didn't see her death coming."

"So she was a client?"

Dia nodded. "So was Cherry. Neither of them were pleasant customers, so I was thankful the others stayed away."

"What do they come to you for?"

She shrugged. "Usual shit. Am I going to find wealth and happiness in my life, that sort of stuff."

The waitress brought over our coffees and a small glass of Coke. A squeal of happiness erupted from the play area, and a white-headed blur was suddenly scrambling over her mother to get to the soda.

"See what you've done?" Dia said, shaking her head in amusement. "She'll be hyper for hours now."

"You say that like it's a bad thing." I grinned as the little girl grabbed the straw and began drinking, a look of pure bliss on her face.

"It is when I have several clients to look after this afternoon." She shook her head. "I saw Alana two weeks ago. She seemed her normal, aggravating self then."

I hadn't yet read the cleanup team report, but the state of decay suggested Alana had been dead for at least a week—meaning Dia had probably seen her just before she'd died. "So you didn't sense anything odd about her?"

"No." She frowned. "Though with Alana, it was difficult to tell. The self-centered are often hard to read."

"Do you know of anyone who might want to kill her?"

She smiled. "She was certainly never on Cherry's Christmas list."

Dia's tone was dry, and I raised my eyebrows. "So the two of them didn't get along?"

"Cherry was more a wannabe Trollop than an official member. I'm afraid Alana delighted in proving to Cherry that she would never be one of them, simply because she wasn't good enough to keep her men."

"Meaning Alana deliberately seduced Gerard James just to prove a point to Cherry?"

"Oh, Alana wasn't the only Trollop to seduce away Cherry's conquests. It's something of a game for them all."

"Then why would Cherry want to be one of them?"

"Because they were the 'in' crowd, and Cherry is desperate to be seen with the right people."

"Even if she hates them?"

"Even if." Dia shrugged. "She is attracted to the power she thinks they hold. She wants that, even if the personal cost is high."

And that personal cost might just give her a motive for murder. "I don't suppose Cherry is a shifter?"

"No, as human as they come."

Damn. Though I should have known better than to hope things would fall into place *that* neatly. "Have you seen Cherry recently?"

"No, not for at least a month." She frowned. "In fact, she left in something of a hurry after our last meeting. She smelled frightened."

"What did you say to her?"

"That an event from her past was not as buried as she thought, and that she needed to be careful about who she let in her door."

I smiled. "That's a warning as clear as mud. As usual."

She shrugged. "Cherry was never very open when it came to readings. It makes it hard to get details."

I raised my eyebrows. "I'm not very open, either, and yet you've been able to read me."

"That's because you're *not* unresponsive to psychic intrusion. You're just very well shielded against it."

"Oh."

She smiled and waved her spoon at my hand. "You want me to do a reading today?"

I snatched my hand out of her way. "No thanks. I've had enough bad news to last me a lifetime."

She laughed softly. "One of these days I'm going to do another reading, and you're going to love me forever."

I raised my eyebrows. "Only if you see true love and kids in my future."

"And what did I say last time? You *will* gain what you want, Riley. It just won't be in the form you have dreamed of."

I rolled my eyes. "How can babies not be in the form I dream of?"

She grinned. "No one said the future was easy to understand."

"And you make a living out of this mumbo jumbo?"

"A very good living," she said solemnly, then chuckled. "I'm just glad most of my clients aren't as skeptical as you."

"I'm not skeptical of your talent—just what it's saying about my future." I took a sip of coffee, and licked away the froth from my lips. "Besides Alana, was there any other Trollop who might be on Cherry's hit list?"

Dia frowned. "For all Cherry's faults, she doesn't seem like the murdering kind."

"Many serial killers don't."

She acknowledged the point with a nod, but added,

"Cherry wanted to be a part of their group. Destruction wasn't in her agenda."

"Well, it's in someone's agenda, and right now, she seems the most likely. Who else did she hate?"

She hesitated. "Enna Free would probably be next on any hate list."

I wondered if the body Kade had gone to check out today was Enna Free. If it wasn't—and she was still alive—then someone had to get to her before the killer cat did. I grabbed my phone and sent Jack a quick message, asking him to haul in both Enna and Cherry, then pulled a piece of banana cake toward me and scooped up a spoonful. It was, as usual, delicious. This had to be the one place in Melbourne where I'd choose banana over chocolate any day. "Don't suppose you'd know where Enna is today?"

"No, but there's an invitation-only charity fund-raiser happening over at Sparkies this evening, and I know some of the Trollops are attending that. Apparently, there's going to be some good man-meat there. Alana's words, not mine."

I snorted softly. "You know, if a man said that about a woman, there'd be an uproar."

"The world is warped," she agreed, then waved her spoon at me. "You want to get into that shindig?"

"If you can get me in, yes."

"Risa, can you get Mommy's phone out of her bag, please?"

The little girl leaned sideways, dug into the patent leather handbag sitting beside her, pulled out the phone, and handed it across. Then she gave me a cheeky grin and said, "Cake, please."

"Come here then, monster."

She scooted around, and I fed her cake while Dia made her call.

"Done," she said, after a few minutes. "And that's enough cake for you, little one."

Risa's pout lasted for all of two seconds, then she scooted back around the table again to finish off her Coke.

"The ticket will be waiting at the door. The cost is five hundred."

I just about choked. "God, I'm glad the Directorate will be paying for it."

"You're just lucky it's one of the cheap functions. Some of the others can be a grand or two."

Thankfully, tonight's event wasn't one of those, because Jack's reaction would not have been pretty. "Have you got Cherry's address?"

"Not on me, but I can phone it through once I get home." She paused, and sipped her coffee. "Would you like a list of all the Trollops?"

"That would be great."

I dug into my bag, then handed over a small notebook and pen. She scrawled in fourteen names, then handed both the pen and book back. "Anything else?"

"What does Enna look like?"

Dia smiled. "I thought you might have guessed that."

I raised my eyebrow. "Blonde hair, blue eyes, and rake thin?"

"Yep. It's their calling card—even when they are naturally dark."

"Men do seem to like their blondes."

She snorted softly. "Like redheads have any reason to complain. Except when they're on a self-imposed diet, that is."

"I've got a feeling the diet might be ending."

"Really? Do tell."

So I told her about Ben and the case we were involved in, and we filled the next hour chatting away like old friends rather than new—something I'd once thought would never happen.

Of course, as much as I would have liked to stay there all day, I couldn't—Jack would have a pink fit—so I eventually headed back to the Directorate.

Jack wasn't in the day-shift office when I arrived, but Kade was sitting at his desk. I tossed my bag on my desk, then walked over to the coffee machine. We finally had mugs rather than those horrible plastic cups, but it didn't make the coffee taste any better. Jack had promised a machine upgrade, but after months of hearing a similar promise when it came to our office area, I had no expectations of it actually happening any time soon.

I slopped some milk into both cups, pressed the coffee button, and shoved the first cup underneath, then glanced over at Kade. "So who was murdered this time?"

He grimaced and leaned back in his chair. "One Cherry Barnes. Thirty-four-year-old divorcée who's been dead for three weeks."

Well, so much for my thoughts about Cherry having all the right motives for murder. "And no one noticed the smell?"

"Apparently not. No one reported her missing, either. Her mom and sister thought she was off on a cruise with some man."

"So who found her?"

"Pest control. They'd been called in because of a sudden influx of rats in the other apartments."

I screwed up my nose and switched mugs. "Don't tell me—"

"Yep, they've been chowing on the body. I don't think the pest controller will be eating for the next week."

"I'm glad I wasn't the one called in." I plonked my butt on the edge of his desk and handed him a mug. "I guess the body was too badly decomposed to tell whether she'd been mutilated or not?"

"She was, but according to Cole, it wasn't our cat. The slashes to her back and stomach are different."

I raised my eyebrows. "Different how?"

Kade shrugged. "He wouldn't be pinned down. I guess we have to wait for the report."

"What about Alana Burns?"

"She'd been slashed on the neck, and there was bruising. She wasn't as cut up or eaten as our second female victim, but both did happen."

"So the violence is definitely escalating." I paused and drank some coffee. It was bitterer than usual, but maybe that was a direct result of drinking the silky smooth stuff at the café. "So if Cherry died three weeks

ago, we might have another male body out there waiting to be discovered."

"Could be. I'm currently going through the cops' un-
solved murder files, just to see if I can find anything."
He reached forward, grabbed a folder, and handed it to
me. "Forensic reports for Gerard James and the shoe
seller. The DNA found at both scenes matches."

"What about Alana Burns? Any DNA found on
her?"

"No. But Cole suspects they'll find plenty on the
body of the second woman. She was bitten a lot."

I opened the folder and skipped the photos, going directly to the reports. At first glance, there didn't seem to
be anything I hadn't already guessed. "So has Cole got
any idea of what we might be dealing with?"

"He thinks it could be a bakeneko."

"A *what?*"

Kade grinned. "My reaction, too."

"So what is it?"

"Apparently, it's a cat with supernatural abilities."

"A cat? So we're not dealing with a human shifter,
but an actual cat who can take human shape?"

Which certainly went a long way to explain the arro-
gance the woman had shown by waving to the witness.
Cats had a huge sense of their own superiority.

"Makes trying to catch this bitch a whole lot harder,
doesn't it? I mean, she really *isn't* going to be thinking
like a regular person." He shook his head, then took a
sip of his coffee. His expression crinkled up in much the
same manner as mine had. "God, that's awful."

"Won't stop either of us from drinking it, though."

"Hell, no." He raised his cup in salute, brown eyes twinkling. "I did an Internet search, and the only thing I could come up with was a couple of Japanese legends."

"I'm guessing they didn't say how to kill this thing." Japanese myths rarely did, for some odd reason.

"No. But they did say that a bakeneko can change its shape into that of a human, and has been known to eat parts of its own mistress in order to shapeshift and take her place."

"Well, some of that criteria certainly fits."

"Yes. But why is it going after these men? Why would a cat—a real cat—want to destroy these people?"

"I don't know, but something has obviously set her off. We just have to try and find out what." I took a sip of coffee and studied the file for a moment. "I wonder if she actually belonged to any of the dead women?"

"Hard to say. She obviously knew the layout of that house pretty well—she ran straight to the open window when she was escaping us."

"Yeah, but I didn't see any cat trays or food bowls, which suggests she didn't actually belong there."

"You think she's a stray the women picked up?"

I smiled. "From what Dia said, the only thing these women pick up is men."

"So why the curiosity over who the cat belongs to?"

"I don't know. It's just a niggle."

He studied me for a moment, then said, "You know, there were food bowls in Cherry Barnes's kitchen."

"Then it might be worth chasing up with the neighbors to see if she had a black cat. Cherry Barnes had good reason to hate her fellow Trollops, so if it's her cat, maybe its seeking revenge on behalf of its dead mistress."

"Yeah, but Cherry wasn't killed by the cat, which means we have yet another murderer to deal with."

"It keeps the day from getting boring," I said lightly, and tossed the file back onto the desk. "Some of the Trollops are going to be at a fancy fund-raising shindig tonight. I'm going to head there and see what I can sniff out."

"You want company?"

"At five hundred dollars a ticket, she can go alone," Jack said, as he came into the room. His bald head positively gleamed under the light of the fluorescents. It looked for all the world like he'd been polishing it. "Besides, you're going to help to round up the other Trollops."

"I get all the fun jobs," Kade muttered.

"Dia gave me a list of their names," I said helpfully, and swallowed my smile as he gave me a dark look. I glanced at Jack, and added, "And she assures me the fund-raiser is one of the cheaper ones, boss."

"Dia runs a multimillion dollar empire. We scratch by on government funds. How's the shoulder?"

"Survivable."

"Good." He handed me a folder. "The report on Vinny Castillo. Thought you might like to see it."

I didn't, because I really wanted to have as little to do with her as possible. But that wasn't an option in my job—I dealt with vampires on a daily basis, and I had a feeling Vinny was going to feature in my life for a while yet.

And God, how I hated those little "feelings" of mine. Especially when they refused to provide any further information.

"We keeping an eye on her?"

"Yep. She's empire-building, no doubt about it." He poured himself a coffee and took a sip. Unlike Kade or I, he made no face. Maybe he preferred the nasty-tasting stuff. "Watch yourself around her. She has a taste for women, and I'm not entirely sure your shields will work against her sort of magnetism."

If our first meeting was anything to go by, he could be right. "Did you find any information on invisible vampires?"

"Not yet, but it's a big database, and unfortunately, not all the early stuff has been transcribed to computer."

"What about the police report on the BDSM murder?"

"I went one better. I sent a forensic crew over to examine the body. The slashes on his body matched those Ivan Lang received before his death."

"Did they say what type of weapon was involved?"

"Something sharp, but not a knife. They didn't think it was animal claws, either."

"Nothing else?"

"Not yet." He glanced at Kade. "What's the status on the murders?"

As Kade updated him, I walked over to my desk and sat down. After the eye scan and signing in, I checked the results of the Aron Young search. Both were still listed as missing, which was interesting. The third one was married, had three kids, and had been working steadily as a chef for the last thirty years. Somehow, I doubted he was our guy, but I flagged his file anyway. Someone could go out and talk to him, just in case I was wrong. After all, it wouldn't be the first time.

I tapped my fingers on the desk for a moment, then pulled up the birth certificates for the two others.

One Aron Young was in his seventies and still listed as human, which meant he probably *wasn't* our man. The Young I'd chased certainly hadn't looked that old, though vampires did tend to retain whatever age it was when they'd undertaken the ceremony. Both Quinn and Jack had obviously been fairly old—for their times—when they'd undertaken it.

The other Young was in his forties, which put him in the right age bracket. Given he was listed as missing, I did a search instead on his parents.

His father, Jonathon Young, had died a month ago. According to the death certificate, the cause was a heart attack, so nothing obviously sinister there. Though why I was expecting something sinister I couldn't actually say.

His mother was still alive, however, and living in Yuroke, a community of small farms on the northern edges of Melbourne. I glanced at my watch and decided there was plenty of time to get out there and back before I had to get ready for the function tonight. I wrote down her address, then signed out of the computer and stood up.

"I'm off to interview the mom of one of our Aron Youngs, boss."

He glanced at me. "Be careful. Until we know what we're dealing with, we don't know how to kill it."

"I doubt the mom is any danger. She's nearly ninety, for heaven's sake."

"Old biddies are mean *and* dangerous," Kade piped up. "Just let me introduce you to Sable's mom sometime. That woman could freeze the balls off Satan himself."

"I do so love the level of conversation I get with you two around," Jack said dryly.

I grinned and got out of there before said conversation deteriorated any further.

It took nearly an hour to get to Yuroke, and another ten minutes to find the right side street and house number.

Mrs. Young lived in a little weatherboard cottage that was barely visible amidst all the gum trees. I drove down the long drive, avoiding as many potholes as I could, my gaze sweeping the old house and the run-down barn that stood to the left of it. The barn actually looked in worse condition than the house, the tin roof rusted and lifting in several places, and the rear corner of the building was broken open to the elements.

The only signs of life were the several chickens that scratched out the front of the barn, and the mangy-looking dog chained to a kennel.

I stopped the car and climbed out. The wind meandered through the trees, making the leaves whisper, and the soft clucking of the chickens added a brighter note to this chorus. There was little noise coming from either the house or the shed. Even the dog was silent, watching me with disinterested eyes.

It looked for the world like this place—and the dog—had been abandoned. Yet there were clothes on the line, and a car parked just inside the lean-to garage on the right side of the house.

I swept my gaze around the buildings once more, then reached back inside my car and collected my gun. I might be dealing with an old woman, but she was an old woman with a crazy son, and just because I couldn't smell him didn't mean he wasn't here. Yuroke wasn't that far out of town, he could easily be using it as a safe house.

I slammed the door closed then walked toward the house. If the old bird happened to be inside and watching, she was doing so extremely quietly. But I didn't think she was. I couldn't smell anyone. Only rubbish and age.

The wooden steps creaked and dipped as I stood on them, and the windows to my left rattled. The whole house was in a state of decay, the window frames rotting and the weatherboards barely holding any paint. Even the door didn't look capable of withstanding much bad weather—it was warped and hanging on a slight angle, so that it didn't look properly shut.

I pressed the doorbell, but didn't hear an accompanying ringing inside the house, so I knocked instead. Even though I didn't use much force, the whole thing rattled.

There was no response. I knocked again, then stepped back and peered through the front window. It looked into a living room and, again, decay was evident. There were newspapers scattered all over the floor, their edges yellowed and curling, and a thick dust lined the top of the patterned sofas and the dark wood of the sideboards. Several cups and plates dotted the coffee table, one with cake that looked rather green. Either Mrs. Young wasn't a very good housekeeper, or the room hadn't seen human occupation for at least a couple of weeks.

"Mrs. Young?" I called out. "Riley Jenson from the Directorate. I need to talk to you."

My voice echoed through the emptiness. No answer came. Not even from the dog.

I grabbed the door handle and twisted it open. The door opened several inches then stuck fast, forcing me to lift it up and over a warped floorboard. Inside, the house smelled as bad as it looked. The air was stale and perfumed with the hint of rubbish and rot.

The floorboards creaked as I stepped inside. "Mrs. Young?"

Still no answer. Nor could I smell any life. I walked down the hallway, checking rooms as I passed each doorway. There were two bedrooms and a bathroom at the front of the house, both a good deal tidier than the living room—although the dust that was so thick in the front room had invaded these rooms as well.

The hall led to a kitchen, and it was obviously here that the old woman spent most of her time. The kitchen was small but tidy, with clean plates and cups sitting in the drainer. The little dining area consisted of a table and a couple of chairs pushed up against the wall, allowing room for a large, well-used sofa chair. A TV stood in the corner of the room.

There was a pile of newspapers at the far end of the

counter. I walked over and had a look at the date. The latest was a month old—around the same date as Mr. Young had died. Maybe his wife had moved out rather than be alone, but why would she leave the poor old dog and the chickens here? It didn't make any sense.

I swung around and saw another door. It probably led into nothing more exciting than the laundry, but I walked over to take a look anyway. My skin began to tingle several feet from the door. I frowned and stopped. Usually I only got that reaction when I was near silver—but why in hell would there be silver in this old house, especially if it housed a family of shifters?

I stepped forward and pressed my fingers against the door. The tingle grew stronger, burning my fingertips. For whatever reason, there was a *whole* lot of silver in the room beyond.

And really, there could only be one reason for that—someone wanted to restrain a shifter.

With some trepidation—and some effort—I pushed open the door. What I discovered was basically a prison. The netting started just beyond the door, and was spiderweb fine. It was made in several layers, so that the overall strength of the net was tripled. Not many shifters would have gotten through it—not without seriously injuring themselves. And even if they had, there was then the silver-coated walls to deal with. That's what I'd been feeling—the back of the door had obviously received the same treatment.

Someone had wanted to make damn sure something—or someone—couldn't get out.

The room itself had been set up like a bedroom. It

had a bed, a small bathroom area, and a TV. There was also a desk and laptop in the corner opposite to the bed. Books and magazines lay scattered about the floor, but not covering the small, stained rug.

My gaze went back to the nets. Was this the explanation for Young's parents suddenly up and leaving Beechworth? Had they discovered that their supposedly dead son was alive, but something of a monster?

Given this room, it certainly seemed possible.

But given the fortifications, how had Young escaped? And why now, if he'd spent a good thirty or so years in captivity?

And where the hell was his mom?

I backed away from the silver room and swung around. There were glass sliding doors at the far end of the small dining area, and these led out into a little patio area.

I walked across, unlatched the door, and walked out. To the right, in a little lean-to at the back of the garage, was the laundry area. To the left were steps, and these led out past the clothesline. The various shirts and undies on the line were a mix of women's and men's, but they looked as if they'd been there for some time. Bird shit decorated the backs of some of the shirts, and fade lines had begun to appear.

I walked down the steps and followed the path, ducking under the clothes and walking toward a little vegetable patch. There were big, fat pumpkins looking ready for the picking, and potatoes and carrots gone wild.

Obviously, this garden had been abandoned long before Mr. Young had died.

The path continued on, and so did I. Trees lined either side, most bearing fruit in various degrees of ripeness. Unfortunately, the birds had gotten to most of it, leaving it half-eaten and rotten.

The path ended in a little sitting area. A large liquid amber tree provided shade, and under this sat a little table and two chairs. To one side, a rose bed that was a riot of color, filling the air with sweet summery scents.

To the other side, a grave.

I'd finally found Mrs. Young.

Chapter 7

I squatted down at the foot of the grave and studied the sturdy little cross that bore her name. It was roughly made, but the painted letters were clear and strong, and the date underneath said she'd only been dead for a couple of weeks.

But the flowers that lay on top of it were fresh. Someone was coming here to look after her grave—and to feed the dog—because he would have been dead by now if not.

I rose and pressed the com-link in my ear, though given the distance from Melbourne, I wasn't entirely sure they'd pick up my signal. The tracker part of the device could pick me up anywhere in Victoria, but the coms section wasn't that strong.

"Hello, anyone listening?"

As expected, no answer came. I blew out a frustrated

breath and walked back down the path, this time heading around the other side of the house. The chickens scattered, running for safety the minute I appeared, but the old dog remained indifferent.

I squatted down beside him and scratched his head. He was little more than skin and bone, his dark, curly coat matted and unkempt. Someone might have been coming back to tend to the him, but they weren't doing a particularly good job.

I rose and continued on to the car. After scrabbling through my purse, I found my cell and dialed the Directorate. Joy of joys, Sal answered.

"What can I do for you, wolf girl?"

"You want to get a team out to my current location? I found a grave, and need an ID on the body within."

"Is this case related and urgent? Because we're stretched."

"Yes to both. Sorry, Sal, but we've a psycho on the loose and we need to stop him. Knowing who that body is will put us one step closer to that aim." Simply because knowing whether it was Mrs. Young or not would give us some idea where *not* to look next.

"I'll see what I can do."

Which was her way of saying she'd do it. "Could you also get the RSPCA out? There's a dog here that doesn't look as if he's seen a feed for a while, and a few chickens that need to be rounded up."

"Someone abandoned their dog? Bastards. I'll get right onto it."

I raised my eyebrows at the anger in her voice. Sal was a dog lover? Who'd have thought? "Thanks, Sal."

I hung up then headed back to the dog, filling up the bowl so he at least had fresh water. Then I grabbed a long bit of wood and went back inside the house.

My skin began to burn the minute I neared that room. I broke off a bit of the wood and jammed it under the door, just to ensure no one could rush up and slam it shut behind me. Then, using the rest of the stake, I pushed the netting aside far enough to step inside. Even though the silver never touched my skin, the room still felt like hell. I was just too sensitive to the metal to be able to stay here too long.

I walked over to the desk and opened the laptop. It wasn't connected to power and the batteries were flat. I reached underneath and shoved the cord into the socket, so the cleanup team could have a look at it when they got here. Then I shuffled through the magazines and books, but they were all computer and mechanical in style, and didn't tell me much about the man who had been reading them. Under the bed I could see glimpses of nudes, so obviously his parents hadn't been recalcitrant in catering to his needs—but again, it begged the question, why lock him up? If he hadn't been crazy beforehand, he sure as hell would have been after thirty of years being locked up in a room filled with silver.

There were several newspapers near the bed, so I walked over and picked them up. Three of them had an article that had been circled in red ink.

The first was about a mugging in Brighton, and I couldn't see any connection to the murders until I read halfway and saw the mention of the eyewitness.

Ivan.

The second—and oldest of them—was about a charity fund-raiser, and came with a photo of several men and women. One of those women was circled—Cherry Barnes.

The third article was tiny, little more than a rave about the hot new chef working at Hot Rabbit. Underneath was a picture of the owner—a big, balding man named Ron Cowden. A big, red-ink cross had been scrawled across his heart.

It wasn't one of the men who had already died. It was someone new.

Shit.

Papers in hand, I carefully edged back through the netting, then dropped the wood and ran to the car and the phone.

"What now?" Sal said, in a long-suffering voice.

"I need an urgent trace on a man named Ron Cowden. He apparently owns a restaurant called Hot Rabbit."

"Why?"

Sometimes, this woman could be a real pain in the ass. Which is why she did it—she knew it bugged me. She could be as big a bitch as me when she wanted to be. "If he's not dead already, he could be the next victim of our invisible vampire."

"Vampires aren't—"

"This one is," I cut in. I glanced at my watch. I'd better get moving, otherwise I was going to be late for my party. "Let me know if you find him. And we might have to bring him in if you track him down."

"It shouldn't be too hard, but I'll let Jack know extra accommodation might be needed."

"While you're talking to Jack, let him know that Cherry Barnes is probably a victim of the invisible vampire."

"Will do."

"Thanks."

I hung up again, then got back into the car and headed home. Rhoan wasn't there, and neither were the school photos from Liander. I grabbed the phone and gave Liander a call.

"Hey," he said, "you missed a great lunch."

"Yeah, sorry about that. Can I ask you a question about the photo?"

"Yep. Fire away."

"Was there a Ron Cowden in it?"

He paused, and paper rustled in the background. "Nope. There's a Jake Cowden, though."

"Could he have been a brother?"

"Maybe. I didn't really have much to do with him."

"Did he have much to do with that bad crowd you mentioned?"

"Not that I'm aware of. He was a fairly quiet kid. Kept mostly to himself."

Well, there goes *that* possible connection. "What about Ivan Lang, Cherry Barnes, or a Denny someone?"

"Denny someone?" Amusement ran through his tones.

"Sorry, I actually don't know his last name." And I hadn't yet even checked out the police report.

"There's a Denny Spalding in the photo, if that helps.

And the other two, as well. Though of course, there's no guarantee that these three are the ones you're looking for."

"You know anything about them?"

"Cherry and Denny, no, but Ivan was fixated on vampires. Said he wanted to take the ceremony and become one, one day."

"He did take the ceremony, but unfortunately, someone cut off his head and let him burn in sunlight."

"Well, that wasn't very nice of them." He paused, and must have taken a drink, because I heard him swallow. "He wasn't a member of the gang, either. But he was one of the few friends Jake Cowden had."

"So what the fuck is the connection between all these people?"

Liander snorted. "Like I'm supposed to know?"

I grinned. "Sorry, just thinking out loud."

"Seems to be a family trait." He paused again, then added, "While we're talking families, I've got a question for you."

"Question away."

"How would you feel about me moving in with you and Rhoan?"

I blinked. Talk about being caught totally off guard! "I think that would be great, but I'd have to ask why you'd want to move into our dumpy little apartment when you have a totally beautiful house of your own?" Not to mention a nifty little apartment above his studio.

"Because I want to ask Rhoan to live with me, and he's just not going to leave you any time soon."

"That's not—"

"That is, even if neither of you have ever talked about it. You're each the only pack member the other has, and I think it's going to be difficult for *anyone* to ever separate the two of you."

"But it's not like we need to live in each other's pockets."

"No, but can you honestly say that if you met your soul mate tomorrow, you could walk away from your apartment and Rhoan to go live with him?"

I opened my mouth to say "of course," then actually stopped to think about it. Rhoan and I might not live in each other's pockets, we might be able to go days— weeks—without seeing each other, but his scent was always around me, completing that part of me that needed pack, needed family. And as Liander had said, he was all I had, all I would ever have when it came to pack.

Even when I had decided to commit to Kellen, the thought of moving totally out of my apartment and away from Rhoan had never really crossed my mind. Yes, I'd contemplated staying with Kellen, but I'd never taken it that one step further. Had never thought that I wouldn't maintain my place here as well as share space with Kellen.

Maybe Kellen had realized that, too. And maybe his problem hadn't solely been with the job and my inability to give it up.

"For a man who plays with makeup, you're surprisingly insightful."

He laughed. "So you've really got no problems with it?"

"As long as you have no problems with the mess."

"I can deal with the mess. I just don't want to deal with spending nights alone anymore."

I smiled. Liander really *was* a catch and a half—not only sweet and loving, but possessing the patience of a saint. I doubt anyone else would have stuck around after all the shit Rhoan had thrown his way, soul mate or not.

I just had to hope my daft brother realized that. Yeah, he loved Liander and yeah, he'd been more committed to him recently than ever before, but he still seemed to want his own space, as well.

"You have my blessing, Liander. When are you going to ask him?"

"Tonight. He's coming back to dinner. I'll hit him with the proposal as soon as he's well fed and happy."

"Fingers and toes crossed for you, then."

"Thanks, I'll probably need it."

"You certainly will." I hesitated, then added, "Just be a little extra vigilant with security for the next couple of days, okay? Until I figure out the connection between all these murders, there is a remote possibility that you could also be on his list."

"You'd have to say *very* remote. I didn't associate with Young or the people who most likely killed him."

"Yeah, but we're not talking about a rational mind here. Promise me you'll play safe."

"Okay, I promise. Now let me go and get ready for my big night."

"Good luck with it," I said and hung up. I stripped

off then headed into the shower. Time to start making myself presentable for my big night, as well.

$\mathcal{D}$usk was crawling in across the sky by the time I pulled into the small parking lot beside Sparkies. The restaurant was all soaring arches, smoky glass, and chrome, and sat on the banks of the Yarra River like some rare jewel.

Melbourne's finest stepped out from chauffeur driven limos and Mercedes—the men uniformly elegant and the women adorned by pearls and diamonds that gleamed and sparkled under the bright entrance lights.

A thief would have had a field day—if he could have gotten past the three security guards standing discreetly in the shadows.

I climbed out of my car, then smoothed down my dress, glad I'd opted for something that wasn't black. Most of the other woman arriving were in autumn tones, which probably meant they were the "in" shades at the moment. My dress followed the simple lines of a modest, V-necked sheath—at least until I turned, revealing the plunging back that stopped tantalizingly short of my butt. And there was nothing autumn hued or modest about its color—it was a lusciously rich emerald that would stand out amongst the autumn tones as fiercely as the brightest of yellows.

The only jewelry I had was my watch, but I didn't need diamonds or pearls to liven the outfit. The red-gold of my hair was enough.

I walked over to the door and waited in line for my turn with the man ticking off guest names.

His gaze met mine, expression polite and blue eyes showing little interest in the proceedings. "Name, miss?"

"Riley Jenson."

He scanned the list, flicked over the page, then nodded. "If you'll just head through that second door to your left, your ticket will be waiting for you."

"Thanks."

He nodded, his gaze already moving on to the next person. A black-suited shifter opened the door with a polite nod as I approached. Inside, the air was warm and perfumed, heavy with the scents of human and nonhuman. I walked down a small hallway until I reached a booth.

A woman with bleached-blonde hair and a fake tan gave me a warm smile. "Here for a ticket?"

"Yes. The name is Jenson."

She shuffled through a pile of tickets, then drew one out. "Riley?"

"That's me." I handed over my credit card. Hopefully, Jack would reimburse me ASAP, because the card had just about reached its limit. I'd discovered a week ago that the man who handmade my wooden-heeled stilettos had just released an autumn range, and I'd gone on something of a spending binge. The pair I wore tonight—a shimmery emerald-colored snakeskin—had been one of five, and the most sedate of them.

The woman in the booth swiped the card—which

was one of the new smart cards, requiring fingerprint confirmation rather than a signature—so I pressed my hand into the machine and got a green-light confirmation.

"You're on table five, Miss Jenson. Just walk down this hall until you see the gentleman in black," she said, handing me back the card, the ticket, and a receipt. "He'll direct you to the right table."

"Thanks."

She gave me another warm smile. "My pleasure."

I continued on down the hall. Music wafted in from the other room, classical and soothing in sound. Voices ebbed and flowed around it, suggesting there were at least a hundred or so people inside.

The door guard gave me a smile as I approached. I handed him the ticket and he scanned it through a machine. As the door swung open, he handed me back the ticket. "Table five is around to the left, in the corner," he said. "Have a nice evening."

"Thanks. I will."

I shoved the ticket into my purse, then headed in. One thing struck me straightaway—Sparkies lived up to its name. Sparkles abounded—in the glint of the ornate chandeliers, in the chrome and glass that reflected back the flickering candles that adorned each table, even in the silver and gold thread that ran through the tablecloths and chairs.

The scents that had been evident outside bloomed to full significance. Human, shifter, and vampire vied for prominence with the flowery assault of perfume and the richer tones of aftershave, creating a cauldron of aromas that had my senses reeling.

How the hell was I going to pick any particular scent out of this?

I blew out a breath and looked around. There were plenty of people sitting at the dozen or so tables that lined the room, but there were also many more standing around the dance floor chatting. Even so, the room looked half empty. Maybe the trendy people arrived fashionably late.

I scanned the table numbers until I found mine. There were a couple of old biddies sitting there, but as they weren't likely to be either Enna Free or my murderer, I wasn't about to head over there until I absolutely had to.

Instead, I headed right, walking around the edges of the room, trying to sort through the riot of scents and track down the one that would lead me to my suspect.

I might as well have been searching for a needle in a haystack.

I was on my way back to my table when awareness hit and sent a heated wave of desire fleeing across my skin.

I stopped, my heart pounding so hard I swear it was going to tear out of my chest. There had only ever been one man who had caused that sort of reaction in me—Quinn O'Conor, ancient vampire, billionaire businessman, and former lover.

I should have guessed he might have been here, because he always seemed to support major charity events like this. But it had been so long since we'd crossed paths that I simply hadn't thought about it.

And if I had, what would I have done?

Not come, a voice deep inside whispered.

Maybe. Maybe not. I was no coward, after all, and I'd faced far worse things than a vampire determined to make me his own—even if he broke my heart and my soul in the process.

I closed my eyes for a moment, taking deep, slow breaths that did little to calm the erratic dance of my pulse, then slowly turned around.

I'd never really believed the line in romance books that said, "their eyes met, and everything else faded away," but that's exactly what happened.

My gaze met Quinn's and everything else—everyone else—disappeared. It was just him and me in the glittery confines of this room, with this amazing sense of awareness burning between us as fiercely as any bush-fire. It was an awareness that had always been there, even from the beginning, and absence had not tempered its flame. It had only made it stronger.

And oh, he looked *so* good. The simple elegance of his black suit emphasized not only the broadness of his shoulders, but the lean power of his body. His night-dark hair was cut short and neat, but so thick and lush that my fingers itched with the need to run through it, as they had months ago when we were still lovers. Being an older vampire capable of standing quite a lot of sunlight, his skin held a warm, healthy tan rather than the pasty white that was common among most of them. And his eyes—his eyes had always captured me the most. They were vast wells of darkness that held his secrets and emotions well in check—too well, most of the time—and yet it was so easy to lose yourself in those endless depths. In all respects, he had the sort of looks that drew the eye time and again. Saying he was good-looking didn't even *begin* to do him justice.

For several more minutes, I did nothing, said nothing, just stood there staring at him, my skin burning and my heart racing.

Then he smiled, and it was such an achingly sweet smile that a shiver ran down my spine and desire spun like a fireball ready to explode all around me.

One touch, that was all that was needed.

One touch, and I was his.

But only a moment, not for eternity. I might want him as I'd wanted few others, but the past between us was laden with lies and mistrust, and it was not something that would ever be brushed aside easily.

He walked toward me, moving with an economy of movement that was both graceful and powerful. But it broke the spell, and suddenly there was noise and people and movement all around me.

I gripped my purse in front of me as if it were some sort of shield and forced a smile. "Fancy meeting you here."

He stopped when there was little more than an arm's length between us. His scent swirled around me, soft and spicy.

"How have you been, Riley?" he said quietly, the lilt of Ireland caressing his voice, sending my already erratic pulse into overdrive.

"Fine, considering. How have you been?" God, we were so polite it was sickening—especially considering all I wanted to do was strip him and make love to him. Right here, right now.

It seems the leash had well and truly broken on my hormones.

"I've been keeping myself busy." He paused, and just for a second, emotion fired his eyes, making them burn as fiercely as the desire that continued to flare unchecked between us. What that emotion was, I couldn't say. As usual, the shields slammed down before I could really identify it. "I heard about you and Kellen. I'm sorry it didn't work out."

I snorted softly, and couldn't help the slight edge in my voice as I said, "You know I'm not believing *that*, Quinn, because you did everything in your damn power to ensure Kellen and I never got together."

He raised a hand, as if to touch my face, then stopped inches away, pausing long enough that I felt the heat of his fingers, then let his arm fall again. Part of me regretted that. Part of me was thankful.

One touch was not what I needed right now, even if my whole body ached with a need that totally refuted it.

"You made your choice, Riley. In the end, I respected it."

"Because you had no other option." I took a deep breath and released it slowly. "Look, I don't want to stand here and rehash the past."

I don't want to redo us. Don't want to deal with any more pain. Just go, just leave, before it all starts up again and I end up in an even bigger mess.

He didn't leave, of course. Whether he'd actually heard my thoughts or not, and whether he was simply ignoring them, I couldn't say. I wasn't consciously trying to use telepathy, but he and I had a link that went beyond psi-talents. So often in the past, he'd made comments that suggested he was reading more of my thoughts than he would ever admit, but he'd never really confirmed or denied it. The only admission he'd ever given was that our sharing blood had allowed us a deeper connection than was usual, and that he could read my thoughts whenever I was sick or in the midst of lovemaking.

Any lovemaking, not just him and me.

That was just one of the things that had torn us apart. That and him trying to change the very essence of what I was.

He studied me, his dark gaze assessing. As if I were some fragile animal he didn't want to spook. I would have laughed if it wasn't so true.

After a moment, he asked, "Would you like a drink?"

"Just a lemonade. I'm actually working a case."

"Oh?" He snagged two drinks from a passing waiter, and handed the lemonade to me. I took the glass, careful not to touch him. The heat from his fingers hit mine regardless, and a tremor ran through my body.

"Yeah," I said, glad my voice sounded normal when my insides were anything but. God, after everything this vampire had done to me, you'd think I'd be over the sight of him. But no, my ditzy hormones were acting like I was a pubescent pup going through her first moon dance. "We think we've got a bakeneko on the loose."

He raised dark eyebrows. "Now there's a creature I've not heard of in a while."

"So you do know of them?" I took a sip of the drink. The fizzy liquid did little to ease the dryness in my throat.

"They're rare. If there's one in Melbourne, you've got real problems."

"Tell me about it," I muttered. "The bitch has killed five people already."

"That's definitely not a good sign." He hesitated, then said, "Come sit at my table, and I'll tell you what I know."

"What about your partner?"

The smile that touched one corner of his lips was sexy, and yet at the same time, almost sad.

"I didn't come with anyone."

"Why not? You're an eligible bachelor who has women falling at his feet and who never has to pay for it, aren't you?"

His soft laugh sent little shivers of delight traipsing up my spine. Good Lord, I had it bad.

"Trust you to quote my own damn words at me," he said.

"That's not answering the question. As usual, I might add."

He gave a slight nod in acknowledgment of the barb. "There was no one in my life that I wished to take to this function." He paused, then added with a slight glint of mischief, "Sometimes, going solo is better than settling for second best."

"Says the man who can afford nothing *but* the best,"

I said dryly, totally ignoring the intent behind the words.

"Ah, but there are some things you can't buy, no matter how much you try." He raised his glass slightly, as if in salute, then took a drink before adding, "It's a lesson I've learned recently, actually."

"Who'd have thought ancient vampires could still be taught things," I said lightly, even as I wondered whether he *had* learned anything, or if it was just another one of those lines, easily said but never really meant. There'd been a lot of those moments between us, too.

And I guess, to be fair, it hadn't been all one-sided. He might have been playing me right from the start, but I'd never really taken what lay between us too seriously. He was a vampire, after all, and he could never give me what I'd spent half my life wanting—kids, and a family of my own.

Except *that* was all out of my reach now, anyway, thanks to the vampire half of my soul and the experimental drugs that were forced upon me.

He swung around and offered me his arm. I hesitated, then slipped my arm through his. It wasn't flesh on flesh contact, but it was still contact, and the desire that rushed through my body left me giddy and breathless in its wake.

He didn't say anything, even though we both knew he was aware of my reaction. He was a vampire, after all, and he'd sense the acceleration of my heart, if nothing else.

We walked across to a table that held a prime position on one corner of the dance floor. He released my arm then pulled out a chair, seating me before sitting down himself. I shifted so that I was I sitting side-on in the chair and facing him. My knees were inches from his thigh, and the heat of his body caressed my skin as warmly as any touch. And I wanted to be touched so badly.

I blew out a silent breath, and tried to get a better grip on my hormones. I might as well have tried to put out a bushfire with a wet towel. "So tell me what you know about bakenekos."

"There's actually not a whole lot I know, because they're so rare." He took a sip of wine, his expression thoughtful. "They are cats—real cats—who somehow gain the ability to take on human form to revenge the death of a much-loved master or mistress."

I raised my eyebrows. "Then they're generally not responsible for the first death?"

"No."

"So why do the legends say that bakeneko are known for eating their masters?"

"Because they *do* eat flesh. Apparently, it allows them to take on that person's human form—a handy thing if they intend to track down and kill those they perceive as responsible for the death of their master."

"All of which the one we have here is doing." I paused to take another sip of the fizzy drink. It was actually a bit too sweet for my liking. "Do they normally have sex with their victims?"

"I've only heard of one or two instances, when the cat has been in heat."

Trust us to get one of the randy ones. "Why would it be scratching the necks of the men it's killing?"

"That could be a form of territorial marking." He shrugged. "Remember, you are not dealing with something that thinks like a human. It may be out for revenge, but it is still a cat, and reacts like a cat."

"A very smart cat."

He made an eloquent motion with his hand. "Of course. Is she just killing men?"

"No. She's been killing women and taking over their identities."

"Which suggests that the bakeneko believes the women played a part in her owner's death. Unless they're cornered, they don't do random."

"Well, the only connection between the ladies seems to be the fact that they belong to a group collectively known as the Toorak Trollops."

"Ah, the high-class hookers themselves."

I raised my eyebrows at the hint of scorn in his voice. "I was told they weren't."

"That depends on your definition of hooker, doesn't it? If they sell their bodies for the high life and gifts, is that not a form of prostitution?"

"They might just enjoy sex. There's nothing wrong with that."

"No, there's nothing wrong with it, even if such wanton indulgence does sometimes offend the stiff sensibilities of very old vampires."

"I'm glad *you* said that."

"If I didn't, you probably would have." He smiled another sweet smile, unraveling a few more threads of control. "However, these women ask for their favors *first*. That, in my opinion, makes them pros."

Well, yeah if you were intent on defining prostitution, asking for payment before the act would definitely be one of the criteria. "So you've had personal experience with the Trollops?"

He shook his head. "Not personally, but I have friends—"

"No," I interrupted, feigning surprise. "You actually have friends? How shocking."

His laugh was soft and warm, filling his dark eyes with mirth and causing that flame of desire to burn even brighter. "Yes, even the control freak has friends."

I smiled. "I'm glad."

"So am I." He reached out again and this time, the palm of his hand cupped my cheek as his thumb lightly brushed across my lips.

One touch.

One single, solitary touch.

And it felt so good that tears briefly filled my eyes. God, how long had it been since anyone had caressed me with any sort of feeling or gentleness? I may have voluntarily restrained my more sexual nature, but a lot of that had been the simple distaste of not wanting just another hand on me. I'd wanted more—had needed more. And with that one simple caress, I knew that I could not let it end here tonight.

I leaned forward and kissed him.

For the briefest of moments, he didn't react. Then his other hand came to my cheek, holding my face gently, tenderly, as he deepened our kiss.

And it felt like I was tasting heaven. Felt like I was coming home after a long, long absence. And the part of me that had died when Kellen walked away came to aching life, fueling the desire that burned around us to even greater heights. Yet despite that fire—despite the urgency that sung through every fiber of my being— our kiss was slow and tender, and so very, very thorough.

After what could have been hours, he groaned—an almost demanding sound that vibrated through my soul. A sound I understood completely. Because, like him, I wanted more than just his lips. I wanted *him*, all of him. Wanted to feel him in my mind, in my body, in my soul.

Which would be a little hard to achieve, given our current location.

He opened his eyes and stared into mine. "What do you want, Riley?"

"I want you." My voice was little more than a breathy rasp of sound, but it didn't matter. He would have heard it had there been a mile between us.

"Just this once? Or do you want more?" He gave me a lopsided smile that made my heart do happy little cartwheels. "I can't change what I am any more than you can. And I prefer not to go any further if this is all there is. I can't do casual when it's you and me."

My gaze searched his for a moment, then I raised my hands, capturing his and lowering them to my lap. "I haven't done casual for months. I stopped having sex after Kellen left."

Surprise crossed his features, but I was relieved to see

that there was no incredulousness. He believed me, when so few others had when I first told them. "How did you get around the moon heat?"

I grimaced. "Well, I couldn't, but aside from those few days, I've abstained."

"I guess that explains the desire that just about blew me off my feet."

"Yeah. Sorry about that."

He laughed softly. "Don't be. It was a nice reaction to get." He studied me for a moment, then said, "You haven't told me why."

I took a deep breath and blew it out slowly. "Because I wanted something more than just the touch of a stranger. I wanted the caring, the emotion, that I got with Kellen. And with you."

"You could have contacted me after the breakup."

"No, I couldn't. I'd told you to go away and give me time, remember. And after the breakup, I still needed that time." To not only recover from the hurt, but to decide what I really wanted. Except it wasn't until tonight, and the kiss we'd shared, that I'd really known. "Quinn, I like what we have. I believe it's good, and I believe it is strong. But I also believe my soul mate *is* out there, which means I still won't commit fully to anyone. Not even you."

"So where does that leave us?"

"In the same old quandary, I guess." I squeezed his hands and then released them. The world felt a whole lot colder without his touch, and my hormones screamed in horror.

He leaned back and picked up his wineglass, his

movements elegant and casual. As if he hadn't shared a mind-blowing kiss only moments before. And yet I could feel the hunger on him, smell his arousal.

He took a sip of the drink, then said, "None of the Trollops are here yet."

I glanced at my watch. It was just after seven-thirty. "I thought this gig started at seven?"

"It does, but the beautiful people tend to arrive just before the main proceedings. Unless they are on the hunt, of course. Then it's a different matter."

"I think most people would consider you one of the beautiful people." But despite the scent of his arousal spinning all around me, he didn't particularly seem to be on the hunt. But then, if a vampire with over twelve hundred years behind him couldn't control his emotions and needs, then who could?

"Was that a compliment? Ms. Jenson, I'm shocked."

"Okay, so I've been a little sparse in my compliments. But then, so have you, buddy."

"Which is very remiss of me. You look stunning in green, by the way."

I smiled. "Compliments that you've been prodded into don't count." I leaned back a little, and crossed one leg over the other, showing a nice amount of thigh. "So what are we going to do, Quinn?"

"I don't know." His gaze went past me. "Marcy Bennett and Enna Free just walked into the room."

I twisted around to look. Two statuesque blonde women stood at the doorway, one dressed in dusky orange that clashed a little too much with her overly tanned skin. The other was wearing the deep red of autumn leaves.

"Enna's the one on the right?" Only a cat would put that color dress with her skin tone.

"Yes."

"Then I guess I'd better go back to work."

I stood somewhat reluctantly. He stood up also, but wrapped his arm around my waist and pulled me closer, his fingers splayed against the bare skin of my back, sending little bolts of electricity tingling up and down my spine.

I licked my suddenly dry lips, and stared into his dark eyes, seeing the hunger there, seeing the need. And not just sexual need. "I thought you didn't want to do casual?"

"I thought you said you'd quit casual?"

I smiled. "Well, yeah, but that doesn't change—"

He placed a finger gently against my lips, silencing me. "I have the presidential suite at the Langham. If you feel like discussing this matter any further, come back there when you finish tonight."

"I'm not sure what time I'm going to be finished working." And I certainly wasn't sure if I *should* go back, no matter what I was feeling or how much I needed him. We'd been through so much, had hurt each other so much, that part of me worried that the cycle would just start up all over again.

I couldn't bear that. There'd been enough shit in my life already. I just wanted a simple, straightforward, caring relationship with someone for a change. No ulterior motives, no hang-ups about what I was or what I did. I just wanted to deal with regular everyday problems in a regular everyday relationship.

And I really wasn't sure Quinn and I could ever have just a regular relationship.

"It doesn't matter what time you turn up. I'm not going anywhere." He bent and kissed me, his lips lingering, teasingly close as he added, "Please come back, Riley."

I took a shuddery breath, and released it slowly. "No promises."

I stepped away, even though all I wanted to do was remain in his arms with all that lean strength wrapped around me. To feel safe and secure and cared for for the first time in what seemed like ages.

"Be careful when you're dealing with the bakeneko. Don't let it get a taste of you."

"The bitch isn't going to get close enough to bite, trust me on that." I gave him a confident smile, then turned and walked away—even though my legs felt like jelly and every step away from him had my hormones screaming in rage.

The glittery room seemed a whole lot noisier away from the quiet oasis that had seemed to surround Quinn and I, and I suddenly wondered if he'd been using his vampires wiles again. Not on me, but on the others in this room. There were a lot of people here, but he was a whole lot of vampire, and it wouldn't have surprised me if he had been keeping the noise and the people at bay while we talked.

Enna and her friend hadn't moved that far from the main entrance, their gazes scanning the room, as if they were searching for someone. Or perhaps they were checking out the talent.

I skirted the room, coming up to them from the left and slightly behind. I was one table away when Enna suddenly swung around, her nostrils flaring as she sucked in air. I hadn't thought she'd gotten close enough to me to catch my scent when we were chasing her earlier, but obviously I'd been wrong. Her gaze zoomed to mine, and an anger that was both derisive and alien flared deep in the blue depths. She bared her teeth and made an odd sort of hissing sound, then turned and ran for the door.

Chapter 8

For a cat who'd only been wearing stilettos for a few weeks, she was damned fast.

I ran after her, dodging tables and people. Some fool in a suit saw her running and gallantly opened the door, then walked away and let it shut, making me waste precious seconds flinging it back open again.

Thankfully, the hallway beyond was relatively clear of people. Enna had already gone through the main entrance doors and swung right, heading toward the river.

I raced after her, startling the doorman by thumping my hand against the door as he began to close it.

"Sorry," he said, but by then I was almost out of earshot.

The night was cold, filled with the scent of eucalyptus and the slightly muddy aroma that was the Yarra River. But the scent of cat rode the night sharply and it was easy to follow. I raced along the footpath, my stilettos creating a sharp tattoo of sound that echoed across the moonlit gardens that surrounded us. Up ahead, Enna's vivid orange form ran on, her arms pumping as fast as her feet. It almost looked as if she was so used to running on four legs that she couldn't quite adjust her motion to two. But it wasn't helping, because slowly but surely I was reeling her in.

Beyond her, the footpath curved around to the left and disappeared behind some trees. I reached for more speed, wanting to grab her before she got to the corner and went out of my sight, however briefly. She was obviously thinking along similar lines, because her speed increased and her arms and legs became little more than a blur.

She could fucking run, I'll give her that. Hell, I had the speed of a damn vampire behind me, and I was only making up little bits of ground.

The corner loomed and she disappeared around it. I was maybe two seconds behind her, but it was enough for her to disappear. I cursed and stopped, my nostrils flaring as I sucked in air, trying to catch both my breath and her scent.

It was there, but not as strong. And lower.

She'd shifted shape.

I did the same and, with my nose to the ground, ran on. The grass was damp under my paws and the scents of the nearby eucalyptus and rosebushes were sharp against the night. Her trail went off the footpath, twining through trees and flowers.

Given the meandering line she was taking, I wouldn't

be surprised if she were trying to mingle her scent with the other aromas, thereby making it harder for me to follow. Obviously, a cat had no understanding just how sensitive a wolf's nose could be.

Her scent was getting stronger, not weaker. I trotted on until I came to the thick, gnarled trunk of a tree and the scent of cat was so strong I was practically drowning in it. I stopped and looked up. Up in the higher branches of the big old elm, two blue eyes glinted back at me.

I shifted shape and said, "Come down, Enna. Or whatever your name really is."

She snarled in reply, white teeth gleaming.

"Climb down, or I'll fucking shoot you out of the tree."

She snarled again, and this time it was a deeper, angrier sound.

Well, the bitch couldn't say I didn't warn her. I opened my purse to grab my laser, intending to shoot the damn tree limb out from underneath her, but at that moment, magic caressed the night. I looked up quickly, had a brief glimpse of a cat the size of a tiger, and then she was leaping down, straight at me.

I swore and dove sideways, hitting the ground with a grunt, tearing the side of my dress and sending my purse flying. I had no idea where the laser went, but it wasn't in my hand when I rolled to my feet. My stilettos chose that particular moment to get stuck in the dirt, so I stumbled a little before I got my balance. From behind came a heavy thump, then footsteps. I swung around in time to see her leap. God, she was *big*. Bigger than a tiger and with paws as large as dinner plates.

I kicked off my shoes, grabbed one in each hand, and ducked away from her leap. She twisted in midair, lashing out with those thick, sharp claws. Several caught my dress, snagging the flimsy material and tearing into skin.

Pain flared as blood began to run down my arm. I hissed and lashed out with a stiletto. The specially hardened wooden tip of the heel scraped down her side, cutting into her flesh and sending blood splattering across the nearby trees and rosebushes.

She growled—a sound so deep it seemed to vibrate through the earth. I shifted my weight, digging my toes into the dirt a little, getting balance and grip as she hit the ground then launched back at me again.

Her lips were drawn back into a snarl, white teeth gleaming. I waiting until the last possible moment, until her claws were almost on me, then dropped low and thrust up with the heel of a stiletto, driving it deep into her belly.

It wouldn't kill her, but a four inch heel shoved in her gut wasn't going to feel real good, either.

Her snarl of rage became a long howl of pain, and then she was running again, her black form quickly disappearing through the trees. I scrambled to my feet, grabbed my purse and the laser, and ran after her.

This time she was even faster. How that was even possible I have no idea. Maybe it was something to do with whatever magic allowed her to change her size.

I followed her scent, ducking and weaving through

the trees, moving so fast they were little more than a blur to me. We were looping around, moving back toward the footpath and the river.

I found my stiletto abandoned on the footpath. The trail ended at the river.

Obviously, this particular cat didn't have an aversion to water. I scanned the dark river, but couldn't see anything or anyone swimming. There were no boats moored nearby, so she couldn't be using those to hide behind. She was simply gone.

I briefly shifted shape to stop my arm bleeding, then pressed the com-link button. "Hello, anyone tuned in?"

"I'm always tuned in," Sal said, voice dry. "Unlike certain werewolves who shall remain nameless."

I grinned. "Gee, I wonder who you could mean?"

"You're wasting my time, wolf girl. Get to the point."

"Well, I just lost the bakeneko's trail—"

"Make a habit of losing your quarry, and Jack won't be pleased."

"She decided to go for a swim in the Yarra and was gone by the time I reached it."

"God, she *had* to be desperate. That river is *unclean*."

And a vampire would know all about unclean. Although, to give Sal her due, she did wash like a regular person, and smelled rather nice for a vamp. So did Jack, thankfully. "She's taken over the identity of one Enna Free, which means the real Enna Free is probably dead. You want to get me her address, and send a cleanup team over there?"

"Hang on."

I walked back and picked up my stiletto. With the

money I'd spent on them, I wasn't about to leave them. And once the blood was washed off, they'd still be totally usable.

"Kade was over there earlier to bring her in," Sal said. "She wasn't home, and he didn't report anything out of the ordinary."

"I'd say she would have already been dead by then." And a horse-shifter wasn't as sensitive to the scent of death as a wolf. "What's the address?"

"Two-nine-one Napier Street, Fitzroy—"

"She doesn't live in Toorak?" I interrupted, surprised.

"Toorak isn't that far," Sal retorted. "And *that* section of Fitzroy isn't exactly cheap, because it's real close to the Brunswick Street shops and nightlife."

Which was mainly human-related. No wolf clubs had opened up in the Brunswick area, so most nonhumans kept away. Except for the vampires, who didn't mind the odd bite on a consenting neck.

"Sounds as if you know the area well."

"I live there. Need anything else?"

"Warn the cleanup team that the bakeneko is wounded and probably pissed off, because I managed to stab her with a shoe. They may have to go in with guns."

"I'll let them know."

"Good. Were you able to track down Ron Cowden?"

"He lives above the restaurant, which is on the city end of Lygon Street."

"Did you find anything out about him? Has he got a brother named Jake?"

"Yes, but the system is still trying to track him down."

"Then give it a kick and make it hurry. This is urgent."

"Everything always is."

True. And it could be that I was barking up the wrong tree, anyway. If this *was* all connected with Young's sudden disappearance at the end of grade ten, then Ron himself wouldn't be a target. And I couldn't imagine his brother being a target, either, considering what Liander had told me.

Still, Young had circled his picture for a reason, so I had to at least check it out.

"Do you know if Kade has rounded up the other Trollops yet?"

"He's having trouble locating a couple of them."

Which wouldn't put him in a good mood. As he'd been known to say—out of Jack's hearing—he'd joined the Directorate ranks for action, not babysitting duties. "I'll probably head on over to the Rabbit after I check Napier Street."

"You don't get extra for all this unapproved overtime, you know."

"You know I do it for the love of the job rather than the money," I said, voice dry.

She sniffed—a disbelieving sound if I'd ever heard one. "Night, wolf."

"Don't let the bedbugs bite," I replied, and hung up on her snort.

I padded back to the car barefooted. Once there, I opened the trunk and grabbed a plastic bag, dumping my shoes in them. I didn't know how useful forensics would find them, but better safe than sorry. Although it would mean I wouldn't get my shoes back for a few weeks.

I shifted shape to heal the wounds a little more, then grabbed a cloth and cleaned the blood from my arm. After slipping on the spare set of practical black shoes I kept for emergencies, I hopped into the car then drove across to Napier Street. It wasn't that far from Sparkies, so it only took me five minutes or so to get there.

Even so, Cole and his team beat me there.

I grabbed my gun and climbed out of the car. "What, have you suddenly grown wings or something?"

He grimaced. For the first time since I'd met him, he actually looked tired. His face was drawn, there were bags under his eyes, and his chin covered by stubble—though if gray stubble could look good, then his certainly did.

"There's only two teams doing the so-called day shift at the moment, and these people you and Kade are chasing are running us off our feet." He swept a hand through his already tousled gray hair and looked at the dark house in front of us. "We were told to go in with guns, so I wasn't expecting you to be here."

"Thought I'd better be, just in case. I had a run-in with our bakeneko and managed to stab her, but she dove into the river and got away. If she's here, she could be hurting and extremely pissed off."

He frowned. "Cats traditionally don't like water."

"Yeah, but traditionally cats can't change into humans or vary the size of their animal, so I don't think the usual rules can be applied in this case." I waved a hand at the house. "I'll go in first and make sure it's safe."

"Try not to destroy too much of the scene," he said dryly.

I smiled. "I'll do my best."

"Good." He hesitated, and amusement briefly lifted the tiredness from his blue eyes. "And may I just say, that's a lovely lot of leg you're flashing there."

I glanced down, and realized that between my tussle with the bakeneko and my shapeshifting, I'd managed to tear my dress from knee to the top of my thigh. Luckily for everyone, I'd actually worn panties tonight, otherwise all the goods would be on show. I gave him a grin and a curtsey. "Thank you for the rare compliment."

I walked past him and approached the wrought iron gate. The house was dark and silent, and I couldn't smell anything more than human.

Once at the door, I grabbed the handle and twisted it. Locked. A quick thump with the shoulder soon fixed that. Obviously, the real Enna Free hadn't been too worried about security, because she didn't even have decent locks, let alone dead bolts.

I opened the door cautiously. The air that rushed out was filled with the richness of jasmine, but underneath it were notes of blood and death.

A clock ticked softly in one of the rooms to the left, but otherwise it was deathly quiet. Literally, in this case. I couldn't smell cat, couldn't sense cat, and didn't think she was here. Just to be sure, I switched to infrared and scanned the rooms for any sign of body heat—large or small.

Nothing.

The bakeneko wasn't here. Only death.

I flicked back to normal vision and walked inside. Moonlight shone through the skylights above, lending the hallway a muted, ghostly brightness. White must have been the color choice for all fashion-conscious Trollops, because the only splash of color in Enna's house was the occasional flare of primary color in the large paintings that dominated a good many walls.

As I got the closer to the kitchen, another scent grew in dominance. Seared flesh.

Enna was laying on the no-longer pristine tiles, which was at least something different from the others. She'd been caught in the midst of frying something, by the look of it, and the deep-frying pot must have tipped over as she'd gone down, splashing across her face and leaving behind huge, watery blisters. Not that she would have had much time to worry about the pain of those—not if the half-eaten mess of her body was any-thing to go by.

I blew out a breath, and tried to ignore the blood and gore scattered everywhere as I walked past the kitchen counter and into the small dining area. I found the bot-tom half of her missing left leg there. Her missing arm was in the bathroom. That window was open—and probably provided an entry and exit point for the bak-eneko.

I shut it then walked back into the other room and stood there, waiting. There was nothing but coldness and the smell of death in the room. The part of me that could feel the dead wasn't picking up anything here at all. Like the all the other murder scenes, Enna's soul was suspiciously absent.

Which, when combined with what the drunken witness had seen, certainly seemed to confirm that the bakeneko was consuming the souls.

Either that, or my talent had decided to go AWOL for some damn reason.

Ignoring the shiver that traipsed down my spine, I turned around and walked out. Cole bent to pick up the black bag at his feet, then said, "All clear?"

I nodded. "The bathroom window was open, so that was obviously her entry point. I shut it for safety, so you'll find my prints there." I hesitated, then added, "Just be aware that she's on the loose and keep your weapons handy."

"I think one of us will smell her before she gets within biting range."

"Maybe, but be careful anyway." I gave him a grin. "After all, I'd hate to see that pretty face of yours all disfigured."

He snorted softly. "Yeah, right."

He walked past me into the house. I turned and headed back to my car. It only took ten minutes to get to the weirdly named Hot Rabbit restaurant, but it took another ten to find parking. This end of Lygon, with its close proximity to two of the most popular wolf clubs and the resulting accumulation of restaurants and coffee shops, was pretty much on the go twenty-four hours a day—and that made finding somewhere to park difficult no matter what the time.

I climbed out of the car and sucked in a deep breath. A riot of aromas assaulted my senses—cooked meats, fresh breads, and coffee mingled with the scents of men and women. Over it all ran the lushness of sex and desire.

While there were still a lot of humans who came to dine in and visit this area, the closeness of the wolf clubs made it a prime gathering area for nonhumans.

And I loved it. Loved the smells, loved the clubs, even though I'd only been here during the moon heat of late. I missed it, too. Missed the freedom and the fun.

But I missed the caress of someone who cared more. And *that* was turning out to be a bigger problem than I'd ever imagined it would be.

I turned away from the clubs and headed for the Hot Rabbit.

As it turned out, you couldn't miss the place. The neon pink sign—complete with pink rabbits that leapt across the board at regular intervals—caught the eye even against all the other competing signs, and the babble of voices and music that flowed out of the place literally assaulted the ears.

The article in the paper had obviously done its work well, because there were a whole lot of people inside. It'd be interesting to see if they kept coming back, or if interest died off in a month or so. Lygon Street tended to have a high turnover of human-accepting dance establishments.

I pushed my way inside. The many scents bludgeoned my senses—perfume, aftershave, and humanity mingling with the heady scent of alcohol and the more luscious aroma of coffee. Either one would do me just fine right now.

The place was done out like an old rock-and-roll bar, and actually reminded me a whole lot of the Rocker, which was only the next block over. Like the Rocker, this place had booth seats that lined one wall, and tables and chairs scattered elsewhere. A dance floor dominated the rear of the room, and it was currently packed—though a lot of people seemed to be chatting more than dancing. But unlike the Rocker, this place had no stairs that led up to a more intimate area.

I made my way through the tables, then pushed through the rows of people waiting at the bar to be served. Ignoring the insults flung my way, I flashed my badge at the nearest bartender.

"What can I do for you?" he asked, barely taking his eyes off the concoction he was mixing.

"Need to talk to your boss, Ron Cowden. He around?"

"Table behind the dance floor," he said, and shoved two glasses of shiny green froth on the bar. "Ten bucks," he added to the woman beside me.

I retreated and made my way around the dance floor. The music appeared louder this close to jukebox, the heavy bass beat pounding through my body and making me want to dance. If this had have been a wolf club, I might have. But it would have been only regular type dancing, not wolf-style.

My hormones might be starved for affection, but my heart still wanted more. And right now, my heart had more will than my hormones.

There were only three tables sitting behind the dance floor, and only one of them occupied. Ron Cowden was even bigger in person than he'd appeared in the photo—a bear of a man with a full bushy beard that was probably meant to make up for the lack of hair up top.

"Ron Cowden?" I said, stopping in front of him and showing him my badge.

He looked me up and down, his gaze barely even lingering on my thigh. Obviously not a leg man.

"Yeah," he said, grinding out a cigarette and almost instantly lighting up again. The foul smoke drifted upward, tickling my nose and making my eyes water.

"That's illegal," I pointed out, taking a step backward.

"It's my fucking restaurant, and I'll do what I please." He sucked on the cigarette for a second, then blew the smoke upward and away from me. At least he wasn't totally inconsiderate. "What can I do for you?"

"I need to know if you had a brother called Jake who went to Beechworth Secondary College."

"Interesting," he said. "You're the second person who's asked me that tonight."

Alarm ran through me. "This other person—was he a man, in his late thirties or early forties, about yea high"—I raised a hand several inches above my own head—" with greasy, stringy hair?"

"Got him in one." He studied me, blue eyes shrewd. "Why is everyone suddenly interested in my brother?"

"The why doesn't immediately matter. Where's your brother, Mr. Cowden? I need to contact him, because he could be in great danger."

"I doubt it. He's dead."

I raised an eyebrow in surprise. "When did this happen?"

"More than five years ago now. Drug overdose, apparently." He paused, and shook his head. "Bit of a waste of air, my brother was. Got into drugs when he was a teen, and never came out of it."

"Was there any particular reason he started taking drugs?" Like witnessing something he shouldn't have? Okay, it was probably a long stretch, but it just seemed odd that Cherry Barnes, Ivan Lang, and Denny Spalding were now all dead, and the one thing they all had in common was being around when Aron Young had disappeared.

"Not that I'm aware of."

"The man who was here before—how did he react when you told him Jake was dead?"

"Well, he wasn't very happy. Thought he was going to slug me, actually."

He was probably lucky that he *hadn't* been attacked. Young didn't seem to be holding on to a whole lot of sense at the moment, and it was actually surprising he was restrained enough *not* to attack the brother of the man he was after.

"He left after that?"

"Yep." Cowden puffed on his smoke for a moment, then added, "Security got the plate number of his van, if you're interested."

"He *drove* here?" Why on earth would a vampire who could fly want to drive anywhere?

And then I remembered that tiny room and the silver mesh that encased it. He might have been able to shift shape, but maybe he never had much of a chance to practice flying. Most shifters didn't gain the skill to change until puberty, so if Young had been a late bloomer, his flight skills would probably be poor—especially if he was a slow learner like me. Maybe that was why he'd fallen to the ground after he'd jumped out of Ivan's window—after being locked up in a small room for so long, he didn't trust his flight skills to get him out of my way in time.

"I'd appreciate the number."

He raised a hand and snapped his fingers. A burly-looking brown wolf appeared. "Yes, sir?"

"Could you get our guardian friend here a copy of the plate number?"

"Straightaway." He took a notebook out of his pocket, wrote down a number, then tore off the sheet and handed it to me.

"Anything else?" Cowden asked.

"No, you've been very helpful." I hesitated, then added, "I'd keep security close, just in case that man returns. He's responsible for several deaths already, and we're not sure what his motives are."

He nodded. I turned to go, then hesitated again. "Tell me, when Jake was in tenth grade at Beechworth, did he ever mention anything unusual happening there?"

Cowden frowned. "Unusual how?"

"Well, did he say anything about disappearances or murders or anything like that?"

"No. I know the cops interviewed him, but they interviewed everyone in that grade after the disappearance of some kid. It shook him up—he was jumping at shadows for weeks."

"But he never said anything about it to you?"

"Nope."

"How soon after that did he start taking drugs?"

He puffed on the cigarette for several seconds. "I'm not really sure. I found him drunk a couple of times after the interview, but I couldn't give you a definitive time as to when he started on the drugs."

"Did he drink before then?"

"He was a teenager. We all drank. Part of the culture, isn't it?"

Well no, but that was beside the point. If Jake wasn't seriously drinking or taking drugs before Young's disappearance, then something *must* have happened for him to start afterward.

But what? That was the million dollar question, and one probably only the investigator at the time would be able to answer. I glanced at my watch. But not now. Though it was barely ten-thirty, a retired police officer might get a little pissed off at being rung at this hour of the evening.

"Well, thanks again for your help, Mr. Cowden. I appreciate it."

"No problem," he said, and got back to his smoke.

I headed back out to my car. Now what? The charity event wouldn't be finished yet, but I doubted the bakeneko would appear back there. She wasn't that stupid. And I certainly didn't want to go back looking like a mess.

But I didn't want to go home alone, either.

Decision time, I thought, but knew the reality was that there *was* no real decision to be made. Because there was only ever one thing I *could* do. Only one thing I *wanted* to do.

I grabbed the phone and dialed Quinn's number. It rang for several seconds, then his warm voice said rather formally, "O'Conor speaking."

"Quinn? Riley."

"This *is* a pleasant surprise," he said, the lilt in voice returning twofold and his tone dropping an octave. "I wasn't actually expecting to see or hear from you at all tonight."

"I need to talk to you." *Need to kiss you, caress you, make love to you.* God, I was making myself hot just thinking about it.

"Right away?"

"As soon as you can get away."

"That can be done immediately. These functions are a duty, not a pleasant pastime." He hesitated. "Would you like to meet for coffee, or shall we just go back to my hotel room?"

I hesitated. I actually *hesitated*. God, Kellen leaving me had done my heart more harm than I'd even imagined. "Hotel room. I need information on the Trollops."

"I hope that's not all you need," he said, low voice sending shivers of delight down my spine.

"Probably not."

"Good. I'll be waiting at the Langham's main entrance in ten minutes."

"I'll be there."

I hung up, flung the phone into my bag, and started up the car. For the first time in ages, excitement buzzed through my veins and I couldn't help the silly grin that stretched my lips.

Yeah, Quinn and I had problems. Yep, we could be bad for each other—but we could also be damn good together. And I needed that right now. I really did.

I made it to the Langham in record time and parked in the underground lot nearby. The rates were a killer, but I didn't care.

Quinn was waiting near the main doors. His warm gaze slid down me, heating my skin to greater degrees, then stopped when it reached my sensible black shoes.

"What happened to the pretty green ones you were wearing?"

"Stabbed a shifter with them."

"That's a rather nasty thing to do." He slipped an arm around my waist and pulled me close. His body pressed against mine, warm, hard, and wonderfully familiar. "What did she do?"

"It was the bakeneko, not an ordinary shifter."

"Ah. Well, it wouldn't have done much good, then. Wooden stiletto heels don't affect bakenekos the way they do us vampires."

His breath ran across my lips, his mouth so close I could almost taste it.

"I know," I said, a little breathlessly. "But she was in

the form of a rather large cat at the time, and that was the best weapon I had."

"I'm gathering she got away?"

"Yep. Which is why I'm here. I need to know more about bakenekos."

"I'll tell you everything I know—just not right now," he murmured, dropping feather-light kisses on either cheek before capturing my lips and kissing me long and strong.

Oh God, it was *so* good.

"Let's go upstairs," I said, a long while later.

He smiled, then slid one hand down my arm and wrapped his fingers in mine. Without another word, he tugged me forward, leading me through the Langham's gold and crystal foyer and into an elevator. It swept us upward, and soon we were walking across the plush carpet toward the presidential suite.

He swept the keycard through the lock, then opened the door and ushered me through. I'd never been in a presidential suite before, and this one wasn't only huge, but it boasted views of the skyline and the city. All the different lights twinkled like rainbow stars, the sheer beauty of them momentarily making me forget my fear of heights. Which was something I'd never thought possible. Maybe becoming a seagull had more benefits than I'd imagined.

I walked across to the plush leather seating, kicked off my shoes, then turned around and watched him stroll toward me. Like before, it was grace and elegance personified, but this time it had an added element. Sheer and utter sexiness.

I licked my lips and saw his gaze follow the movement. Smelled the sudden, delicious rise of desire. "I really need a shower first. I'm all sweaty and horrible."

A smile teased his lips and creased the corners of his dark eyes. "I'd like to say you could never be horrible, but I've seen you in a coffee-deprived state." He gave a mock shudder. "Horrible doesn't even begin to classify it."

I grinned and didn't deny it. "Which way to the shower?"

"This way." He caught my hand again and led me through a bedroom bigger than my entire apartment, then into a bathroom that was all white marble and gold elegance.

He reached into the huge double shower and turned on all the jets. Then his gaze met mine, and a sexy smile teased his mouth. "You know, of course, that you haven't a hope in hell of showering by yourself."

I arched an eyebrow, and said saucily, "Who said I wanted to shower by myself?"

He laughed, and it was such a warm, free sound that tremors of delight ran across my skin. Then he wrapped an arm around my waist and pulled me against him again. His body was warm and hard against mine, and his erection rubbed my belly erotically. I wished we were naked, wished it was skin on heated skin rather than silk and fiber.

And then all thought disappeared as his lips came down on mine. We kissed, exploring and remembering the taste and feel of each other so slowly and sensually.

"You need to be naked," he said eventually, his

mouth so close to mine that I felt the movement of his lips.

I kissed him lightly, then said, "You're quite capable of handling that task."

He smiled, dark eyes shining with amusement and desire. "So I am."

He skimmed his hands up my waist to my shoulders, then hooked the material with his thumbs and gently pushed the straps down my arms. The dress shimmied down my body and pooled at my feet. Once I stepped free, he picked it up and tossed it toward the chair in the corner.

"Almost there," he murmured, kissing my lips, my neck, my throat. His tongue lingered on the pulse point at the base of my neck for a moment, and his desire surged, scorching my skin. Then his kisses ran down my body, until he reached my breasts. He kissed one nipple, then the other. I shuddered in delight, arching a little to offer him greater access. He chuckled softly, and caught one nipple with his teeth, nipping it lightly then suckling it. I moaned, and the desire that was already burning through my system became an inferno that seared the very air.

His lips left my breasts and moved down my stomach. I shuddered, enjoying the sensual exploration even as I wished he would *hurry*.

He slid his fingers either side of my panties and pushed them down my legs. I stepped out, and he tossed them in the general direction of the dress. Then he kissed my thighs, and the junction between them, before rising and stepping back. His gaze took in my breasts, my curves, my legs, and he sighed.

"Glorious," he said, his gaze rising to mine again. In the dark depths longing echoed. And a longing that spoke of months, years—centuries, even—not just minutes. Once that would have scared me, but not now. Now, I finally understood it. "Absolutely glorious."

But it wasn't his words that had my silly heart doing strange things. It was the way it sounded when he said it. It was the longing and the loneliness I saw in his eyes given voice.

"My turn," I said, and proceeded to strip him— slowly and deliciously—allowing plenty of time for my fingers to slide across his skin, remembering the contours of his golden body, the feel of all that lean muscle. It was good to be able touch him again, to tease and arouse him as his scent swirled around me, filling every breath and making my soul sigh in pleasure.

When we were both finally naked, I caught his hand and pulled him under the water. The needle-fine water was hot, but I barely even felt it because of the heat in my own skin.

"I had a dream just like this, once," I said, as he grabbed the soap and began washing my back and butt.

He raised an eyebrow, dark eyes sparkling with the same sort of heated desire that was running riot through me. "Who said it was a dream?"

A smile teased my lips as I raised an eyebrow. "I was asleep. That makes it a dream."

"There is no such thing as sleep when our minds are able to connect so intimately."

He continued to wash me, his movements slow and sensual. Between the heat of the water and the heat of his hands, I was pretty much ready for anything.

"So it wasn't a dream?"

He shrugged, a movement so eloquent. "It was desire and fulfillment captured on a field only telepaths with a deep connection can reach. Nothing less, nothing more."

"It was a *whole* lot more, let me tell you."

He smiled and kissed my lips. "Would you like that dream to become a reality?"

"Please," I whispered.

"Your wish is my command."

He turned me around so that, as in the dream, my back was against the hard heat of his body, his erection nudging my butt as he began to wash my breasts and belly. The scent of lavender touched the air, filling every breath, as tantalizing as the scent of sandalwood and man.

And oh, it felt *good*. Better, even, than in the dream, and that had been delicious enough.

But now, as then, the sensation of being caught between the heat of his body, the drum of the water, and the caress of his hands was nothing short of torturous.

I grabbed the soap from him and turned around. His beautiful body gleamed like sculptured pale-gold marble in the half-light of the bathroom, the water reverently caressing every muscle, every curve. I followed the water's lead, soaping every marvelous inch, until he was quivering with desire and his breathing was as fast as mine.

"Enough," he murmured, taking the soap from my hand and putting it back in the holder.

I wrapped my arms loosely around his neck and kissed him. He pressed me back against the wet, cool tiles, his mouth hungry against mine, the heat of him flowing around me, through me, burning my skin, and contrasting sharply with the coolness seeping from the tiles.

"God, I missed you," he said softly. "Missed this."

"So did I."

It came out little more than a pant of air as he slid so very slowly into me. For a moment we simply stood there, his body pressed against mine, in mine, filling me, liquefying me, the water pounding our flesh but doing little to dampen the heat that burned between us. His dark gaze came to mine and, in the ebony depths, I saw the spark of determination flare. This vampire wasn't going to be sent away again without a fight. Wasn't going to let *me* go again without a fight.

But that was okay, because there was nowhere else I wanted or needed to be. Not now, and not in the immediate future.

He began to move, slowly at first but gradually getting faster, until it was all passion, heat, and intensity. Until I was drowning in the storm of it but loving every minute. And as before, the sensual heat of our dance had our spirits combining, making this more than one moment of mere intimacy, more than mere pleasure. It made us one in a way that went beyond anything I'd ever experienced with anyone else. Even Kellen.

His movements became fiercer, more urgent, and so

very wonderful. The rich ache grew, flaring across my body, becoming a kaleidoscope of sensations that washed through every corner of my mind. I couldn't breathe, couldn't think. I could only feel. Then the shuddering took hold and I gasped, grabbing his shoulders, clambering up his body to wrap my legs around his waist and push him deeper still. Pleasure exploded between us and my orgasm ripped through my body, shuddered through my soul. He came with me, but as his body flowed into mine, his teeth grazed my neck. I jerked reflexively when they pierced my skin, but the brief flare of pain quickly became something undeniably exquisite, and I came a second time, the orgasm shuddering on as he drank briefly from my neck.

When I finally remembered how to breathe again, I opened my eyes and stared into his.

"That was even better than the dream."

"Reality often is."

I smiled. "The reality right now is that I'm beginning to resemble a prune."

He laughed and turned off the water. I stepped away from him, then squeezed the water from my hair. He handed me a towel so thick and lush my fingers got lost in it, then began to dry himself with another. It was, I thought, as heat stirred anew, a delicious sight.

I shoved my hormones back into their box and began to towel myself dry. "I could really do with a coffee right now."

"And here I was about to suggest we retire to the bed and continue our re-familiarization process there." He flung his towel around my shoulders and tugged me close. "Because there's still lots of you I'm hungry to explore and remember."

And there was lots of me that wanted to be explored and remembered...

I let my towel drop and pressed myself against him. He was more than half ready to go again, and it sent a shiver of delight traipsing across my skin to know that he was as hungry for me as I was for him. "There's nothing to say we can't have coffee *and* bed. I'm versatile. I can share my pleasures."

"I've heard that about you," he said, tone serious but ebony eyes alight with amusement. "But I'm not convinced. Perhaps you need to demonstrate this versatility."

My grin was all cheek, all dare. "Any way you want me to, vampire."

He laughed, a low rich sound that had my hormones flipping with glee, then he grabbed my hand and tugged me toward the bedroom. "With a challenge like that, it could be a very long time before we surface."

And it was.

But God, it was *good*.

*O*ne thing about being in the presidential suite, I discovered, was all manner of food being available on call whenever you wanted it.

I sat cross-legged in the middle of the bed, the tray in front of me holding a hamburger with all the trappings, a hazelnut coffee in the biggest mug the hotel could find, and chocolate coated strawberries that were as sweet and delicious as they looked. Right now, I was alternating between them and the burger, and getting some very disapproving looks from Quinn. He might have proved in the last few hours that he wasn't as old-fashioned when it came to lovemaking as I'd thought, but it seemed he still had a few hang-ups about the way food should be eaten.

Not that he'd actually eaten anything for a very long time.

He'd retreated to the other side of the massive bed and was half under the sheet, his back resting against the padded head rest. He was sipping a red wine and I could smell the tartness of it from where I sat.

I took another bite of the burger, practically moaning as the patty and its juices filled my mouth, then said, "So tell me how to kill this bakeneko."

"You need to kill her body."

"That goes without saying, doesn't it? I mean, killing a body stops most things."

He raised his glass in salute of my point. "However, the bakeneko is *not* most things. She is now a creature of magic, and that magic not only gives her the ability to remold her form, but also provides extreme speed and power. She will not be an easy kill."

Few bad things were. "Do we need to kill her any specific way?"

"Cutting off her head should work." He took another sip of wine. "If the spirit is caught in dead flesh, it will leave this world and never return."

"So the spirit itself is never actually killed?"

He shook his head. "But she cannot inhabit the flesh of another. With her body gone, she must move on."

Well, at least that was something. I gulped down some coffee, discovering it was as delicious as the rest of the feast. "No souls have been present at the murder scene, and we have a witness who swears he saw the creature sucking at a victim's mouth. I think she's ingesting the souls—is that possible?"

"Very possible, especially if her attacks are escalating." He took a sip of wine, then added, "Every soul she consumes strengthens her, but it also fuels her anger and madness. That's another reason to be very careful."

"Do bakenekos live on souls?" I shuddered at the thought.

"'Live' is perhaps the wrong word. They don't need souls to survive, even if it does strengthen them. They simply enjoy the pain and the suffering of ripping a soul from its dying body."

"So it's all part of the ultimate vengeance?"

"Yes."

"Then I guess it's a good thing we're rounding up the remaining Trollops." I popped a strawberry in my mouth and munched on it. "I have a list of fourteen names—would that be all of them?"

"I only know of fourteen, so yes, more than likely. I could check the list if you want."

I smiled at his tone. "You really don't like them, do you?"

"It would be more accurate to say that I don't like the dishonesty of what they do." He contemplated me for a moment, dark eyes suddenly serious. "You know my feelings about werewolves and their sexual beliefs, but at least werewolves are honest about their needs. There are never any lies or half-truths, and that I can admire."

I sighed and put down my burger. The time had come for the discussion we'd both been avoiding. "You can't change what I am, Quinn. Can't change the *way* I am."

He put his wine on the side table and sat up a little straighter. The sheet slipped down his stomach and pooled around the top of his thighs, revealing tantalizing glimpses of short, dark hair.

"I learned *that* particular lesson the hard way. And the months we have been apart were—" He hesitated, and looked at me. In the ebony depths was an echo of the bleak loneliness I'd seen earlier. "Hard."

"It didn't have to be that way, you know."

He gave me a lopsided smile that had my heart doing odd little flip-flops. "I know. But as you've noted on a number of occasions, I am a very old vampire who likes to get his way."

"Trying to change the very essence of what I am was way out of line."

"I know, and I have had more than enough time alone to regret it, believe me." He shrugged one shoulder. "I did what I thought was best for us. I wanted a chance, Riley, and you didn't seem to be giving me one."

"I was giving you as many chances as Kellen. I saw him no more than you. You were the one playing games. You were the one who kept on pushing and pushing and pushing."

"And you were the one who refused to consider that a soul mate might be anything other than a werewolf," he snapped back, the slightest touch of anger in his voice.

There was nothing I could say to that, because the accusation was true. Finding my wolf soul mate was a dream I'd lived for for as long as I could remember, and it wasn't one that I could give up easily—even now, when much of that dream had already been shattered to dust and blown away by fate.

He sighed, and it was a sound of frustration. "I can't let it end here, Riley. There's just too much that's good between us."

I picked up my coffee, cradling it between my hands and letting it warm my fingers. "Do you remember Dia?"

He frowned. "The clone? The one whose baby we rescued?"

"Yes. She once asked me a very interesting question."

A dark eyebrow arched. "And what might that have been?"

I took a sip of coffee, then said, "She once asked if a being with two souls can have just the one soul mate."

Understanding, and perhaps just the slightest hint of joy, flitted through the ebony depths. "Did you ever come up with an answer?"

"No." I gave him a lopsided smile. "And given the shit fate has been throwing my way of late, I'm not entirely sure I'll *ever* uncover the answer. But the point she was trying to make is the same one you've been making—I'm not just a wolf. I'm part vampire, as well. It's entirely possible that the two halves of my soul have different expectations and different needs."

"Entirely possible," he agreed, his voice solemn but a delicious mix of desire and relief burning in his dark eyes. "And any other—shall we say, less cultured—vampire would be tempted to say 'I told you so' here."

I laughed and threw a strawberry at him. He ducked out of its way, and the strawberry hit the lamp on the bedside table beside him and bounced off into the middle of the room.

I uncrossed my feet and rose to retrieve it. There was no point in wasting a perfectly edible strawberry, after all. "I still believe I have a wolf soul mate out there somewhere, Quinn, so it won't ever be just you and me."

"But will you continue be the free and easy wolf that I first met months and months ago?"

I padded across the carpet, my toes getting lost in the thick fibers. "Hey, you fell for that werewolf, so she can't have been too bad."

"She wasn't. And she still isn't. But I've always desired more than being just another number on speed dial."

I snorted softly. "You were never on speed dial."

"Well, *that* makes the situation even worse." His voice was dry, but amusement lingered near his lips. "As I keep saying, what we have deserves more than that."

I bit into the strawberry, catching the bits of chocolate that flaked off with my free hand. "I think we need to go back to the very beginning and start again. I think we need to date, and learn to be friends, before we decide on anything else."

"And forgo sex? After the sex we just had? Are you crazy?"

I laughed. "I am not suggesting we forgo sex. I'm just suggesting we include all the other regular relationship stuff, as well. We've never really had that, you know."

He sobered. "And a good part of that was my fault."

"Yep," I agreed, then laughingly ducked the pillow he threw at me. "Hey, at least I never said it was all your fault. I've come that far."

"I suppose I should be grateful for small mercies."

"You should," I said in a haughty tone, then laughed softly. "I don't care who was to blame, Quinn. I just want to start all over again—and this time, I want to try and make it right. Or as right as you and I could ever be."

"And hearing *that* makes my old heart want to dance with joy."

I snorted softly and walked back to my side of the bed to grab my coffee. But as I did so, pain hit—pain so deep it felt like my heart was being ripped out of my chest. The world was suddenly spinning, turning, falling, and I couldn't think and couldn't breathe. There was only pain, mind-numbing pain.

Only it wasn't mine.

It was Rhoan's.

Chapter 9

I hit the floor hard and lay there for several seconds, my breathing panicked and my heart beating a million miles a minute.

Something had to be terribly wrong with Rhoan for me to be getting this sort of reaction. And yet it didn't feel like he was in danger. Didn't feel like he was hurt in any way.

"Riley?" Quinn was suddenly next to me, his hands gliding over me, looking for wounds or hurt when there wasn't any. "Riley, what's wrong?"

"Rhoan," I gasped, somehow pushing to my hands and knees. The dizziness hit again and fear flooded me. God, what was going on? "Something has happened to him."

Quinn grabbed my waist and hauled me upright. "Can you get dressed? Where's your phone?"

"Yes, I can, and in my bag."

He spun and walked into the living room. I staggered to the bathroom and hurriedly put on my clothes. The world spun again and I grabbed the corner of the shower to keep upright. When it eased, I found my shoes then ran out to the living room.

Quinn was on my phone. "There's no answer from Rhoan, either at the apartment or on his cell phone."

"He wasn't at home. He was at Liander's—" I stopped, and horror ran through me. Oh *God*, had something happened to Liander?

Please, don't let it be Liander.

I grabbed the phone from Quinn and quickly dialed Liander's number. There was no answer and the answering machine didn't come on. And he always—*always*—turned that on when he went out.

"We need to get to Liander's."

"I'll get my pants and my keys—"

"I'll drive—"

"You can't," he said, almost savagely from the other room. Not anger *at* me, but anger *for* me. "Not when you're getting input from whatever it is Rhoan is going through. You'll be putting your life—and others—at risk."

Keys rattled as he grabbed them, and then he was beside me again, wearing pants and carrying a jacket, but no shirt. He cupped his hand under my elbow as we walked toward the elevator. As the doors swished closed, I rang the Directorate.

Sal answered. "What now, wolf girl?"

"I need Rhoan's location immediately."

"Hang on." Keys tapped in the background, and the computer beeped. "He's on the move, heading down Epson Road."

"What's the nearest cross street?"

"He's just turned into Bangalore Road."

Heading for Liander's house, not his workshop and loft. "Tell Jack something has happened to Liander. Tell him Rhoan might need restraining."

"Will do." She hesitated. "You heading there now?"

"Yes."

"Be careful, wolf girl."

"He's my pack-mate," I said, and hung up.

The elevator reached the parking area and the doors swung open. Quinn grabbed my arm again, and together we raced toward his Porsche.

"Where's Liander's place?" he said, spinning the back wheels as he took off fast.

"Kensington. Enter from Epson Road."

He nodded and the car's speed increased. Lights and buildings zipped by, but I didn't really see any of them. I was too busy worrying.

"Any idea what the problem is?" Quinn asked, after a few minutes.

"Maybe, but I'm hoping to God I'm wrong."

"Why?"

"Because we've got a serial killer on the loose, and Liander might just be one of his targets."

"Again, why?"

I glanced at him. His questions were short and sharp, his concentration on the road and the few cars that were on the road at this hour.

"Because our killer seems to be going after people who once shared a school year with him. We have no real idea why, other than the fact that the killer disappeared after an altercation with some of the kids in that year."

"And Liander was one of those kids?"

"Yeah, but he didn't have anything to do with the killer or the kids who apparently did him in."

"So the killer is a vampire now?"

I hesitated. "Well, he smells like a vampire, but he's invisible in the daytime and able to walk around in sunlight without harm. And I think he was some sort of shifter before he was turned."

"No vampire is that immune to sunlight—even the very old ones."

"Well, he's not very old, but I chased him out into the street and the bastard didn't burn."

"Then he's not a vampire."

"What is he then?"

"He could be a dozen different things." He hesitated. "The fact that he becomes ghostlike in the daylight makes me lean toward a bhuta."

"A what?"

"It's a type of vampire that can come about after someone suffers a violent death. They supposedly don't live on blood, but rather intestines and excrement, and they have no physical body in daylight. Only at night."

That description certainly fit what I knew of Young. "They may have no physical body, but they can still pick up things and use them as a weapon in daylight."

He glanced at me. "You've already had an altercation with it?"

"Yeah, it jumped me. I wasn't expecting an invisible vampire." I glanced at the window, noting the location and knowing we were almost there. The knowledge didn't do anything to ease the tension in me. It only increased it. "Do these bhuta die like regular vampires?"

"Only if you catch them at night. They're impossible to kill during the day."

Great. Just great. "God, I hope something hasn't happened to Liander."

Quinn took one hand from the wheel and reached across to squeeze my knee. His hands were warm against my skin, his touch comforting—even if it didn't ease the sick fear sitting like a lump in my stomach.

"Liander's ex-military. He can fight. He'll be okay."

I licked my lips and looked away from the caring in his eyes. Not because I didn't want to see it, but because I was trying to be strong and any sort of understanding and caring right now just might make me cry.

"I'm a guardian," I said softly, "and this thing almost whipped my ass."

"Because you weren't expecting it—"

"Liander mightn't be, either." My one hope was the fact that I *did* warn him to be careful. *Please, please, have been careful, Liander.*

Quinn swung into Bangalore Road so fast the tires squealed and the smell of burned rubber briefly invaded the car.

"Be careful of the speed bumps," I said, just a second

too late. The car went flying across the first one and came crashing down on its nose.

"Thanks for the warning." Quinn's voice was dry, but he didn't ease the speed perceptibly until we reached the next bump.

God, we were close, so close . . . part of me wanted to get out and run, to just get there and know. My stomach was tying itself up into knots and sweat was beginning to trickle down my spine. I didn't think I've ever been this afraid of anything else in my life.

We round the corner and Liander's street came into view. "Park over there." I pointed to the parking bays on the right of the road as my gaze traveled down the line of cars there.

Rhoan was already here, and he'd left the car in such a hurry the driver's door was still open and the keys were in the ignition.

Oh God, oh God . . .

Quinn pulled into one of the free parking spots. The car had barely stopped when I scrambled out and ran, the sound of my shoe heels hitting the road surface echoing across the silence of the still sleeping night.

There were no lights on in Liander's three story terrace house, nothing to indicate there was anything wrong. The front door was open, though—and while it wasn't busted down or damaged in any way, that wasn't a good sign. Liander was too security conscious to leave it like that. And I doubted Rhoan would have left it open. If the door *had* been closed when he'd gotten here, he probably would have busted it down in his anxiety to see what the problem was.

I would have if the situation had been reversed.

I ran through the gate and up the steps. Quinn was a warm, dark presence behind me, but as I ran through the doorway, he stopped.

I twisted around to look at him. He grimaced. "Liander's never invited me in, so I can't cross the threshold," he said. "But go find your brother. I'm here if you need anything."

"How would the bhuta have crossed it? I sure as hell can't imagine Liander inviting him in."

"He didn't need to. Bhutas don't operate under the restrictions that hamper most vampires."

"More fucking wonderful news." I spun and continued on into the darkness.

There was no sound in the house. The scent of roast lamb and spicy vegetables lingered on the air—evidence of the dinner Liander had planned. His scent, soft and masculine, filled the house. Rhoan's warm spices and leather scent was absent, but I could feel the heat of his presence. He was upstairs.

I grabbed the handrail and began to climb. My footsteps made little sound against the thick carpet, but it wouldn't matter. Rhoan would know I was here, the same way as I knew he was here.

I reached the first floor—the one that held the bedroom. The silence seemed to get thicker, and while the air still held the rich scent of cooking and Liander, something else began to invade it.

Fear.

Blood.

Energy caressed my mind, a tingling of warmth that

stirred the fibers of my soul, intimate in a way that went beyond touch, beyond sex. Quinn, pushing lightly at my shields, wanting to talk to me, wanting me to open the psi-door we'd developed as a means of communication.

I dropped several layers of shields, and said, *Nothing yet. Rhoan's on the top floor but I have no idea where Liander is.* I hesitated, then added, *I can smell blood.*

So can I. There's not a lot of it, though, so that is at least one good thing. But there is only one heartbeat on the top floor. If Rhoan is up there, then it has to be his.

Then where the hell is Liander?

I don't know. Just be careful. The anger I can feel is fearsome.

He's my brother, Quinn. He's not going to hurt me.

Being blood kin doesn't always protect you. Not when there's this level of fear involved.

I licked my lips and climbed to the next floor. This one was basically one huge open area that Liander used for an office area, and it was wrapped in darkness just like the lower floors.

And while there was no sound, the smell of anger and fear thickened, and it was all twined up in Rhoan's leathery scent.

"Rhoan?" I said softly, pausing briefly on the top step and looking around.

"He's gone. We had an argument, and now he's gone."

The voice that rose out of the darkness was a frail shadow of its normal self. Fear lashed at me, thicker and stronger than before.

"What do you mean by gone?" I stepped into the

room, then stopped. Moonlight filtered in through the windows at either end of the large room, lending enough brightness to highlight the smashed furniture, scattered paperwork, and the blood splattered across the wall.

Oh God, oh God ...

I closed my eyes and took a deep breath. Liander couldn't be dead. Rhoan wouldn't be talking if he were. The shock of a soul mate's death often left the living partner in a catatonic state—something that Ben had basically confirmed when he talked about the death of his mate.

I took another few steps forward, and finally saw Rhoan. He was kneeling near what used to be Liander's main desk, though now it was little more than splintered remains. Evidence to the fact that he really *had* put up a major fight. But he was fighting something far stronger, far faster, than him. Something that didn't even operate under the normal rules governing vampires.

He'd lost, but he wasn't dead. That was something to hold on to, something to work with, at least.

I walked closer, and saw that Rhoan was hugging something to his chest. Something that was white, but stained dark in patches. Patches that smelled a whole lot like blood.

No, no, no, I thought, and took a deep shuddery breath to calm the ever rising fear.

"Rhoan," I said. "He's not dead. We need to get out there and find him."

He finally looked at me. His gray eyes were wide and

shocked, filled with a pain that went soul deep. "He's hurt. He's dying."

"But he's not *dead*." I forced a sharpness into my voice. I needed to get past the shock, the hurt, and the guilt; needed to goad him into action. "Liander wouldn't be sitting there hugging a bloodied shirt if the situation were reversed. You're the fucking guardian. Start acting like it!"

He surged to his feet and threw the bloodied shirt at me. "Smell that! *Feel* it! That's *his* blood on the shirt. *His* fear! Whatever came for him, he couldn't handle it alone. And he was military-trained." He shoved a hand through his thick, red hair, then spun away. "I wasn't here, Riley! I should have been and I wasn't."

I caught the shirt one-handed. The blood was thick and sticky to the touch, an indication that it wasn't very old. And the smell of sweat and fear lingered—telling signs, considering I'd never known Liander to be afraid of *any* physical threat.

I tossed the shirt on the tipped-over chair and said, "This is no time for recriminations, Rhoan. He's alive. Let's start from there and try to find him."

"I can't." The words were torn from him. "I can feel he's in trouble, I know he's hurt, but I can't feel *where* he is. It's not like you and me."

"Then we find him the old-fashioned way—through good old-fashioned detective work."

"How? We don't even know who or what did this to him."

"Actually, we do."

He swung around to face me, and the sheer fury in his eyes was knee-quaking.

Be careful, Riley. He's not thinking straight right now and he's looking for something—or someone—to take his anger out on.

Tell me about it. I held up my hands—a useless gesture if he actually decided to attack. "One of the cases I'm investigating involves what Quinn tells me is a bhuta—a vampire with no physical body in the daytime."

"What has this got to do with Liander's disappearance?" His voice was flat and cold, and his eyes had gone from resembling anything human to something that only saw death. Only wanted death.

The look of a guardian. The look of a killer.

I'd only seen it a couple of times, and it certainly wasn't something I'd ever expected to see aimed my way.

I raised my chin a little and met his gaze defiantly. Perhaps not the best move when facing a wolf on the edge of madness, but I couldn't afford to back down, either. If he smelled or saw any sort of weakness in his current state, he might just attack anyway.

"I'm not entirely sure how Liander's involved, but Aron Young—the bhuta in question—seems to be intent on tracking down and killing anyone who was in the same class as him in tenth grade."

"And Liander was?"

"Yes. I did tell him to be careful, Rhoan, but I really didn't think he'd be in danger—"

I didn't get any further and I never even saw the

punch. One moment I was standing there, the next I was flying across the room. I hit the wall with enough force to knock a hole into it, then slithered to the floor.

I felt him move: a furious force coming straight at me. Battling stars and the need to throw up, I flung myself sideways, grasping the leg of a nearby shattered chair, then swung with all my might.

The blow hit him just below the left knee. There was an almighty crack as the chair leg broke, but the force of the blow knocked him off his feet and onto his back. I grabbed another chair leg then scrambled to my feet, sniffing back the blood beginning to run from my nose as I jumped onto his stomach, pinning his arms with my knees and thrusting the chair leg under his chin.

"Bitch," he muttered, his eyes still glazed and furious, his body bucking like a bronco.

"Enough," I yelled, and pressed the leg a little harder against his neck. He was wheezing, struggling to breathe, but I didn't let up the pressure. I couldn't when he was in this frame of mind. He wasn't even seeing *me*. He wasn't seeing anyone or anything except Liander laying bloody and hurt somewhere.

"Rhoan, *look* at me. This is stupid—we need to find Liander, not fight."

He still wasn't listening, too consumed by the grief wrapping around him. He continued to struggle, forcing me to grip tighter with my legs to even stay on top of him.

Blood dripped from my nose, splattering across his face and lips. He licked automatically, and suddenly his movements stopped.

"You're bleeding," he said, as the coldness began to seep from his eyes.

"Well, I fucking wonder why?" I swiped at my nose with an arm. "Are you going to hit me again? Or are you finally over your little hissy fit and ready to do something useful?"

"I didn't mean—" He stopped. We both knew he *did* mean. "I'm sorry."

"So you fucking should be." I tossed the chair leg aside and got up. "You might want to shift shape. I think I did some damage to your leg."

"Yeah," he said, wincing as he tried to move it. He shifted shape, laying there in wolf form for several seconds before changing back to human form. He climbed to his feet and grimaced. "Better, but not great."

I couldn't feel sorry for him. I might understand why he'd lashed out, but that didn't mean he was getting any sympathy. Especially when my jaw was aching and my nose was throbbing.

"First things first," I said. "We need to find the old school photo Liander was going to give me, and check all the names on it. We need to know if it's just Liander he's snatched, or whether he's taken them all."

"That's downstairs on the coffee table." He spun and headed for the stairs. The anger still bubbled in him, thick and strong, but at least it now had direction. "He was showing me before we had our argument."

I followed him down. "What the hell were you arguing about this time?"

"He wanted to move in with us."

"So?"

He looked over his shoulder. "You knew?"

"He asked for my permission first." I raised a hand to my jaw, massaging it lightly. It hurt to talk, but it didn't feel like anything was broken. Maybe he'd pulled his punch at the last moment. "Don't tell me that's what you argued about."

"I don't know if I'm ready for that yet."

"You're never ready for anything he wants, Rhoan." I hesitated, then added harshly, "And now you may very well not have to worry about it ever again."

He stopped and swung around violently. "That's unfair—"

"No, what you're doing to *him* is unfair. He's your soul mate, Rhoan. Dammit, why won't you just start treating him like it?"

"Because of this! Because of things like this!"

I looked at him incredulously. "Why has him being kidnapped got anything to do with your relationship?"

"It's what could happen to him. I'm a guardian—"

"That's just a fucking excuse, Rhoan, and you know it."

"How can you say that when you lost Kellen for the very same reason?"

"Kellen left because he didn't want to sit at home wondering if each night was going to be the night I didn't come home. Liander's accepted that possibility and is willing to live with it."

"But I'm *not*. If I commit to him, if we do the moon ceremony, and then something happens to me, he dies. And I don't want that. I couldn't live with that."

"Death isn't always the end result of the moon

bond." Although I had no proof of that. Ben might have survived the death of his soul mate, but they hadn't sworn their love on the moon. Maybe that *was* the difference.

"I don't care." He spun around and clomped down the stairs. "I refuse to risk full commitment."

"But he's not *asking* you to risk it, Rhoan. He's just asking to move in with us and become part of our family. Why is that asking too much?"

"It's a risk—"

"Life itself is a goddamn risk! As Liander being caught by a serial killer proves."

He muttered something under his breath. I caught the words "bitch" and "ridiculous," and smiled. "This bitch is going to kick your ass to kingdom come if you don't start acting sensibly where Liander is concerned."

He snorted softly and strode across the living room, snatching an old photograph up and thrusting it in my direction. "This is it."

I took the photo from him and then looked around. "Where's the phone? My cell's in the car."

He pointed to the left, then crossed his arms, his nostrils flaring. "Why is Quinn here?"

"Because I was getting emotional hits from you, and it was shaking me up so badly I couldn't drive." I picked up the receiver and dialed Jack's number.

"I suppose I should be grateful he couldn't pass the threshold, or my ass would be history."

"Too right it would be," Quinn commented calmly from the doorway. "You're too old to be acting like a petulant child."

"Christ, first my sister tells me off, then her lover." He paused. "How come you two are together again? When did that happen?"

"We are not together, as such," Quinn said. "Not yet, anyway."

Rhoan raised an eyebrow as he glanced at me. "Funny, because you have his scent all over you, which kinda indicates you *have* been together."

"Having sex doesn't mean we're together. It just means we were horny," I answered, then said, as Jack picked up the phone, "Boss, we've got problems."

"Sal told me. You and Rhoan okay?"

"Yeah, we survived the encounter. Rhoan's thinking a little more clearly now."

I looked at Rhoan as I said it. He grimaced, and thrust a hand through his hair. His body was still taut with tension, and the smell of his anger and frustration stained the air. He was in control, but only just.

"What about Liander?"

"He's missing. I think Aron Young might have him."

"Why? What is his connection to the other men Young has murdered?"

"As far as I can see, the only connection between any of them is the fact they all did tenth grade in the same school as Young. It's not much."

"For twisted minds, it often doesn't have to be. What do you need?"

"I need a trace on a van and the following names. Liander's not dead yet, so he's been snatched rather than killed outright. Young knows we're onto him, so maybe he's gone for the rest of them too. Maybe he's planned on one big killing party."

"It's possible. Give me the details."

I read the names out, then added the plate number the bouncer had given me. "I'm about to head on over to Vinny's. She tasted him, and I'm sure knows more than what she's saying. I think it's about time she anted up."

"Just be careful," he warned. "Emos don't have to be touching to suck emotion from you. She and her crew can drain from a distance if they wish."

"She wouldn't want to try it on Rhoan right now. Trust me on that."

"I can imagine." His voice was dry. "You sure you two are unscathed?"

"We can walk, we can talk, and we can certainly throw a punch or two. We're fine."

"Good. I'll contact you as soon as we have any info."

"Thanks, boss."

I hung up.

"So who is this Vinny?" Rhoan said.

"An emo vamp who has set up camp in one of the abandoned government housing towers. I mentioned her before, remember?"

"No." He frowned. "When?"

"After the premiere—when you and Liander came home pissed."

Darkness ran across his face, and he took a deep, shuddering breath. "Yeah, I remember. Let's go see this Vinny, so that there *is* a next time."

I gave him a hug, and his arms wrapped around my waist, holding on to me briefly. I could smell the fear on him, smell the pain. Feel the quivering in his limbs that was a mix of anger and the need to hit out, to hurt those responsible.

Vinny had better *not* try anything on my brother.

I pulled back. "Quinn should drive, in case you get any more hits from Liander."

He nodded and thrust a hand through his hair again. "It's gone quiet on that front."

"He's okay, Rhoan. You'd know if it were otherwise." I turned and headed for the door, so he couldn't see the worry in my eyes. Him getting nothing from Liander was *not* a good sign.

It meant he was getting weaker, that the link between them was fading.

He couldn't die. *God, fate, and whatever else might be up there watching—please don't let him die.*

Quinn was no longer at the door. I led the way down the street, following his scent, and heard an engine start up. Rhoan's car, not Quinn's. There was more room in my brother's car.

Quinn reversed out of the parking spot then stopped to let us in.

"Where to?" he asked, glancing at me as I climbed into the front. His eyes were alight with anger and concern, and just a hint of hunger. He might have fed off me earlier, but the smell of blood was on me, and it was teasing his vampire senses to life.

I gave him the address, then sniffed back the blood still running from my nose. "Sorry," I said, when I could.

He shrugged and shoved the car into gear, taking off

so fast the tires squealed. "I am old enough to control my hunger, Riley. And there isn't that much blood." He glanced at the rearview mirror. "Though there deserves to be."

"Try losing someone you love and see how you react," Rhoan retorted.

"I have. And people died because of it. My point, however, is that Liander is *not* dead, and you should not be acting like he is."

"For fuck's sake, did you *have* to bring him along?"

For all the annoyance in Rhoan's voice, Quinn's gentle chastisement seemed to have some effect. The scent of fear retreated a little, and the anger and determination came to the fore. Hopefully, it would sustain him through whatever the next few hours had to offer.

Hopefully, those hours *wouldn't* contain death. Not Liander's death, anyway.

We sped through the darkened streets at breakneck speed, Quinn's sharp reflexes getting us through red lights and what traffic there was with equal ease.

The shattered sides of the old government housing block came into sight. Spots of light gleamed here and there, but mostly the building was dark. My gaze was drawn to the top floor. No lights shone there. But then, Vinny's room had been draped in heavy velvet and it was unlikely light would show anyway.

Quinn drove over the footpath and right up to the main doors. When he stopped the car, we climbed out. The scent of vampire spun through the air, thick and cloying.

"There's a lot of them in there," Quinn said, distaste touching his expression as his gaze swept the building.

"At least forty," I commented.

"How in the hell can one vamp control forty fledglings?" Rhoan asked in disbelief.

"She's not a blood vamp." I pushed through the shattered front doors. Footsteps scattered and the slight taste of fear touched the air. I glanced at Quinn as I began to climb. "Why are they retreating? They didn't last time I was here."

His smile was decidedly dark. "Last time you were here, you weren't accompanied by one of the old ones."

"They can tell what you are?"

"No. I'm letting them *know* what I am. Trust me, in an emo's nest, it's always better to advance warn what sort of trouble they'll be getting into should they try any tricks."

Rhoan frowned. "What sort of tricks are emos likely to get up to that would be different to a blood vampire?"

Quinn glanced at him. "They feed off emotion. Therefore it is to their benefit to amp it up where possible."

"Ah." Rhoan considered this for a moment, then said, "So my anger and fear for Liander is something she'd likely play with?"

"Most likely. If she doesn't take heed of the warning."

I glanced back at him. "Is that warning going out telepathically?"

He nodded. "And emotionally. I'm empathic, remember."

He was also something else entirely—something

that wasn't just vampire. Though his mother had been human, his father came from a race known only as the priests of Aedh—beings who were more energy than flesh, and who were seen by humans as being tall, golden, and winged. They were, in fact, the race that had apparently instigated the legends of angels. I didn't know a whole lot more than that, but I had a sneaking suspicion that the skills inherited from his father were coming into play, as well.

After all, Vinny didn't seem the type to be scared by the presence of an old one—but an old one who was something that no longer existed in anything other than myth? Yeah, that would shake her overly confident little world.

We reached the top floor. A different girl guarded the door, but like the previous girl, she was dressed casually and again had a suspicious bulge on her right hip. Unlike the previous guard, this girl also looked worried.

"We're here to see Vinny," I said, stopping little more than a foot away from her. Her scent was orangey, but underneath it ran fear.

Not of me, not of Rhoan. Of Quinn.

She licked her lips and said, "Vinny is rather busy—"

"If Vinny doesn't want a busted door, you had better open it," I said.

Her gaze went blank for a moment, then she said, her voice several octaves lower than it had been moments ago, "The old one stays outside."

"The old one will rip this place apart if you do not open this door, Vincenta." Though Quinn's voice was still decidedly mild, there was a hint of steel underneath that was warning enough to anyone with sense.

Vinny had sense.

The guard stepped back and opened the door. Quinn held out his hand and said, "Give me the gun."

The note of command was in his voice and the girl obeyed without question. Quinn pocketed the weapon, then waved us on.

Rhoan went through the door first. I followed, my gaze sweeping past the velvet lushness to come to rest on Vinny's cozy little setup at the far end of the room. Like before, she was attended by several toga-clad teenagers but, unlike before, their tension was something I could taste. There was no caressing, no languid eyes or secretive little smiles.

How many weapons did they have hidden under their outfits? More than a few, I suspected.

"I do not appreciate my home being invaded like this," Vinny said, her voice as frosty as her expression. Her gaze barely even touched me or Rhoan, but rather centered on the man who walked behind me. "It is outside vampire custom, as you well know, old one."

"Vampire custom is adjustable according to the circumstances," Quinn replied, voice dry. "A fact you'll learn if you live long enough. Which is a debatable event at the present moment."

The air filled with sudden murmuring, and the anger of many different minds seemed to lash at my senses.

"Is that a threat, vampire?" Her voice was soft. Deadly.

Quinn merely smiled. "Simply a fact, Vincenta. I am

not, however, the one you have to fear in this little trio. Though I can be, if you wish it."

Her gaze flicked to Rhoan and myself, seemingly dismissing Quinn for the moment. "Why are you here uninvited, wolf? Have you caught the bastard who murdered Ivan yet?"

"No, but we will. Because you're going to tell us everything you know about him."

She smiled and leaned back in her chaise lounge. "You know the cost of information."

I didn't get a chance to answer. Rhoan simply stepped forward, wrapped a hand around her pale neck, then yanked her off the lounge and into the air.

The toga-clad vamps behind the chair blurred into action, some leaping across the leather lounge at Rhoan, others whipping out weapons.

I didn't move. I didn't have to.

Rhoan casually battered away the two that attacked him, then swung the dangling Vinny in their direction. "Shoot, and she dies. Move, and she dies."

"You can't—" Vinny's voice was hoarse and, while vampires didn't actually need to breathe, her face was going an interesting shade of red.

"Oh, I can," Rhoan said, voice all calm iciness. The voice of the killer, not my brother. "We guardians have the power to kill pests on sight. The question that has to be answered now is whether you're a pest or not."

"I can't—" She stopped, gasping for air like a fish out of water.

I glanced at Quinn, and opened the link between us. *Is she faking it?*

His amusement rolled down the psychic lines. *Hell, yeah. She could win an Academy Award with this performance.*

One of the toga-clad teenagers shifted slightly. Energy whispered down the link, a mere echo of the power that Quinn flung across the room at the kid who had moved.

"Stop," he said, voice holding the steel of command. The kid froze and his eyes went wide. As wide as his mistress's suddenly were.

"And drop that weapon," Quinn continued. "All of you, drop your weapons."

Weapons clattered to the floor. Every kid had at least two.

"Kick them under the chaise lounge, out of reach."

They did so. I glanced at Vinny. For the first time, there was fear in her eyes.

"Ready to be a help rather than a hindrance?" Rhoan asked softly.

She nodded. Rhoan lowered her back to the ground, and eased his grip on her neck. "Now, be pleasant and answer Riley's questions."

Vinny licked her lips, then said, "What do you want to know?"

"Why is Aron Young kidnapping and murdering those who were in tenth grade with him?"

"As I told you before, he seeks vengeance for his death."

"Why now, though? Why not in the years immediately after his death?"

"Because he was unable to get out before now."

So he *had* been kept prisoner by his parents. "How did he get out?"

"His mother—she was sick. Her heart or something. She let him out."

And then she'd died, and he'd buried her rather than let her rot where she lay. I guess even evil bhutas had one soft spot. "Tell me where he is."

"I gave you an address—"

"One address," I cut in sharply. "Vampires intent on foul deeds always have more than one hidey-hole."

I'd learned *that* the hard way.

Amusement flitted briefly through her eyes. "That is true. I cannot, however, give you that information, because I do not have it."

Shit. I was *so* hoping that Vinny would give us the easy answers, but I guess I should have known better. Fate was never one for giving me the quick way out.

"Is there anything else you can tell me about him? Anything that might help us find him?"

She considered me for a moment, then said, "Try his home. I tasted memories of it in his thoughts."

"We have people in his home. He's not there."

"Which home, though? I do not speak of the home after his death, but rather the home when he lived. The place where it all started."

Beechworth. But how would he get that many people up there, let alone keep them contained? Beechworth was a good three hour drive from Melbourne. There were eighteen teenagers in that school photo, which meant there could still be fifteen on

Aron's hit list. That was a whole lot of people to hunt down. A whole lot of people to control.

And then I remembered the plate number I'd gotten from Ron Cowden. Young owned a van, and that could certainly carry a number of people.

"Let her go, Rhoan."

He glanced at me. "We got everything we need?"

"I think so."

He released her and stepped back. Vinny retreated to the safety of her chair, but her toga-clad fledglings didn't move to comfort or caress her. Quinn was still holding them immobile.

The scary thing was, it didn't even seem to be much of an effort.

"You are no longer welcome here," Vinny said, her gaze sweeping us and eyes dark with anger. "Please leave."

I turned and followed Rhoan and Quinn toward the door. But as I neared it, Vinny added, "I could have been a powerful ally, Riley. It is a shame you have chosen the other path."

I turned to face her. "I have shared wine with old ones and dark gods. A young emo vamp is a long way down the ladder of the things I fear."

She smiled her cold smile. "It is good to know even guardians get things wrong."

"Oh, I get lots of things wrong, but there's one thing you should always remember." I met her cold gaze with one of my own, and saw something flicker through the brown depths. Just what that was, I couldn't say, though it wasn't fear. *That* scent had not been one she could claim through this whole event, even though it had been in her eyes. Which made me wonder if even that had been nothing more than an act. "I always bring down my enemies, Vinny. And you might want to consider whether you really want to be that."

And with that, I turned and walked out the door.

Chapter 10

"That was a threat even Jack would be proud of," Rhoan commented, as we climbed back into his car. "Looks like he's going to make a proper guardian of you yet."

"Bite it, brother." I didn't even *want* to contemplate actually having to back up my words if Vinny decided to make trouble for us all.

"Where to next?" Quinn asked, as he started up the car and drove off.

"Beechworth, obviously," Rhoan said, then glanced at me. "If you believe what she said was the truth."

"I do. You want to ring Jack, and see if he can get us an address? And ask if he's had any luck with those names in Liander's photograph. I'll give the cow a call, and see if she can patch me through to the guy who used to be the cop there."

"You know," Quinn said conversationally, "for a woman who didn't want to be a guardian, you're sure doing a whole lot of guardian-type organizing."

"You can bite it, too, vampire."

"Oh, I have, and it tastes divine."

A smile tugged at my lips. "How about you concentrate on driving, seeing as we're going so fast?"

"Ah, but I'm old, and with age comes versatility. I can now manage to do two things at once. As I believe I demonstrated earlier this evening." He raised an eyebrow as he glanced at me. "You enjoy it, don't you?"

I smiled. "Sex? Vampire bites? Yes to both."

"You know what I mean."

I sighed. "Yes. There are still lines I won't cross, but I can't *not* do this job anymore. The thrill of the chase is highly addictive, I'm afraid."

"Oh, yes," Quinn said softly. "It can be *very* addictive."

The odd note in his lilting tones caught my attention. "You were a cop sometime in the past?"

"I was a cazador."

I raised an eyebrow. "And that is?"

"Cazadors are vampire enforcers. They were policing the vampire world for the old ones long before the Directorate ever came into existence."

"I've heard tales of them," Rhoan said, with the phone to his ear. "From what I understood, not all of them were on the side of the angels."

"Unfortunately, that is true." Quinn shrugged lightly. "It is very difficult not to become addicted to the kill rather than the hunt if you do it for a long time.

Especially if you're a vampire. That's why cazadors are now employed for no more than a couple of decades. The risks of addiction are far less that way."

So they still had them? Meaning there were worse psychos out there than what the Directorate dealt with? That was a scary thought. "Even if they are only doing the job for a few decades, wouldn't the craving to kill still become a problem?"

"Vampires learn very early on in their rebirth to control their darker desires. It generally takes a lot of time—and bloodshed—to break that training."

I studied him for a moment, seeing the darkness beneath his serene expression. Seeing the sorrow. Once it would have worried me to know what he was feeling, but not now. Maybe I'd grown up. Maybe I was simply more accepting of the gifts and intuitions that were mine. After all, even if they now kept me in this job, they also help me survive it. "Who did you kill?"

He didn't meet my gaze. "Someone who didn't deserve to die." He hesitated, then added softly, "Someone I loved."

"Then she had no contract out on her?"

"No. But she was good friends with someone whose house was slated to be cleaned." He glanced at me then, and the brief bleakness in his eyes left me in no doubt that the cleansing had been total—every man, woman, and child. "She was at their house when I went in there to fulfill the contract. I didn't even see her—didn't even realize what I'd done until afterward."

"That's when you gave up life as a cazador?"

He nodded. "When I came out of the killing haze,

there I was, covered in her blood, with her broken body at my feet." In his dark gaze I saw echoes of a pain that still wasn't healed, even though I suspected this had all happened a very long time ago. "I swore to never again kill on somebody's order. It is a vow I have kept to this day."

Which wasn't to say he *hadn't* killed. I'd seen him do it more than once, and had no doubt that, even after that event, he had a history littered with bodies. He was a very old vampire, after all, and none of them were saints.

Even the ones who were descended from angels.

"How long were you a cazador?"

"Two hundred years." A humorless smile touched his lips. "I was *very* good at it."

"After two hundred years, you'd expect nothing less than expertise." I hesitated, then asked, "So how long ago was all this?"

"I was a little over three hundred when I started."

So it was over seven hundred years ago that he quit. "Three hundred years was a decent age for a vampire to reach back then, wasn't it?"

"There have always been older ones, but yes, the past was a bloody place to survive." He grimaced slightly. "Humanity might not have had the numbers that it has today, but it had a whole lot more superstition, and a tradition of killing anything it didn't understand."

"So why weren't the old ones cazadors? I would have thought the older the vampire, the better cazador they'd make."

"True. But also, the older you get, the more you appreciate the years and your life." His smile regained some warmth, and amusement crinkled the corners of his eyes. "Like all Hollywood and literary myths, the one about old vampires mourning what they are or regretting their long existence has very little to do with reality."

"And yet there must be some who do kill themselves, because in most myths there lies a kernel of truth." Even the worst of the werewolf myths had the occasional grain of truth behind them. Besides, he himself had once believed that an old friend had walked out into the sunshine because a love affair had gone horribly wrong.

Of course, *that* had turned out to be little more than a cover story spread by a madman intent on creating an army of clones, but why would he have even believed it if it had never actually happened before?

"Indeed it does happen, but rarely." He glanced at me, the warmth in his eyes growing stronger. "And before you ask, no, I have never loved anyone that much. Even if I did, I doubt I would contemplate such a thing."

"Because you never give all of yourself to one person?"

"Because I love life too much." He gave me an amused look. "And you're a fine one to talk about never giving all of yourself to one person."

"Hey, I tried. Not my fault it didn't work out." Not my fault he'd made demands that were just impossible for me to obey—even if I *had* been able to. "Besides, I *will* commit when my soul mate finally decides to make his appearance. Until then, I'll just have to muddle along as I am."

"Okay," Rhoan said from the backseat. "Enough chitchat. Jack says eight of those fifteen names have gone missing in the last six hours. There were witnesses to two of the kidnappings, and both gave descriptions matching Aron Young. One of them also gave a description of the vehicle—a white van that matches the plate number you asked Jack to trace earlier. Jack's currently trying to patch into the satellites to track him."

I twisted around to look at him. "So the eight were definitely taken, not killed?"

"Yes." Hope had dawned brighter in his eyes. "And we've got an address for the house he lived in at Beechworth. Apparently, it's just outside the town itself."

"No indication as to the current owners and whether it's occupied?" Quinn asked.

"The current owners have no relationship to Young, apparently. He's tried ringing the listed number, but there's no answer."

"Young wouldn't be up there yet, anyway." After all, he'd only taken Liander little more than an hour ago. "Besides, there's no guarantee that *is* where he's going."

"We'd better hope it is, because otherwise Liander's a dead man."

"Give him more credit than that," Quinn said softly. "He's a fighter, and he has something worth fighting for. You."

Rhoan gave a soft, derisive laugh. "He might have decided otherwise after my stupid behavior tonight."

"Well, with any sort of luck, you'll get the chance to fix that." I gave him a dark look, and added, "And you had better."

His smile was wan, but there nevertheless. "It's like that old cliché says—you never know what you've got until you almost lose it."

"Just make sure you tell Liander *that* when we finally rescue him."

"I intend to, trust me." He blew out a breath that didn't seem to do a whole lot to ease the tension still evident in his body.

I resisted the urge to say "you'd better," and asked, "I don't suppose Jack found the files for Young's disappearance?"

Rhoan snorted softly. "Apparently it's regular procedure for regional police offices to purge computer files after twenty years. They have a hard-copy record, but it's still being found."

"Just as well we can go straight to the source, then." I dragged my phone out of my pocket, and pressed the button to ring the Directorate. "Has Jack got any other information about the house Young used to live in?"

"He's going through the council records for house approvals. He'll let us know if he finds site or floor plans."

"What can I do for you, Riley?" Sal said.

I shoved the phone to my ear, and said, "I need to be put through to a Jerry Mayberry. He used to be the local police officer up in Beechworth. He's retired, but apparently he's still living up there."

"Hang on, and I'll see what I can do." She put me on hold, and tinny elevator music blasted me. I winced and shifted the phone away from my ear.

"How is the cop going to help us?" Rhoan asked.

I glanced around at him. "He was the cop on duty when Aron Young disappeared. He might be able to tell us a little more than what was reported in the papers."

Sal came back online. "Okay, I found an address and a phone number. You want me to patch you through now?"

"Yes. Thanks, Sal."

"Hang on, then." I went back on hold for a second, then there was a click, and the phone was ringing.

And ringing.

Come on, come on, I thought, then glanced at the clock and realized I was actually ringing at an ungodly hour. The poor man was probably tucked up nice and warm in his bed.

Eventually, a gruff voice said, "Hello?"

"Is this former sergeant Jerry Mayberry, from the Beechworth Police Station?"

"That would be me."

"Mr. Mayberry, it's Riley Jenson, from the Directorate. We're investigating several murders that appear to be linked to an old case of yours, and I was wondering if you could help me with some details."

"I'll try, but my memory is not as sharp as it used to be." He hesitated. "The Directorate, you say? Which section?"

"Guardian division, Mr. Mayberry."

"Martin Bass still in charge there?"

I smiled. There was nothing wrong with this man's mind. Nor, I suspected, his memory. "There's no Martin Bass working in the guardian division, sir. Jack Parnell has been in charge for the last eight years or so."

"Ah, yes." His tone softened a little. "What case we talking about?"

"Aron Young's disappearance."

"Ah. That was a strange one."

"In what way, Mr. Mayberry?"

"We had evidence of rope marks on a tree limb, we had blood splatters we believe came from the victim, and we're sure he was killed. But we never found a body and none of the kids would talk."

"But you think they knew something?"

"Oh, yeah. Half of them were drinking or taking drugs within weeks of Young's disappearance."

"How many kids we talking about?"

"Seven. They were good kids at heart, but a little wild. They tended to egg each other on when in a group situation."

And that was when a lot of bad things had happened. Peer pressure could be an incredibly powerful thing, especially when you were a teenager and trying too hard to fit in. As I suspected Young might have been. "What do you think might have happened?"

"Probably an initiation gone wrong. We had a gang problem at the time—most of the kids were in one, except for a couple of the wolf cubs. These seven represented the rowdiest of them."

"So initiations were common, as well?"

"Hell, yeah. Usually it was something simple like stealing a street sign or getting their head flushed down the toilet, but Harvey's mob believed in testing the strength and commitment of their inductees."

"How?"

"We had one kid crack his head open with a rock. Apparently he'd been told to hold it above his head for several hours—starting at noon, in mid-summer."

"They sound like they were a bunch of charmers." And if *that* was a sample of their stunts, then it wasn't hard to imagine them slipping into more testing—and more dangerous tasks. "Who's this Harvey you mentioned?"

"He was gang's leader. A real tough nut, with a mean streak a mile wide. He definitely *didn't* have a heart of gold."

"What happened to him?"

"He was found in the bush not far from where Aron Young was last seen. He'd been dead a few days by the time his body was discovered and the animals had gotten to him. His guts had been eaten away."

A chill ran through me. Bhutas fed on the intestines of the dead, and it seemed a little too coincidental that the man in charge of the gang just happened to be found that way. So why didn't he kill Denny back then? Or Ivan? Or even Cherry Barnes? Why wait until now?

"What did the coroner say?"

"There was a large contusion on the side of his head, but there was no indication of a struggle or other injuries. The coroner said he probably slipped and smacked his head open, and died as a result of blood loss and exposure."

And I was betting the blood loss had more to do with his guts being munched on than any head wound. "Time of death?"

"Ten o'clock, give or take an hour."

Bhutas could walk in daylight, so it definitely *wasn't* beyond the realms of possibility that Young was behind Harvey's death. "How soon after Harvey's death did Young's parents move out of town?"

"You're not thinking they were involved, are you?"

"No. Just curious."

He paused, and in the background a kettle whistled. "It wouldn't have been more than a week or so afterward that their house went up for sale. We did question them, by the way, before we got the coroner's report. They both had water tight alibis for the day of his death."

Of that I had no doubt. It was their son who wouldn't have, I bet.

So were they responsible for stopping Young's rampage before he could even fully begin it? Was he the reason behind their sudden decision to move? "Where exactly was Harvey's body found? We may need to go up there and have a look at the area."

"We didn't miss anything." His voice had sharpened slightly.

"I'm not saying you did, Mr. Mayberry. We just have new evidence about Young's disappearance, and it may help us understand it better if we see the area."

"Oh," he said, sounding mollified. "He was found in

Historical Park, near where the gang used to meet. It was a clearing surrounded by granite outcrops and black cypress, which made it something of a natural amphitheater."

"You can't give me anything more direct than that?"

"Well, it was past the old powder magazine building, down near Spring Creek. You'll know it when you see it."

Great. We could be wandering around for hours. Which we didn't have. "There's nothing else you can tell us about the case? Any odd tidbit that might not have made the report but instinct said might be related?"

He hesitated. "Well, there were two kids I swear were witnesses—"

Witnesses. Puzzle pieces suddenly began clicking into place. "Not Jake Cowden and Ivan Lang?"

"The very ones. Like the wolf cubs, they tended to be loners, but they often used to sneak off and spy on the gangs. Cowden used to e-mail me photographs every now and again, which were often quite helpful when we were investigating minor incidents."

"Did he e-mail you anything about Young?"

"No, but he reported his camera missing the next day, and he was sporting quite a shiner. Ivan looked pretty messed up, too."

"But they never talked?"

"Refused to. Cowden started drinking not long after that, though."

"What about Cherry Barnes?"

He snorted. "That one was more trouble than she was worth."

"In what way?"

"She was Harvey's girlfriend, and a real tease. Harvey was always getting into fights because of her."

And she'd grown up to become a wannabe Trollop. Oddly appropriate. "Thanks for your help, Mr. Mayberry."

He grunted. "If you do find out what happened to Young, I'd appreciate a call."

"Will do, Mr. Mayberry." I hung up.

"Anything?" Rhoan asked.

"Maybe." I shoved my phone back into my pocket and repeated what Mayberry had told me. "I think it's highly likely Young will be going back to the scene of his death, rather than where he used to live."

"He'll probably think it'll be safer," Quinn commented. "After all, he knows the Directorate is onto him, and he also knows you can trace his home addresses. But finding the location of his death more than twenty years after the event is a different matter."

"I still don't understand why he's doing all this now," Rhoan said. "Why didn't he finish the lot of them when he finished off Harvey?"

"I suspect because his parents discovered what he was doing and stopped him. They had him locked up for years, remember."

"Being locked up in a room filled with silver wouldn't exactly enhance his sanity prospects, either," Quinn commented.

"No." I glanced at the clock again. "We need to be up

there before dawn so we can have a chance of killing the bastard. How fast does this baby go?"

"Let's find out, shall we?" Quinn said, pressing the accelerator firmly. The car took off with a throaty roar.

"This isn't a sports car," Rhoan said dryly, "so just watch the shudder when you climb over one twenty. It'll do your arms in."

"One twenty won't get us into Beechworth before dawn, will it?" I asked.

"No."

"Then don't worry about the shudder and just get this rust-trap moving."

Quinn glanced at me, amusement touching his lips and glinting in his dark eyes. My hormones did a happy little dance, but I shoved them back down and told them to behave. Now was not the time.

"Your wish is my command."

Rhoan snorted. "The day either of us believe that is the day we fall over dead."

"Who asked the peanut gallery for an opinion?"

"No one," Rhoan snapped. "So shut up and drive, my friend."

For a change, Quinn did exactly as he was told.

Maybe there was hope for him yet.

Red fingers of light were beginning to scrape across the sky by the time Quinn stopped the car beside the old stone walls that surrounded Beechworth's powder magazine building.

I climbed out the car and sniffed the air, my nostrils

flaring as I sampled the aromas within. The predawn air held a chill that felt like ice, but underneath it ran scents of eucalyptus, earth, and the freshness of water.

And underneath all *that* was the hint of fear.

Fear that was thick and strong, and coming from more than one source.

People were alive out there. Hopefully, Liander was still one of them. I grabbed my phone and dialed the Directorate, asking the cow to call in ambulances and any medical help she could find close by.

"I can hear heartbeats," Quinn said softly, as he came around the front of the car. "They're a ways off, so it makes it hard to define just how many."

"But there's definitely more than one," Rhoan said, closing the car door softly. "And that's good news for those of us needing some right now."

I squeezed his arm lightly. "How are we going to attack this?" I glanced at Quinn. "And how are we going to kill something that's not only invisible, but all but invincible in the daylight?"

Quinn glanced at the red-flagged sky. "We have a good half-hour before the sun actually rises. We need to attack him before then, or we'll be forced to wait until the following night."

"Waiting is *not* in my plans at this particular moment in time," Rhoan said, voice flat. "So do we attack as one, or as individuals?"

"Together," I said. "I've seen him fight. He's fast and he's strong, regardless of the fact he's been locked away for years."

"Insanity often gives people an edge." Quinn glanced

at Rhoan. "I'll find and protect Liander and the other hostages. I'll leave the killing to you two. You're here officially. I'm not."

And Jack could sometimes get cranky about involving civilians in cases—unless, of course, he did it himself. I looked at my brother. "Don't suppose you've got an arsenal in the trunk?"

He grimaced. "No. I removed the guns and locked them up before I took the car to the car wash this afternoon."

Obeying the rules, as usual. Whereas I would never have even washed the car, let alone obeyed Jack's safety rules about where to store weapons when not on duty. Which would undoubtedly get me in trouble one day, but on *this* day, it would have been a boon.

"So you've no weapons at all?"

"I've some stakes."

I glanced at Quinn. "Will they work?"

"If you stake him while he's visible, they will."

"Then stakes it is," Rhoan said.

He walked to the trunk and fetched a couple, then handed two to me and flexed his shoulders. "Let's go."

His gray eyes had become cold and dead. The eyes of the hunter. The eyes of the killer.

I glanced at Quinn. He gave me a smile that was a nice mix of confidence and desire, then turned and melted into the semi-darkness. I switched to infrared and watched him run toward the tree line, then turned and followed my brother.

While I couldn't hear heartbeats like he and Quinn, I was still a wolf, and the scents of sweat and blood and fear that rode the air were unmistakable. And they were getting stronger.

As the granite outcrops began to grow more numerous, and the eucalyptus gave way to black cypress, Rhoan paused, pointing to the right then holding up five fingers. I nodded, but wondered if Young would actually give us that much time. He was a vampire after all, and he could hear heartbeats as well as either Rhoan or Quinn. No matter how caught up he was in his whole revenge scenario, he'd realize eventually that we were here.

I made my way through the trees and the shadows, stepping carefully but quickly, keeping low where possible. It was tempting to shift to wolf shape, because she was quieter and far more deadly in the forest. But if Young happened to see me and attack, my wolf would be at a distinct disadvantage. Teeth against fist and feet—especially when they had the speed of a vampire behind them—was never a good thing.

The blood and fear scents were growing stronger, and with them came the sound of voices. One of them I recognized. Liander.

He was *alive*. I briefly closed my eyes and said a silent thank-you to fate.

And yet the knowledge didn't ease my tension one little bit. Because there was another voice riding the wind besides Liander's, and *that* one didn't sound particularly calm *or* sane. I eased up on the speed and, using a rock as cover, peeked out into the clearing.

Liander and another man were tied by their wrists to a huge branch that overhung the clearing. Both men had been stripped naked, and their feet hung several inches off the ground. It had to be hurting to be suspended like that, but there was little evidence of pain on Liander's somewhat battered features. His body was littered with bruises, evidence of the fight he'd put up and the pain Rhoan had felt, but the thin man hanging beside him was almost unmarked, except for his wrists. Though I suspected the bloody condition of those were not through anything Young had done, but rather his desperate writhing to escape.

I had no idea where the other captives were. They certainly weren't in the clearing, but then, the van Young had driven up in was nowhere in sight, either. Maybe he was keeping everyone else tucked away to play with another day. Quinn would find them, and keep them safe. I doubted if even a bhuta would have much hope against someone who had spent two hundred years as a vampire assassin.

I couldn't see Young, but I had no doubt his was the other voice I'd heard. Part of me wanted to rush out there right now, to grab Young and pummel him senseless for what he'd done to Liander and the other man. But there were still two minutes of Rhoan's five to go, and I had no doubt my brother would pummel *me* if I didn't do exactly what he asked. Besides, not only was he the senior guardian here, he had a whole lot more at stake. I silently blew out a breath and settled in to wait.

And I was betting the two minutes would seem like an eternity.

I've found the van and the other people who were kidnapped, Quinn said.

I hesitated, fearing the worst, then asked, *Are they all alive?*

Yes. Beaten and bloody, but alive. I won't move the van because Young will hear it, but you can be sure he won't get near these people again.

That was *one* vow I had total faith in. *Thanks.*

Just be careful, Riley.

Now you're starting to sound like Jack.

His warm laughter ran through my mind. My lips curved into a smile, but it quickly faded as Young came into view. His thin face contorted with rage and lank hair slapped at his back and shoulders. His hand struck his thigh in time with his movements, and with every blow the scent of blood became stronger. I frowned, concentrating my gaze on his hand and seeing for the first time the sheer length of his fingernails. They had to be a good inch long and were razor sharp. Every time he slapped himself they were tearing through the fabric of his stained jeans and into his flesh.

He didn't seem to notice. Or care.

The image of Ivan's back rose—the torn and blood-ied strips of flesh that hadn't appeared cut by a knife or a whip. Was that how Young was killed? I hadn't thought to ask Vinny that question.

"You have no idea what these people did to me."

Young's voice was high and uneven. He continued to pace the length of the clearing as he spoke, slapping away at his thigh. The scent of blood continued to grow, and so did the mad spark in his eyes. Working himself up to the task almost at hand, I realized suddenly.

"And you have no idea how they wrecked my life."

"No one can understand what you've been through," Liander said, his voice very calm and very even despite the pain he had to be in. "And you have every right to be angry."

He was trying to empathize with Young and diffuse the situation. Worth a try, I guess, but Young wasn't your everyday madman. He'd had more than twenty years to fantasize about his revenge, and I very much doubted that a calm, sympathetic tone would help.

"Those bastards left me for dead. They sliced me open and left me for *dead*." Blood splattered wetly now when he slapped his thigh, and his teeth had begun to protrude from his lips. "But I didn't die. I found a way to live, and I *will* have my revenge. On everyone."

"If you didn't die, then you weren't meant to. Fate obviously had other plans for you."

As Liander spoke, his gaze went from Young to the trees surrounding the clearing, and I knew then he was aware that we were here. God, I hoped Young didn't come to the same realization.

I glanced at my watch. Still thirty seconds to go.

I shifted my weight from one foot to the other and tried to stifle the growing sense of anxiety.

"But not everyone here was responsible for your death, Aron," Liander continued, still in that soft, calm tone. "Not everyone deserves to die."

Young swung around and stalked to Liander, his face inches away and spittle flying as he said, "No one *here* lifted a finger to help."

"It's hard to help when you don't know anything is—"

"*Everyone* knew what that gang was doing," Young said, cutting Liander off, "and no one did *anything*. For that alone, you deserve to die. *All* of you."

And with that, he raised his bloody claws and slashed at Liander's stomach.

I thrust to my feet and ran into the clearing. But I was slower, far slower, than my brother. Liander's skin had barely begun to split and bleed when suddenly Rhoan was there, a howl on his lips and murder in his eyes.

He hit Young full force and the two of them went flying, hitting the ground yards away and tumbling into a tree. I swerved around them and kept running toward Liander. His stomach was still opening and there was blood and bits and God knows what else beginning to spill from inside him.

"Why does the cavalry always arrive too late?" he said, the amusement in his cracked voice not hiding the pain suddenly evident in his expression and his eyes. I threw the stakes down and grabbed him around the hips, trying to take the weight off his arms with one arm, while I thrust my free hand against his bloody stomach. Only my grip slipped in all the blood, and suddenly my fingers were *inside* him.

Bile rose, but I swallowed hard and jerked my hand free, ignoring the metallic reek of blood and the stench of fear—fear that was mine as much as his—and grabbed as much of his innards as I could to stop them falling out any further.

"Quinn," I screamed, not even taking the time to

open the link between us. "I need a knife and some help here."

From behind me came a scream. A thick, high-pitched scream that didn't even sound like it had come from a human throat. Rhoan's, not Young's.

He knew Liander was dying.

They were soul mates, and he could feel it.

No, no, *no*.

The fighting behind me increased. I wanted to look, wanted to know that my brother was okay, but I didn't dare. I needed to look after his lover first, because without Liander, I'd have no brother.

"I'm not dying," Liander whispered, his skin so pale and body shaking. "I won't die on you, Rhoan. I promise."

He couldn't keep that promise. Not if we didn't get help soon.

God, where were the fucking medics?

Where the hell was Quinn?

I'd barely even thought that, and he was there.

"Hold him," he said, and something silver flashed up high. Liander was suddenly a deadweight in my arms, and I grunted softly, holding him against me, my body trembling with the effort of not letting him drop.

Quinn freed the other man and lowered him to the ground, then stepped over him and came back to me.

"Okay, I've got him," he said, and suddenly Liander's weight eased away from me.

"Careful," I said, panic in my voice. "There's bits of his insides leaking from the wound."

"Small intestines, probably." He wasn't looking at

me, but rather Liander, gently feeling his upper abdominal area. "Is that tender?"

Liander shook his head. Quinn grunted. "Hopefully, no liver or spleen damage then." He glanced at me. "I saw a first aid kit in the car. Run and grab it."

I couldn't figure out how the hell a first aid kit was going to help but I didn't argue. I simply got up and ran. Rhoan was fighting like a madman, and the real madman was getting beaten to a bloody pulp.

Rhoan had no intention of killing him fast. No intention of using the stakes laying nearby on the ground just yet. Young was going to *pay*.

I couldn't feel chilled by that. I really couldn't.

I reached the car, flung open the door, and saw the kit on the backseat. As I grabbed it, I heard the sirens and hope ran through me.

They'd get here in time to save him.

They would.

I had to believe that. For Rhoan's sake, and for mine.

I ran back to the clearing as fast as I could and dropped down beside Quinn. Liander's skin was pale and clammy looking, and his breathing seemed rapid.

"Shock," Quinn said. "Has the kit got sterile bandages?"

My fingers were shaking so hard it took several attempts to open the kit. "Yes," I said, looking at him.

"Open it and give one to me."

I did, adding, "It's moist."

"Perfect." He covered the leaking intestines with it. "Is there a large abdominal or universal dressing in there?"

"There's a thick bandage."

"That'll do."

A scream hit the air, a thick sound of pain that went on and on, and vaguely sounded like words. *My eyes, my eyes . . .*

Rhoan, still bent on revenge. I closed my eyes and said, "Rhoan, end it. Liander needs you here." I looked up at Quinn. "There's an ambulance on its way."

"Then get up there, and get them down here fast." His voice was grim. "We need to get him to hospital."

I got up and turned around. Saw Rhoan grab Young by the neck and snap it sideways. There was a crack and Young went limp. Not a killing blow, because broken necks didn't kill vampires outright, but it was certainly disabling.

I closed my eyes. "Finish it, Rhoan."

He looked at me briefly, his bloodied face free of emotion, his gaze still that of a killer. Then he turned, grabbed a stake, and plunged it into Young's heart. Young screamed, but the sound was abruptly cut off as blue fire erupted from the wound, spreading rapidly across Young's body, consuming and destroying.

Rhoan watched dispassionately for a moment, then turned away. His gaze went past me and his face crumbled, and suddenly he was sobbing and running toward Liander.

I resisted the instinct to grab him, comfort him, and ran to find the only hope Liander had.

Chapter 11

Twenty-four hours later, I was sitting in a waiting room in a Melbourne hospital, holding my brother's hand and hoping for the best.

Liander had lost a lot of blood and was now in emergency surgery to fix cuts to both his bowel and small intestines. He might be a werewolf, but there were some wounds that even a werewolf needed help to heal.

Rhoan hadn't said a word since we'd arrived. Other than acknowledging Liander's parents as they'd come in, he simply held my hand and stared at the wall, a blank expression on his face.

Not allowing himself to think.

Not allowing himself to feel.

It some ways, the very lack of emotion scared me, simply because I knew it was all there, bottled up, ready to explode should the worst happen. And I wasn't entirely sure the four of us would be able to contain his wrath and grief if Liander did slip away.

I hoped Ben was right. Hoped that he *wasn't* an exception to the rule, and that losing a soul mate didn't necessarily mean death. I didn't want to lose my brother—and especially not like this.

I swallowed the bitter taste of fear and pushed the negative thoughts away. Liander would live. He'd promised, and he wasn't a man to make such promises lightly.

Quinn came back into the waiting room, a tray of coffees in his hands. He placed it down on the small table in front of us, then offered one to Liander's parents. Yann, a heavier-set version of Liander himself, shook his head, but Raina—another silver wolf—accepted a cup gratefully, a small smile of thanks breaking the worry etched into her lined features.

Quinn held a cup out to me and I took it gratefully, sipping at the hot liquid and wincing a little at its bitter taste. Hospital coffee was on par with the muck we got at work.

"Rhoan?" Quinn said, offering him one of the remaining plastic mugs.

"No thanks."

"Rhoan—" I said, but he cut in sharply.

"No!"

His voice cracked with a mix of worry and barely repressed fury—everything that wasn't showing on his face. I squeezed his hand. I could only imagine what he was going through, and as frustrating as his reactions were at the moment, they were also totally understandable.

Hell, there was no way known I would have been as calm as he currently was if it had been *my* soul mate out there in the operating room.

Quinn sat back down beside me, pressing his warmth against my side and helping to battle the chill threatening to overwhelm me. He, like me, smelled of old blood, but my scent was also mixed with the aroma of fear and dried sweat, and it was decidedly unpleasant. As was my dress, which had become stiff and uncomfortable with all the dried blood on it. I plucked at the material lightly with my fingers. It was yet another dress that would end up in the trash. This job was playing havoc with my wardrobe. And my life.

God, please, let Liander be okay.

I took another sip of coffee, then leaned against Quinn a little more, resting my head lightly on his shoulder. He didn't say anything, simply wrapped his arm around my shoulder and hugged me.

It was good that he was here, and not just because his mere presence had an oddly soothing effect. Quinn was convinced Liander would pull through, and that conviction rolled off him like a blanket, smothering the flames of panic that might otherwise be present.

But I was also glad that he was there for me. Glad I had someone that I could lean against when I needed to. There hadn't been a whole lot of people I could say that about in my life, and the fact that I was feeling it now, with Quinn, made me realize that no matter what the difficulties were between us, we had to give this a fair go.

I might be an independent, stupid bitch at times—

okay, most of the time—but even I needed someone to turn to occasionally. Someone who wasn't my brother or his lover.

My phone rang into the silence. I took a breath and blew it out slowly. I knew without looking that it would be Jack.

"I need you on the job," he said when I answered.

"Jack, we're still at the hospital—"

"And we've still got a killer running around loose," he cut in. "I'm sorry, Riley. I know you want to be with Rhoan, but I need one of you here. Kade's good, but he hasn't got a wolf's tracking skills."

"What about Iktar?"

The spirit lizard had come through training the same time as Kade, but had been floating between day shift and night. He apparently had a few qualms about working with vampires—and the night shift was all vampires—but at the same time, day shift had proven something of a hassle for him. Humans might be used to the presence of shifters and vampires, but the sight of a spirit lizard, with their featureless faces and tendency to run around naked, had caused more than a few shocked reactions. Besides, Iktar's skills were most useful in the in-between times of dawn and dusk. If there was a hint of a shadow around, a spirit lizard could simply disappear—and more completely than a vampire could shadow at such times. Which was a very useful skill to have when you were tracking down psychos.

"I had him rounding up the remaining Trollops last night," Jack said.

"So they're all safe?"

"There's a Jenny Franklin and a Joan Hawkins who are currently unaccounted for, but there's no sign of violence at either of their homes. Relatives have been unhelpful."

Not so great. I hesitated. Stopping the bakeneko was a priority, I knew that. But so was my brother. So was stopping him if anything went wrong. "Jack—"

"It's not a request, Riley. It's an order. Don't make me come and get you."

I blew out a breath. I knew when I was defeated—and I definitely *didn't* want a scene at the hospital. Not when my brother was so fragile, mentally.

"I have to go home and change before I can do anything."

"Do it, then meet Kade in Toorak Road."

He gave me the full address, and I frowned, "Isn't that a parking lot?"

"Yeah. Another naked male has turned up, this one found on his car on the top level."

On? *That* didn't sound good. "I gather he's in the same state as the others?"

"Worse."

I wanted to ask what could possibly be worse than what we'd already seen, but I had a bad feeling I'd know the answer soon enough. Besides, I *had* seen worse. Many times. It seemed bad men and women didn't have a whole lot of respect for the human—and nonhuman—condition. "Crap."

"Yeah." He paused. "I talked to some of the other women last night. All the murdered men were Cherry

Barnes's former partners. And all the murdered women were the next lovers of those men."

Which is basically what I'd guessed after talking to Dia. "So unable to reach her mistress's actual killer, the bakeneko is exacting revenge for what she sees as betrayals of her mistress's trust. And she's killing the women first so she can take their form and then kill the men?"

"It would appear so."

And if it hadn't have been for the bakeneko's catlike sense of self-superiority, we might never have realized who was behind all the murders. "Did the cuts on Cherry's body match those found on Ivan and Denny?"

"Yes. She appears to have been Young's first victim."

"Meaning it was Young who set the bakeneko off in the first place?"

"Yes," Jack said grimly. "Keep your com-link open, Riley. I want to know where you are at all times."

"Will do." I hung up and looked at Rhoan. "I have to go."

He didn't even look at me. "I'll be fine."

I didn't believe it. Not one little bit.

Quinn squeezed my shoulder lightly, then removed his arm. My world seemed colder without it. Just for an instant I wondered if he was using his vampire wiles again, then wanted to smack myself mentally. Besides the fact that my shields had grown substantially since he'd last tried that, I honestly didn't think he'd do such a thing when we were still sorting out what was going to happen between us. He might be a very old vampire and set in his ways, but he wasn't stupid.

"There's been a murder?" he asked softly.

I nodded, then opened the link between us and said softly, *Will you look after Rhoan for me? I know it's a huge favor, but—*

He leaned forward and stopped my words with a kiss. And oh, what a kiss.

It's not such a huge favor, he said after a while, his breath warm and soft against my lips. *Rhoan was a friend long before we got together. I'll keep him safe for you, have no doubt about that.* Out loud, he added, "Be careful."

It felt like a weight had been lifted from my soul. I smiled and touched his face lightly. "I will."

He kissed me again, then added, "Ring me when you finish. We've things to discuss."

Things to discuss, decisions to make. But there was one decision that *didn't* need to be made. Quinn was back in my life and I was more than happy about that. But in what capacity he stayed there remained to be seen.

I let my fingers slip down his cheeks and across his lips. He kissed my fingertips lightly, sending a tingle right down to my toes. I sighed, but forced myself upright. I wanted to stay, not just for my brother but to soak up the warmth and strength that was Quinn, but I was a guardian, and there were people out there dying.

"Take care when dealing with the bakeneko," he added, dark eyes filled with concern. "Remember, she's consumed a number of souls now, and that will make her both fast *and* deadly."

"Hey, I took out a god of death—how bad can a bak-eneko be after that?"

He didn't say anything. I touched my brother's shoulder lightly, then left. And the feeling that I'd just tempted fate sat like a weight in my stomach.

*T*he top floor of the parking lot had been cordoned off with yellow tape and watchful cops. Blood rode the wind, thick and fresh, and somewhere ahead Kade was speaking, his rich tones bringing a smile to my lips.

A smile that wasn't likely to stay there given the apparent extent of the blood. This was going to be *nasty*.

I flashed my badge at the officer guarding the top-floor entrance, then ducked under the tape and walked up the ramp. One of Cole's men—the bird-shifter—was bagging something that looked suspiciously like a chunk of meat, and I paused.

"Is that what I think it is?"

He glanced up, his expression neutral but his brown eyes afire with anger. "Yeah."

So it *was* an arm. Or what remained of it, anyway. The bakencko was definitely getting more violent with every kill.

"Stop this thing, will you?" he continued, zipping the bag up with more force than necessary. "I don't want to see what it does next."

"Neither do I." My voice was grim. I glanced up the ramp as Cole's voice rode the air, then glanced back at the bird-shifter. "Do you actually have a name?"

"People call me Dobbs."

"First name, or last name?"

"Friends don't use my first name."

And neither would his enemies, if that tone was anything to go by. "Thanks, Dobbs."

He nodded and got back to the gruesome task of collecting the smaller bits of flesh and fat globules that were still scattered about.

The wind hit me full force as I entered the top floor, blowing me back a step before I realized it. I shivered and collected the flyaway ends of my coat, quickly zipping it up. Thank God I'd had the chance to change—my blood-soaked dress would have left me frozen.

Kade and Cole were squatting near the rear of a blue Toyota four-wheel drive. Even from this distance, it was evident that neither man was happy.

I walked across, my boot heels clicking briefly against the concrete before the sound was rushed away by the wind. Neither man looked around, though both would have been aware of my presence.

"What's up?" I stopped behind Cole and bent to peer under the car. Something that resembled a bloody mess of flesh lay about halfway down.

Not the torso that matched the arm. That arm had been male. This mess was female.

Although I could really only tell that by the pretty gold charm bracelet that was somehow still attached to her visible arm.

"Two victims?" I said, hoping to God I was wrong.

"Two victims," Cole confirmed, rising and stripping off bloody gloves. "We think this one is unrelated."

I straightened and met the icy-blue of his gaze. "As in wrong place, wrong time?"

"Unfortunately, yes."

"That's uncharacteristic, isn't it? I mean, she had witnesses when she did the shoe seller in the window, and she made no move against them."

"Given we are not dealing with anything remotely human, who's to say what is, and isn't, characteristic?" Cole motioned me to follow him.

I glanced at Kade, who was still studying the body intently, then spun and followed the wolf-shifter. I saw the second body long before we reached it. His torso was sprawled across the trunk of the sports car and there was a look of pure terror frozen on his face. Or what remained of it.

That expression said that this was a man who'd experienced the depths of hell in the midst of one of life's greatest pleasures.

I stopped and silently cataloged his injuries. The blood loss from the scratches alone would have been deadly enough, but she'd also ripped him apart limb by limb, leaving only his torso and head on top of the car's trunk.

I closed my eyes and fought the bile that rose up my throat. It wasn't as if I'd never seen bodies pulled apart like this before. I had, but that didn't mean seeing it again now made it any easier. I doubted it ever would.

"God," I said, voice thick.

"Yeah," Cole said. "I think she must have taken cat form to get out of here, because she would have been covered in blood after all this."

I dragged my gaze away from the body and looked around. "There would have to have been screams from both the victims. Surely someone heard them?"

Cole's expression was grim. "The local boys are interviewing the shopkeepers and the patrons. I doubt we're going to get anything."

"Then how was the body discovered?"

"A bit of the woman was flung over the side of the building. It hit a kitchen hand from the restaurant next door as he was dumping bags into the trash."

"Anyone talked to him yet?"

"I think he's been sedated." Cole grimaced. "He'll probably have nightmares for weeks, poor kid."

"He's not the only one." I rubbed my arms lightly, then stopped as power began to caress the air and an odd tingle raced across my skin.

Excitement surged. It *wasn't* just the escalation of the violence that was different with this crime scene.

"What?" Cole said softly.

"There's a soul here." My gaze darted around the parking lot, but I couldn't see anything that resembled the wispy smoke of a soul. Of course, the wind might be tearing any manifestation apart before it was fully formed.

"Whose soul?"

"I don't know." I spun around and took several steps toward the rear wall. The wind was less frantic here, and just for an instant, a wisp of smoke stirred in the shadows holding court in the corner.

Who are you? I asked. I'd learned not so long ago that my ability to sense and hear souls had stretched into being able to converse with them telepathically, as well. Not that there was ever anything resembling whole conversations between us. The ability to talk from beyond the grave seemed to take a lot of strength, and many souls did little more than speak a word or two before their presence disintegrated and they moved on.

But maybe *this* time, one word might be all we needed to stop other innocents getting mauled by the bakeneko.

I took another step forward, and the chill in the air suddenly increased. Whoever it was, they were close by. Had to be. The presence of a soul in this world always seemed to drag me too close to the fierce cold of the underworld.

Again, smoke stirred in the shadows. Just a wisp, a bare outline—nothing that would even be defined as ghostlike. But it was there. The power of it spun all around me.

Who are you? I asked again.

For a moment, there was no response, but the energy in the air increased, until it felt like fireflies dancing across my skin.

Why? Came the reply. So soft. So confused. And very definitely female.

No one knows why this creature is so destructive, I said, hating that I had to talk to her, hating that I had to feel her pain like this. Yet in some odd way, it was probably helping her. She'd have no answers at all if I wasn't here. *You weren't its intended victim. You were just in the way.*

The chill in the air increased, and with it came a sense of anger. *It was not my time.*

She mightn't have thought so, but fate always had other ideas on such things. *Can you tell me anything about the creature?*

She was fast. The sense of energy increased, until the tingling on my skin felt like fire. Very briefly, a wispy face formed in the shadows—a thin pretty face with wide lost eyes. *She took my bag. My phone. My car keys.*

She took your life, too, but I kept that thought to myself. I had no idea if souls could feel shock, but this one showed every sign of going through that right now. I didn't need to make it any worse for her.

What is your name?

Maria. Maria Kennedy-Smith.

Is there anything you can tell me about the person who did this to you?

I knew her. But it didn't seem like her.

The chill in the air was beginning to fade, and the shadows once again swallowed her wispy features.

What was her name?

Jenny Franklin.

One of the missing women. So if her body wasn't in her apartment, where the hell had the bakeneko killed her?

Why would she do this?

The thought was almost a wail. I shivered and rubbed my arms. *It wasn't her. It was a lookalike. Jenny's dead, too.*

The energy was almost gone, the fire on my skin little more than a caress of warmth.

Get whoever it is, came the thought. *Stop her*.

Then she was gone, heading back into whatever realm her soul was destined for.

I blew out a breath and turned around. Cole was watching me with a concerned expression. "You know, I didn't notice it before, but you almost seem to fade when you do that. It's as if they're sucking the life from you."

I rubbed my arms. "I can feel the chill of the other side through them. So maybe it *is* sucking something out of me." Who really knew? It might be a talent Jack intended to use to its full capacity, but it certainly wasn't one that the Directorate had seen much of. My teachers were magi, not other people who shared the same skill.

"If it is, then be damn careful. You might reach a point where returning becomes difficult."

I repressed a shiver at the thought, and forced a grin. "What's this? Caring about a guardian? Is the world about to end?"

He snorted softly. "Did I say I cared one way or another? Woman, you're reading me all wrong." His blue eyes held a twinkle that took away the harshness of his words. "Now, what did the damn soul say?"

I smiled. The guardian-hating, werewolf-despising shifter actually *cared* what happened to me. He mightn't lift a finger to help me, but he *did* care. It was a nice to know, because even if I teased him endlessly and gave him hell, I did actually like him.

"Her name was Maria Kennedy-Smith. Her killer was Jenny Franklin, who's one of the Trollops we haven't yet gotten into protective custody."

"And now won't. Past evidence would have to say she's well and truly dead by now."

"Yeah." I dug my phone out of my pocket. If we could trace Jenny's car, we might just find the bakeneko's trail. I glanced around as Kade walked up. "You found something?"

"The bakeneko is mad."

I snorted softly as I pressed the button for the Directorate. "You don't need empathy to know that."

He gave me an annoyed look. "No, I mean she's going mad. There was no taste of insanity in what she did to Gerard James. There wasn't even insanity in what she did to the shoe man. But there was an insane amount of anger in that last woman's apartment and here—" He hesitated. "Here there is just violence for the sheer pleasure of it. She might have had a motive to begin with, but that has long since gone."

"So she's just killing for the sake of killing now?"

"I would say so."

"Fuck." I blew out a breath, then added, "Jenny Franklin was one of the women you were supposed to take to the safe house, wasn't she?"

"Yeah, but we checked her house and there was no sign of her. She hasn't reported in for work, either. Last I heard, the liaisons were chasing up the location of a couple of exe's, to see if they could shed any light on her whereabouts." He studied me for a minute, then said, "Don't tell me the remains under the car are her."

"No, the remains belong to Maria Kennedy-Smith. Her soul wasn't sucked up by the bakeneko, which is why I know the cat had Jenny's form."

Kade looked at Cole. "Why would she waste a perfectly good soul like that?"

"Maybe it was a last minute killing. Maybe she needed to get out before she was discovered." Cole shrugged, then looked at me. "Yell if you have any further questions."

He spun and walked away, picking up a set of fresh gloves before moving back to the body under the car. I looked away. I didn't want to see him retrieve what was left of Maria. Not when her anguish and pain was still fresh in my mind.

"What can I do for you, wolf girl?" a familiar voice said into my ear.

"Kade said a trace was being put on Jenny Franklin's car. Do you know if that's come through yet?"

"Hang on, and I'll check." She paused. "Okay, she owns a white Porsche, and it's currently parked in Lygon Street."

Which was a long street with lots of clubs and restaurants. It could take forever to find the bakeneko there. "Is there anything in Jenny's history that could give a clue as to why the bakeneko has gone there?"

"One of her exe's owns the Lygon Towers, and lives on the top floor. We've tried contacting him, but there's no answer."

If he also happened to be one of Cherry's exe's, then there was probably very good reason for him not answering. Like, death at the hands of a bloodthirsty, sex-crazed cat. "Send me the address."

"Will do. Oh, and Jack just said to make sure tracking and sound is on."

"Jack's a nag." I hung up and flicked the small button in my ear, turning on the tracker and the sound. They'd hear me if I yelled for help, but I couldn't actually hear them unless I flicked the button again.

Kade was frowning. "Why would the bakeneko go straight from one kill to another? From what I've seen of cats, they tend to sleep off a kill."

"Maybe that's what she's doing. Maybe she figures it'll be safe to hide out in the apartment of one of Jenny's exe's." I shrugged. This thing was a cat, so who really knew how its thought processes worked? "But the Porsche is parked there, so that's where we go."

He grinned and flung an arm around my shoulder, his fingers casually brushing one breast. Even through the thickness of my coat and sweater, I felt the heat of that caress. But then, I knew just what those clever fingers could do. Unfortunately, they wouldn't be doing anything clever to *me* any time soon, and not just because we had an insane killer to catch.

"You know I'll follow you anywhere," he said, amusement enriching his warm tone. "I'll also do you anywhere, but you won't let me."

"Once you've seen Jack really angry, you'll understand why," I said wryly. "In the meantime, you have to drive. At least that'll keep your hands busy."

"I drive an automatic. There's plenty of scope for my hands to play."

I snorted softly and stepped out from under his arm. "You're incorrigible."

"I'm a horse-shifter. We have sex on the brain."

"Let's try to concentrate on catching our killer, huh?"

He shook his head sorrowfully. "You're just no fun anymore."

"Oh, I'm still party central, it's just that you're not on the invite list anymore." I pushed him lightly toward the ramp. "Lead the way, horse man. We have a killer to stop."

$\mathcal{T}$he apartment building belonging to Jenny's ex was set right in the heart of busy Lygon Street, and close to the Blue Moon. The heavy thump of old rock-and-roll music ran across the incessant hum of traffic and brought a smile to my lips as I climbed out of the car.

I hadn't been back to the Rocker since they'd switched to more modern music to attract the younger crowd on the weekends, but it was nice to know they hadn't totally abandoned the old-style music that had made them one of the more popular wolf clubs. Maybe I could start visiting them again, now that my version of celibacy was basically over.

But even as that thought crossed my mind, doubt stirred. Was I really ready to dive headfirst into being a free and easy wolf again? Part of me whispered yes, but another part—the part that still ached—said no. I had Quinn and, right now, that was enough.

Especially considering Quinn himself was more than able to break my heart again.

I turned and studied the building in front of me. It was modern in style—all glass, metal, and sharp angles—and, to my eye at least, there was nothing appealing about it. Not even its closeness to the wolf clubs would have enticed me to live here. Even from the outside, it just didn't feel "open" enough.

Kade led the way into the building, and an elevator swept us up to the top floor. There was only one door on this floor, but ringing the doorbell got no response.

"You want me to break in?" Kade asked, a "dare me" smile teasing his lips.

I raised an eyebrow. "I thought your wild youth was spent breaking into old cars, not homes and apartments."

"No, I said I'd done some things that would make your hair curl." The teasing smile stretched, becoming sexy enough to curl my toes. "Why do you think I ended up in the military? It was either that or jail."

"So those wild ways caught up with you?"

"Actually, my dad caught up with me. He was a cop. Bad move, having a cop for a dad, I can tell you."

"I can imagine." I waved a hand at the door. "You sure you can get this open? Electronic locks have gotten a whole lot tougher since your wild days."

"Yeah, but I've always kept my hand in. Just in case." He got what looked like a small black box out of his pocket and pressed it against the key-reader. A second later, there was a beep and the door clicked open.

I gave him a deadpan look. "You carry an electronic lock picker in your pocket?"

"Saves breaking down doors and getting a sore shoulder."

"You do know they're illegal, don't you?"

He grinned. "Doesn't stop the bad guys, and it won't stop me."

I shook my head and pulled my laser from its holster. "You ready?"

He raised his eyebrows as he pulled free his own weapon. "Sweetheart, I'm always ready."

"Heard that about you stallions." I pushed the door open and stepped quickly into the room. The living room was large, white, and pristine, with modern furniture that matched the modern feel of the building.

And it wasn't empty, I realized, as the smell of cat and death hit.

The bakeneko *was* here.

Chapter 12

I didn't have time to warn Kade.

I barely even had time to spin around in the direction of the scent when a huge black paw hit me, knocking me across the living room and sending me smashing into a wall. The plaster dented under the force of the impact and the laser went flying from my hand.

I hit the floor just as hard as the wall, and pain flared across my back. I ignored it, and swiped irritably at the warm liquid spilling from the slashes on my cheek.

But the scent of blood that filled the air wasn't only mine. Kade had managed to move away from the doorway, but he'd been backed into a corner by the bakeneko and his right arm was shredded so badly I could see strips of bone in places. He'd had time enough to grab a metal chair from the dining area and that was the only thing standing between him and the bakeneko's bloody fury. But the metal was having trouble standing up to the force of the creature's blows, with huge dents marring the various struts.

I had no idea where his laser was. Like mine, it had obviously been sent flying when the bakeneko attacked.

She was *massive*—a big black monster who stood at shoulder height with the horse-shifter. Her paws were the size of damn plates, and her claws were thick and brutally sharp.

We needed to get rid of her—fast.

I scrambled to my feet, then had to thrust my hand against the wall as dizziness hit. I shook my head to clear it, sending droplets of crimson scattering across the pristine whiteness, then spotted a laser on the floor and dove left to grab it. I wrapped my finger around the trigger, making the weapon hum, but I resisted the urge to fire. Kade was right behind the bakeneko, which meant I couldn't take a shot. Not when the power of these things could shoot holes through concrete walls and still kill someone on the other side. Even if I moved around to the other side, it wouldn't help. She'd sense the movement and shift to counter.

The bakeneko snarled and raised a paw for another swipe at Kade. I sighted on it and pressed the trigger. The blue beam shot out, but, as I'd feared, the bakeneko saw it and moved. The beam missed flesh, piercing the thick window beyond the two of them and disappearing into the gray day.

The creature roared—a sound thick with fury—then, surprisingly, she spun and leapt for the same window. I shot again, but the bitch was moving too fast and the shot did little more than singe hair from her back before shooting another hole through the glass, further weakening it.

Kade dove forward, trying to grab the creature's tail, but there was so much blood on his hands that he couldn't get a grip.

The creature hit the window headfirst. The glass shattered, the thick shards glittering as they followed the creature out into the chill afternoon.

"Shit," Kade said, running to the broken window and staring out.

I quickly joined him. My stomach rebelled instantly at the drop, but I shoved the old fear away and concentrated on our quarry. The big cat was tumbling tail over head toward the concrete, but at the last possible minute seemed to find her balance and landed on all fours. We were five floors up, but the damn bitch didn't even seem to notice.

In fact, she didn't even appear to be limping as she ran up the street, her presence causing squeals of panic as people scattered to get out of her way. I raised the laser but didn't dare take a shot—the bakeneko was moving so fast there was no guarantee I'd get her. But I sure as hell would get *someone* down there.

"Well, at least we know how she got out of James's office." I slapped the laser against Kade's chest, then scrambled up onto the sill. "I have the tracker on. Follow me in the car."

"I didn't think you could fly—"

"I can't," I snapped. "At least, not very well. But not very well might just make the difference here. Go."

He went, though his expression very much suggested he expected to find me splattered on the pavement when he got down there.

I took a deep breath, then reached for the magic deep in my soul, holding the gull shape in my mind and feeling the power of it surge through my limbs, twisting and changing my shape.

In gull shape once more, I spread my wings, then closed my eyes and jumped. For a moment the sensation of falling was so overwhelming that panic surged, then I remembered the need to actually *fly* and began to pump my wings. Felt the surge of air rushing past my feathers and the sensation of falling ended abruptly.

I opened my eyes and saw the pavement sweep by inches from my belly. Relief slithered through me, though the reality was that smashing against the pavement had been a close thing, and only emphasized the need to go back to Henry and practice this flying thing a whole lot more.

I swept upward, gaining height so I could see past the buildings and traffic, and spotted the bakeneko in the distance. She was little more than a blur of black, her presence more notable through the wave of pedestrians that were scrambling to get out of her way. She raced around a corner, moving away from Lygon but toward Rathdown Street, then swung left and kept on running.

I followed, wondering where the hell she was going and hoping like hell she didn't go too far. The muscles in my wings and chest were beginning to ache already. I might be fit, but I wasn't *flying* fit.

I couldn't see Kade's car, but he might have been

caught in traffic. Not all Directorate cars had sirens, which made dashing through red lights something of a hazard.

I just had to hope that he *was* near. That he was following the tracker okay. I didn't want to face this thing alone.

It raced on, a black blur that seemingly felt no weariness. Shops and apartments gave way to a mix of cafés, small houses, and warehouses. Rathdown Street came to a junction and, for the first time, the bakeneko paused, nose in the air. Undoubtedly tasting the breeze for any sign of followers. I hoped I was already high enough up to avoid being scented, because I just didn't have the energy to climb any farther.

Her form began to shimmer, shift, until a tall, blonde woman stood in place of the black cat. She hitched the torn shoulder of her bloodied dress back into place then more shimmering took place, and the dress itself changed, until it was no longer torn or bloodied. Which meant it was part of the magic rather than a reality. Interesting.

Her shoes had disappeared when she'd shifted the shape of her dress, and she was now barefoot as she padded across the road. She walked quickly through the park, skirting a wooden fence before moving into the parking lot of what looked to be an abandoned warehouse. I circled around to watch, though the effort of holding my wings still enough to glide made my limbs tremble.

The bakeneko raised a fist and casually broke down the door, then disappeared inside. I flew around the perimeter, looking for other possible exits. There were plenty of windows and doors in the place, but after five minutes of circling, there was no further sign of her. Maybe she intended to hole up here—she had no reason to run any farther, after all, because she thought she was safe. Although we weren't dealing with anything that remotely thought the way a human did, so who knew what it was actually intending?

I continued to circle, watching the exit points for any sign of movement, but the building remained silent. A few minutes later, I saw a blue Ford pull up. Kade exited and looked up at the sky.

I swung around and headed toward him, shifting shape as I neared the ground. It took several stumbling steps to gain any sort of balance, and then it only happened because Kade grabbed my arm and held me upright.

"God, you're trembling."

"Yeah, flying really isn't my style." I shook my limbs in an effort to ease the ache. It didn't actually help much. "The bakeneko has holed up inside the warehouse."

Kade's gaze went past me, and he frowned. "There's lots of exit points. If we go in, she can escape very easily."

"Yeah." I touched my ear lightly. "Riley to Directorate."

"We've been listening," Jack said. "I've got two birdshifters on the way. They'll watch the outside while you two go in."

"ETA?"

He paused, then said, "Two minutes. Iktar will be there in five."

"Tell him to take the main front entrance. We're going in through the parking lot." I paused, then added, "And tell him to be careful. This thing is big and bad."

"Then you be careful, too."

"You know me. I'm always careful."

His disbelieving snort rang in my ears.

I hesitated, then asked, "No word from the hospital?"

"None yet, I'm afraid."

Damn. The knot in my stomach tightened a little bit more, but I did my best to push the worry aside. I had a killer to catch, and if I didn't dedicate all my attention to it, I might just end up in hospital right alongside Liander.

That would *really* make Rhoan's day complete.

"So we're going in?" Kade asked.

"We have no choice."

He handed me a laser, then pulled the other one free from the waist of his pants. A dangerous place to shove it, I would have thought. "And help is coming?"

I glanced skyward. Two brown dots were soaring high up. I couldn't help the sliver of envy at the ease of which they did that. "Our eyes are in the sky. Iktar will be coming in around the front."

He pressed the laser's trigger lightly and the weapon whined as it charged up. "Let's go, then."

I switched my laser on, then followed him across to the building, keeping as low and as close to cover as possible. Hopefully, the roar of traffic going up and down nearby Brunswick Road would mute the sound of our steps.

With the doorway reached, I pressed my back against

the grimy brick wall, feeling the chill of it seep into my spine. Beyond the smashed door, the warehouse was dark and silent. No creaks, no wind moaning through broken glass, nothing that seemed spooky or out of place.

Yet I was spooked regardless. Probably because I knew what lay in wait.

I met Kade's gaze. He held up three fingers, then pointed to the left. I nodded and silently counted. At three, I slipped in the doorway, laser raised and held at the ready as my gaze swept the room.

Silence met me. The air was thick with the scent of oil and age, the walls grimy and slick looking. The room itself was filled with shadows, despite the light filtering in through dirty windows. Perfect conditions for a black cat who wanted to remain unseen.

There was a concrete ramp to my left and a walkway that went up and around the room. Several doorways led off into deeper darkness from this. To the right was a set of high double doors. They were solid looking and padlocked, so the bakeneko hadn't gone that way.

I glanced back at Kade and motioned him in. He moved to the right, nostrils flaring as he made a sweeping motion with the gun.

"She knows we're here."

Though he kept his voice to a whisper, his words seemed to slide off the walls as sharply as a bell being rung. Or maybe it just seemed that way because I was so damn tense.

"I can sense amusement coming from the general direction of door number two."

"I would have thought she'd be angry more than amused."

"Well, a human probably would be, but this thing isn't human."

Very true. I blew out a breath, then quickly moved up the ramp and across to the first doorway. The deeper darkness looked unwelcoming. Despite the fact that Kade had sensed amusement coming from the direction of the other doorway, the smell of cat was coming thick and sharp from this one. Maybe the two corridors were linked farther in.

Maybe it was all part of the bakeneko's plan. After all, cats delighted in toying with their prey.

Kade halted beside me. I motioned toward the door and gave the low signal. He nodded.

I blinked to switch my vision to infrared then went in fast and low. Nothing moved in the corridor. Several doors led off it, but all of them were closed. A set of double doors waited at the far end. I centered my laser on it, then nodded a go-ahead.

Kade came in and moved quickly but quietly to the first doorway. With his back to the wall and laser at the ready, he wrapped his free hand around the handle then thrust the door open. Nothing jumped out at him. He checked the room visually, then glanced at me and shook his head.

I scampered to the next doorway and repeated his actions while he watched the double doors. There was nothing in the small room but rubbish and broken furniture. The other two remaining rooms were also empty.

Which left us with the double doors and whatever lay beyond them.

The cat smell was no sharper than before, and yet my skin tingled with awareness of her presence. Maybe it was fear, maybe it was my clairvoyance trying to send me a warning I really didn't need, but either way, we had no choice but to continue on through our chosen route.

I glanced at Kade and half-motioned that I'd go through first, but froze as footsteps whispered across the silence.

Human footsteps, moving gently away.

Then laughter, soft and mocking.

The bitch *definitely* knew we were here.

I stepped forward and kicked the door open. On the other side, nothing but the darkness of a large room was revealed. I waited until the door had whooshed back toward us, then dove through the opening, coming back up onto one knee and quickly scanning the room. No bakeneko. Just her scent riding the heavy, musty air.

"She's definitely playing," I said softly, as Kade came through the door.

"I don't care what she does, as long as we kill her at the end of it." He nodded toward the stairs at the far end of the room. "She gone up that?"

"Smells like it."

"Then let's go."

He led the way, his footsteps echoing across the silence. There was no point in being silent any longer. She knew we were here, and given a cat's hearing had to be as sharp as a wolf's, she would probably hear us regardless of how quiet we were.

We raced up the steps and ended up in a corridor that was long, thin, and even darker than the room below. There were eight doors leading off the corridor, and a larger, double set waiting at the far end.

"This place is a fucking maze," Kade muttered, disgust in his voice. "Though our quarry seems to have run straight toward the door at the end."

"'Seems' being the operative word," I said, not trusting the fact that it was slightly open one little bit. I drew my gaze back to the nearest rooms. "Though infrared isn't bringing up any life-heat close by."

"The bitch is here *somewhere*, so let's go find her."

He strode forward, seemingly free of the fear that was twisting my stomach. It was weird. I mean, I'd faced things far worse than this bakeneko, and yet I was practically shaking at the thought of confronting her.

Maybe it was simply the knowledge of what she could do.

Being dead was one thing. We all had to go sometime, after all. But being dead and having your soul *eaten* was another matter entirely. I wasn't at all sure that I believed in reincarnation, but I sure as hell wanted my soul to hang around and find out.

We moved forward as before, checking each room thoroughly before continuing on. Despite my fears, there were no traps waiting in any of them.

But the cat smell was getting stronger.

Which meant we were getting closer.

I stopped at the ajar door and glanced at Kade. He

pointed at me, then to the right, and raised five fingers. I nodded and sucked in a breath, releasing it silently as I counted.

At five, we kicked out the doors and ran through—me to the right, Kade to the left.

The room was large and filled with windows, but the light seeping in was yellow and dusky. There were plenty of shadows for a cat to hide in.

Out of the corner of my eye I saw movement. I twisted around and sighted, the whine of the laser cutting through the silence as my finger pressed against it. I released it when I saw that it was something small and furry with a very long tail.

Not a cat. More likely a rat.

I blew out a breath and continued on, keeping to walls and running low. Kade was on the other side, keeping pace with me simply because I wasn't moving at vampire speed. The whine of his laser was a sharp echo of mine.

Again, something moved in the shadow. I swung the laser around, but it was only another rat, scampering along the wall.

Which was odd. We weren't anywhere near the rats to scare them, so if they were running from the cat, why couldn't we damn well see her?

Even under infrared, there was no sign of life other than the rats.

Then it hit me.

The bakeneko could change sizes. Why wouldn't she be able to go smaller than a tabby as well as larger?

I stopped and swung round.

Saw something big and black emerging out of the shadows where the rat had just been.

"Kade! Behind you!"

I fired the laser even as I screamed the warning, but the bakeneko was moving way too fast. She'd consumed a lot of souls, and now she was faster than anything I'd ever seen before.

It didn't matter. I kept hitting the trigger.

And kept missing.

Kade twisted around and fired blindly. The shot scoured the creature's side and she screamed—a high sound of fury that made my ears ache.

Then she was on him, her sheer weight and speed flinging them both backward, until all I could see was a fighting ball of black and brown.

I swore and raced across the room. They were still rolling, tumbling, across the filthy concrete floor, but Kade had somehow managed to get his hands around the creature's neck. The corded muscles in his arms were evidence enough of the strength he was using to try to strangle her, but he seemed to be achieving little more than holding her wickedly sharp teeth away from his throat. And all the while, her claws were ripping at him everywhere else.

I couldn't risk a shot. Like before, I could kill Kade as easily as I could kill the bakeneko. So I reached out and grabbed her tail instead.

"Hey, bitch, try tackling someone in your own species group for a change."

I hauled back as hard as I could, and ripped her away from Kade. But she came away fighting, twisting around and slashing with her claws. I ducked the blows and flung her sideways with all my might. Then I fired the laser.

This time, I hit the bitch.

The bright beam scoured another trench down her side then flung itself toward a rear leg, slicing through flesh and sinew. The burnt smell of fur and skin tainted the air, but even as I pressed the trigger to fire again, the bakeneko was on the move, her speed seemingly unhampered by the wound.

Kade, bleeding from a dozen different wounds, scrambled to his feet and ran to the left. He swooped up his laser and pressed the trigger, but with the creature running at full speed, neither of us were having much luck. She crashed through the door at the far end of the room and disappeared.

"She's playing hide-and-seek," he said. Blood poured down his arm and both legs, and his stomach had several deep slashes. When combined with the still raw—but no longer bleeding—wound he'd received in the apartment, he wasn't a pretty sight.

"You'd better shift shape to stop the bleeding," I said, "Iktar should be here by now. Go find him while I track the creature."

"Fuck that." He snorted softly. "You think I'm going to let you go after that thing alone? You've got rocks in your head, sweetheart."

I might have rocks, but I was swifter and faster than he was. I was also less injured. "Kade, we need help to bring her down."

"Iktar can track emotions as well as I can. He'll find us quick enough. Move, Riley."

There was no point in arguing. *That* was obvious not only in his tone, but in the anger in his eyes. He wanted to bring this creature down *bad*.

I ran forward, following the scent of cat and burnt flesh. Power shimmered across my senses as Kade shifted shape to stop the bleeding, then the sound of his footsteps echoed as he followed.

We crashed into the next room. The bakeneko was nowhere to be seen, but there were several shimmers of life crouching in the corners.

"The bitch is playing rats again."

I raised the laser and fired at the nearest nest. High-pitched squeals met the assault, and those rats I didn't kill went scattering.

One of them was faster than the rest, and it was running—changing and growing, until it once more resembled a big cat. And she was running straight at Kade again. We fired, the twin beams of blue cutting across the grimy shadows, missing the bakeneko but cleaning up everything else. Windows, walls, rats.

She launched herself in the air, her body little more than a blur of black.

"Kade!" I screamed, a warning he didn't really need.

He threw himself sideways, but the giant cat's paw hit him mid-leap, sending him flying straight at one of the grimy windows. Glass shattered, then Kade was gone.

I swore and fired the weapon, keeping my finger on the trigger and sending a continuous beam the bakeneko's way. The laser grew hotter in my hands, until it was almost impossible to hold, but it didn't do much good. The bitch was moving faster than any vampire, and while I left a trail of burnt and smoking brick, plaster and debris, the bakeneko remained whole.

As the red light began to flash on the weapon, warning that its charge was failing, I backed toward a wall and looked around for another weapon.

Unless I wanted to slap her senseless with a dead rat, there wasn't much here.

The laser finally gave out, the bright beam dying with little fanfare. I shoved the overheated weapon away and flexed my fingers. It looked like I'd have to do this the hard way—at least until Kade and Iktar got here.

The bakeneko finally stopped moving, her form shifting as she took on human shape again. But it seemed to take her longer than before. Maybe the energy she was expending was finally taking a toll.

"You," she said. "I shall eat. Your flesh smells sweet."

Her voice was low and oddly scratchy—the voice of someone not used to controlling vocal cords. It made me wonder how she'd kept up the facade of being Alana Burns for a whole night. But there again, maybe there'd been no need for her to say much. She'd been with a politician, after all, and they were notorious for loving the sound of their own voices.

I shifted my stance a little, my weight on my toes so I could move fast if needed. Although I was more than happy to keep her talking until the cavalry came to the rescue—in fact, I had to—I couldn't risk letting her escape. There'd been too many deaths—and too many souls lost—already.

Besides, I'd rather fight with words than fists. I had enough scars as it was.

"So why me?" I said, watching her eyes and ignoring the satisfied smile teasing her lips. "Why not the man you threw out the window? He tastes a whole lot better than me, trust me on that."

"He is not a pale one. It is the pale ones I must kill." She began to walk toward me, the lazy smile on her lips growing. A cat playing with its prey.

I flexed my fingers, trying to ease the tension winding through my muscles. "Why only us pale types? That hardly seems fair."

"Pale women killed my mistress. She hated them, and they killed her."

"Your mistress was killed by a vampire out for revenge. Her death had nothing to do with any of the other people."

Or me. But I don't think the bakeneko cared. Her quest for vengeance had slipped into outright lust for murder.

She was halfway across the room now, her strides long and rolling. There was no tension in her shoulders, no sign that she expected any sort of fight—like she expected me to be a quick and easy kill. And maybe I would be—this bitch might not be stronger than a god of death, but she was certainly faster.

"No," she said. "They took everything from her. They stole her life, so I steal theirs."

"And the men you killed?"

"She hated them. Hated what they did to her." A languid smile drifted across her lips. "I used them like they used her."

Like a cat should talk about behavior when they treated the whole world as underlings. "She was a Trollop. How else would they treat her?"

The bakeneko frowned. "I don't know this word."

"It means she was little better than a filthy cat in heat, and she was treated as such."

The bakeneko's eyes darkened. "For that, I rip you apart slow—"

The words were barely out of her mouth when I leapt at her. I had to—catching her by surprise was my only real hope of doing some serious damage. I had time to see her eyes widen slightly, then I hit her head-on, knocking her down and sideways. We both hit the ground hard, but I rolled to my feet quickly and hit her again, one foot smashing her in the face and mashing her nose flat, the other catching her in the throat. She staggered back, making a gurgling sound, the smirk disappearing under a cloud of anger and pain. I hit the concrete and again pushed upward. The bakeneko's shape was shifting again, becoming a cat from the feet up. But the shapeshift wasn't as fast as before, so maybe the constant fighting and the wounds I'd inflicted on her were beginning to take their toll. Even so, I didn't want to see her in cat shape. Paws that could become the size of buckets held no appeal at all. Not when I had to fight against them, anyway.

I swore and lunged forward, grabbing her arm and twisting it with all my might. She snarled, a sound that came out only half human, then slashed at me with a hand that was partially clawed, ripping through my coat and down into skin. I gritted my teeth against the scream that careened up my throat, but held on to her arm and gave it another twist. Bone shattered and suddenly her left arm was hanging useless. One less weapon to worry about.

She hit me again, knocking me sideways. I staggered several steps before I caught my balance. But by then, she'd attained her full cat shape. And she was leaping straight for my throat.

I dove out of reach and rolled to my feet, then twisted around, lashing out with one booted foot, smashing the heel across her mouth. Flesh and bone gave way under the force of the blow and blood flew.

She snarled again and lashed out with her claws, scraping down my leg and deep into flesh. Pain flared, thick and hot, but I ignored it, spinning again and smashing another blow into her mouth, this time dislodging teeth.

She screamed in fury and launched at me. I had no time to run and met her leap head-on, grabbing her throat with one hand and clawing at her eyes with the other. The breath whooshed from my lungs, leaving me gasping as the bakeneko's back legs clawed at my flesh and her fetid breath washed across my face.

We rolled across the cold concrete, my grunts mingling with her snarls as we punched and clawed at each other. My thumb found her eye socket and I dug deep, desperately trying to blind her. She screamed, the sound deafening, and shook her head from side to side, desperately trying to dislodge my grip. I dug deeper and deeper, until fluid gushed over my thumb and I hit bone. With a quick sideways flick, I tore the eyeball from the socket.

She roared and suddenly her broken teeth were in my flesh, gnawing at my arm. Sweat rolled down my face and white-hot pokers of pain began burning up my arm and into my brain. I drew my legs up, desperately trying to get my feet under her belly before she bit down into bone.

She ripped her head sideways, out of my grip, taking a chunk of flesh with her. A scream burned up my throat, but with it came anger and a desperate strength. My feet found purchase underneath her and I heaved with everything I had, sending her flying up and over my head.

I scrambled to my feet once again and backed away, blood dripping from my fingertips and splashing across the concrete.

The bakeneko hit the far wall and righted herself, her weight on three legs and the right side of her face bloodied and battered. There were strips of flesh—my flesh—hanging from her mouth, and her tongue came out, gathering them inward, before she swallowed.

A bizarre sort of smile stretched her broken features, then her form was shifting once again. Only this time she didn't become a blonde.

This time, she became me.

And she was perfect.

Perfect.

Aside from the fact that she had a broken arm rather

than shredded legs and a chunk out of her arm, I might have been staring at a perfectly clothed reflection. Obviously, whatever magic allowed her to change could hide bloodied clothes or a gouged eye, but it couldn't heal a broken limb. It was nice to know that some shifting magic remained constant across species.

"I will walk out of here, guardian. I will walk away with no one being the wiser."

I flexed bloodied fingers and shifted my feet. "Like hell you will."

And with that, I leapt at her. If she remained in human form, I had a chance. But it wasn't my only chance. Iktar and Kade *had* to be close.

She sidestepped fast, but her speed seemed to be restricted by either her human shape or her wounds, and I hit her hard, my boot sinking deep into her side and sending her flying.

I swung round. The bakeneko had regained her balance, but rather than attack, she ran backward. I ran after her, wondering why the fuck she was suddenly retreating when the bitch was so confident of a win.

A second later, I had my answer.

The door behind her was torn off its hinges and two figures appeared, one little more than a shadow and the other blood covered and battered.

"Shoot her!" the bakeneko screamed, her voice my voice. "Blow her fucking brains out!"

Neither man hesitated.

They both raised their guns and fired.

Chapter 13

Only they didn't fire at me.

They fired at the creature wearing my face.

One bright laser beam sliced through her legs, the other through her neck. There was a brief moment when shock registered, then her head parted company from her body and all three bits plopped to the floor.

I stared at her for a moment, unable to believe it was over so suddenly, then wiped a trembling hand across my face and met Kade's gaze as he limped toward me. "How did you know?"

He gave me a smile that was all aching weariness. "She's not missing her left little pinky. You are."

"Then you're both more observant than me, thank God." I hadn't even fucking noticed.

He wrapped a bloody arm around me and dragged

me into a hug that was so damn fierce and comforting I felt like crying.

"You're a mess," he said, after a while.

"Now there's a case of the pot calling the kettle black."

"You both should go to the hospital," Iktar commented.

I looked around Kade's arm, and saw him lightly toeing the bakeneko's body. As he did, smoke began to rise, twisting and curling skyward. It swirled around its human remains, finding shape and solidarity. Briefly gaining the form of a cat.

She turned, and her ghostly gaze met mine. She didn't say anything, simply bowed, then her form broke apart and began drifting skyward before disappearing completely.

"She's gone," I said, and wondered what sort of afterlife things like her went to.

Iktar glanced at me, his body fading into the shadows and featureless face unreadable. "It is always best to be sure."

And with that, he aimed the laser at her heart and shot the hell out of it. Spirit lizards believed that the soul resided in the heart, and that by destroying the heart you destroyed the soul, preventing it from moving on. In this case, he was too late, but I doubted it would have made a difference anyway. Souls seemed to rise from the whole, not just from the heart.

"He's right," Kade commented. "We should take ourselves to hospital and get checked out."

"*You* can take yourself there. I'm going home to shower and eat." Although I'd have to shift shape and stop the bleeding first. Not to mention help start healing the missing chunk out of my arm.

But after all that, I *would* head to the hospital—to hold my brother's hand and wait for Liander to wake.

"You *are* bleeding rather heavily, you know. I mean, I'm loving the hug, but between the two of us we're creating quite a puddle."

I laughed and stepped back. He was right—there was quite a bit of blood at our feet.

"Then get ye to the hospital. Sable will kick your butt if you haven't got the strength to pamper her the way she deserves to be pampered."

"Too damn right." He touched my torn cheek lightly. "Do you want a lift?"

I shook my head. "I'll take Iktar's car. He can grab a lift back with the cleanup team."

"The cleanup team do not like me," Iktar commented.

I grinned. "Well, you will show off your party trick at inappropriate moments."

And having seen that trick myself, I could totally understand their aversion. I mean, a penis he could retract into his body was bad enough, but being able to produce barbs along it as well was just . . . gross.

"Hey, they asked," he said. "Not my fault."

I smiled and shook my head. Iktar didn't sound too depressed about not being liked and I had to wonder if he'd done it deliberately. Our spirit lizard got a kick out of not only shocking people but alienating them.

Their culture had this weird belief that the fewer friends you had, the more powerful you were. Of course, they also believed family was all that mattered, and that I could *totally* understand.

Kade leaned forward and kissed my uncut cheek. "Today was fun."

"You have a very odd definition of fun," I said, voice dry. "And kissing is against the rules."

"Like you care about the rules." He gave me a salute good-bye, then spun on his heel and walked out.

I walked over to Iktar and held out my hand. "Keys?"

"In the car."

"Thanks."

He nodded, then his all-blue gaze met mine. "This job will kill us all, won't it?"

I hesitated, then nodded. "Probably. None of us is immortal, Iktar."

His gaze went back to the bakeneko's body, then he nodded slowly. "I guess it's as good a way of going as any."

"Oh, I think getting old and slipping away peacefully surrounded by friends and loved ones would be a hell of a lot better than this."

His gaze came back to mine. "But you and I are not destined for that, are we?"

"Probably not." I squeezed his shoulder lightly, his flesh cold and clammy under my fingertips, then walked away. I didn't want to think about a future I might not have. I just wanted to get to the hospital and make sure my present was alive and well.

*

*L*iander's surgeon walked in an hour after I arrived back at the hospital.

Yann and Raina stood up immediately, but Rhoan didn't move, his expression carefully neutral but the tension in his body suddenly sharpening.

"How did the operation go?" Raina asked, her normally warm tones thin and high. Shaky.

The gray-haired surgeon gave her one of those smiles doctors all over the world seemed to use. The one that said everything was fine, even if things were going to hell and back.

"We repaired the bowel and the small intestine damage, but we can't one hundred percent guarantee we've gotten all the fecal matter out of his abdominal cavity, so we'll have to keep an eye out for infection. For that reason, we've confined him with light silver to stop him from shifting."

"But silver will kill him—"

"And by shifting, he could accelerate the infection as much as the healing, and that could be dangerous. We need to give it a day or so to be sure." The doctor gave her his best professional smile. "We don't use enough silver to kill, just restrain. It'll burn, but he'll heal from that and be fine."

"Oh, thank God," Raina said, raising one hand to her chest.

The surgeon hesitated, then said, "He did lose a lot of blood, and we'll have to keep him in the hospital for a little longer than we normally would for a wolf, just because the risk of infection *is* a lot higher, but I think he's going to be fine."

"That's excellent news, Doc," Yann said gruffly.

The surgeon smiled. "I wish all my patients were as tough as this young man. I don't like losing patients."

Which in itself said just how close Liander had been to death.

"Can we go see him, Doctor?" Raina asked.

The surgeon hesitated again. "Only two of you. And only quickly."

"Thank you, Doctor."

He nodded and spun on his heel. "This way."

Raina squeezed her husband's hand, then followed the surgeon. Yann didn't move. "Rhoan?" he said, voice sharp.

Rhoan looked up quickly. "Yes, sir?"

"You'd better get in there, boy, while the surgeon is feeling kindly."

Hope flitted briefly across Rhoan's tired features. "But he's your son—"

"And he's your soul mate. And I know he'd probably be more comforted by your presence than mine. Go, son. Go see him."

"Thank you," Rhoan said, and scrambled after Raina. He wrapped an arm around her shoulder and walked down the hall with her.

I smiled at Yann. "Thank you."

Yann waved the comment away. "Your brother is probably the only reason Liander held on. That was a bad wound, lass."

"I know."

His gaze briefly slipped to the raw wounds still visible on my arm and my face. "I guess you do."

He sat back down. I leaned against Quinn's shoulder, and finally allowed myself to relax.

Liander was going to be okay, and so was my brother.

Maybe fate wasn't such a bitch, after all.

A day later, the doctors confirmed Liander was out of the woods. They'd moved him out of intensive into a general ward, but they still had him restrained. Apparently, they wanted to give it one more day before they allowed him to shift and accelerate the healing.

But at least with him now in a general ward, Rhoan could finally sit by his side and hold his hand. That was what he'd been doing for the last twenty-four hours, and Jack appeared to understand. He hadn't hassled Rhoan once about getting back to work.

Maybe it was just *my* love life he couldn't show any sympathy for.

I handed Rhoan a coffee and a burger, then sat down beside him. For the first time in days, he actually looked relaxed. I took a sip of the bittersweet liquid, tried to pretend it was hazelnut *and* nice, then said, "So what are the plans, then?"

He unwrapped the burger and took a bite, then washed it down with the muck they had the cheek to call coffee. "Once he's cleared to leave, I plan to take him home and look after him."

"His home, or our home?"

He met my gaze and gave me a tired half-smile. "Our home. It's what he wants."

My heart did a happy little dance for Liander, but part of me couldn't believe Rhoan really meant it—that he wouldn't change his mind sometime down the track, and break his lover's heart all over again. "What about what *you* want?"

He took another bite of the burger, then shrugged lightly. "You were right before."

I raised my eyebrows. "This is a first. Not me being right, because I usually am, but you actually admitting it."

He snorted softly. "Enjoy it while you can, because it won't happen again."

"Oh, I'm sure it will. Me being right, that is."

He grinned and leaned sideways, hitting me lightly with his shoulder. Coffee slopped over the edges of my cup, splattering my jeans. "Hey, careful. It may not be good coffee, but it *is* coffee, so let's not waste it."

He shook his head and finished the burger. After tossing the wrapper in the trash, he said, "I was always so scared about making a commitment and then dying, leaving Liander to cope alone. I never really thought about the opposite happening."

"We all have to die sometime, Rhoan." But may it be many, many years away, and not on the job, as Iktar had stated.

"Hell, yeah, but you and I, we have a higher rate of succeeding than most others."

"You know, that's a really depressing line of thought when I'm sitting in a hospital filled with sick people and ghosts." I took a sip of coffee, then added, "So because you've suddenly realized that Liander is as vulnerable to death as you and me, you're letting him live with us?"

"And I'm going to share more of myself with him. I'm going to try and give him what he wants, up to a point, because he deserves better of life and better from me."

I smiled. "Well, that's true."

He snorted softly. "You are such a bitch, sister."

"Had a great teacher, brother."

He shook his head. "I won't do the ceremony. I can't. I just *can't*. Not with what we do, not with what we face. But I can give him everything else he wants."

Not doing the ceremony wouldn't save Liander from hurt or pain or worse if Rhoan died. Not if what Ben said was true. But I wasn't about to give my brother another reason to push Liander away. Not when he was finally getting everything he wanted.

"He's never wanted the ceremony, Rhoan. All he's ever wanted is you."

"And that's the whole problem, sis. I love what I do. I love the adrenaline rush of it." He hesitated, then added softly, "I'm addicted to it. I *need* it. I can't completely give it up, not even for Liander."

And he wasn't talking about the killing. He was talking about the sex.

"I never knew."

His gaze met mine. "Liander does. I told him a while ago, when he basically told me to give up other men or he'd walk away."

"So that's why you've been behaving yourself."

"Everywhere except work. He understood, Riley. He really did."

"He's an amazing man."

"And as I've said all along, I don't want to lose him." His gaze went to his lover. "And especially not like this. If one of us has to die, then let it be me."

"Let it be no one in this little family unit," I said softly. "I think we've coped with enough shit in our lives already."

"Ain't that the truth." He looked at me for a moment, then touched a hand lightly to my still scarred arm. "The hole is gradually healing."

"Yeah, thankfully." Though it *was* taking its time, it would heal and probably without much of a scar. I was going to end up with one on my face, though, at the point where one of the bakeneko's claws had dug the deepest. But at least it wasn't in the middle of my face nor was it that big. I could live with it.

Especially given what could have happened.

"But you still look very tired. Maybe you should go home and rest."

"Brother, I look better than you do."

"Yeah, but I didn't lose buckets of blood and then refuse to let the hospital do something about it."

No, he'd almost lost something worse. His heart. His soul. "You know I hate hospitals."

"And I'm giving you the chance to get out of one."

I studied him for a moment, then said, "Are you sure you don't want company?"

"I'll be fine. Liander will be fine. All is good. Go home and rest."

I leaned forward and kissed him. "Thanks. Just make sure you eat, bro. You're going to need all the strength you can muster to look after Liander when he comes home."

He snorted softly. "And you think I'm a bad patient. Wait until we get *him* home."

The anticipation was there for the world to see, and I smiled. "Bringing him home has a nice sound to it, doesn't it?"

"Yeah," he said, and flicked my nose. "Go."

I went.

*D*usk was settling in by the time I got home. And resting against the front door of our apartment, waiting for me, was a clear plastic container containing a single red rose.

As a cure for tiredness, it was pretty damn fine.

With a smile teasing my lips, I walked into the apartment, tossing my bag and keys aside before sitting down on the arm of the sofa to read the little note.

I really would like to start again, it said, *and I'd like to take you to dinner. Our first official date. No strings. Nothing expected. Just you and me, finally getting to know each other.*

There was no signature or name, but it didn't need one. It could only have come from one man.

And it seemed Rhoan wasn't the only one who finally had something to look forward to.

With a silly grin stretching my lips, I all but ran over to the phone so I could ring my vampire.

Tempting Evil

Half-werewolf and half-vampire, Riley Jenson is now an agent with the DOR – the Directorate of Other Races. However, trusting her superiors and lovers barely more than she trusts her worst enemies, Riley plays by her own set of rules.

Her latest mission: to enter the heavily guarded pleasure palace of a criminal named Deshon Starr – a madman-scientist who's been messing around in the gene pool for decades. With two sexy men – a cool, seductive vampire and an irresistibly hot werewolf – vying for her attention, Riley must keep focused. Because saving the world from Deshon Starr will mean saving herself from the trap that's closing in around her...

Dangerous Games

In Melbourne's urban underworld, there's a place for every fetish and fantasy. But for Riley Jenson, one such nightclub has become an obsession. Riley, a rare hybrid of werewolf and vampire and new agent for the Directorate of Other Races, hasn't come in pursuit of pleasure but of an unknown killer who's been using the club as his hunting ground.

Leave it to Riley to find the only ticket into the heavily guarded venue: Jin, a deliciously hot-bodied bartender who might just provide the key to unmasking a killer unlike any other in the Directorate's experience. Taunted by a former colleague gone rogue, Riley follows Jin into a realm of pleasure she could never have imagined but as danger and passion ignite, a shocking mystery begins to unravel one where Riley herself becomes the ultimate object of desire...

Embraced by Darkness

Just when Riley Jenson thought her life was getting back on track, fate throws another curve ball. The alpha of her estranged pack – and the man who tried to kill her by throwing her off a mountainside – demands her help to find his missing granddaughter.

Riley would love to refuse, but if she does, her mother dies. And if that isn't enough, something is tearing humans to shreds, and it's up to Riley as an agent for the Directorate of Other Races, to track down the killer before another soul is embraced by darkness…

Praise for Keri Arthur:

'Keri Arthur's imagination and energy infuse everything she writes with zest' Charlaine Harris

'Keri Arthur skillfully mixes her suspenseful plot with heady romance in her thoroughly enjoyable alternate reality Melbourne' Kim Harrison

'Strong, smart and capable, Riley will remind many of Anita Blake, Laurell L. Hamilton's kick-ass vampire hunter…Fans of Anita Blake and Charlaine Harris' Sookie Stackhouse vampire series will be rewarded' *Publishers Weekly*